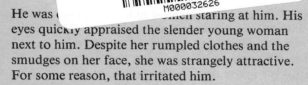

Nick

He was c... ...en staring at him. His eyes quickly appraised the slender young woman next to him. Despite her rumpled clothes and the smudges on her face, she was strangely attractive. For some reason, that irritated him.

''You must be the little city girl from Chicago who wants to play cowgirl for a summer,'' he said flatly.

Lindsay was taken aback by his tone. ''Do you think a person has to be raised in a log cabin in the middle of nowhere to know how to ride?'' she retorted indignantly.

''Listen, we see a lot of city slickers out here who think they're hot stuff on a horse, when maybe only one in a thousand knows anything about it.''

''Well,'' she replied coldly, ''maybe I'm that one in a thousand.''

Dear Reader,

Spellbinders! That's what we're striving for. The editors at Silhouette are determined to capture your imagination and win your heart with every single book we publish. Each month, six Special Editions are chosen with *you* in mind.

Our authors are our inspiration. Writers such as Nora Roberts, Tracy Sinclair, Kathleen Eagle, Carole Halston and Linda Howard—to name but a few—are masters at creating endearing characters and heartrending love stories. Their characters are everyday people—just like you and me—whose lives have been touched by love, whose dreams and desires suddenly come true!

So find a cozy, quiet place to read, and create your own special moment with a Silhouette Special Edition.

Sincerely,

The Editors
SILHOUETTE BOOKS

JESSICA BARKLEY
Into the Sunset

Silhouette Special Edition

Published by Silhouette Books New York

America's Publisher of Contemporary Romance

For my parents, for their love and support from
the time I started writing in grade school;
for Dave and Amber, for being my inspirations for
Nick and Sundance; and for my grandma, who is
somewhere up in heaven with her buttons busting.

SILHOUETTE BOOKS
300 East 42nd St., New York, N.Y. 10017

Copyright © 1987 by Jessica Barkley

ISBN: 0-373-09406-X

First Silhouette Books printing September 1987

America's Publisher of Contemporary Romance

Printed in the U.S.A.

JESSICA BARKLEY

lives on a small farm in Wisconsin with her husband, their daughter, five horses, fifteen cats and one dog. An avid reader, Jessica also enjoys traveling and distance riding. She has been writing stories since grade school, and although she has published several magazine articles, her true love is romantic fiction.

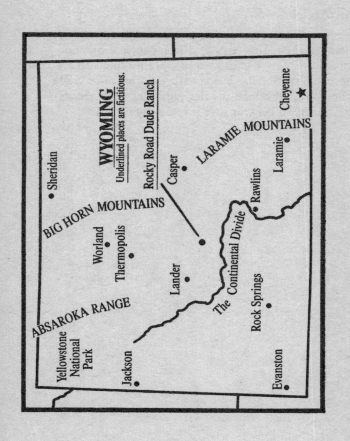

WYOMING

Underlined places are fictitious.

Rocky Road Dude Ranch

Cheyenne

LARAMIE MOUNTAINS

Laramie

Casper

Rawlins

Sheridan

BIG HORN MOUNTAINS

The Continental Divide

Worland

Thermopolis

Lander

Rock Springs

ABSAROKA RANGE

Yellowstone National Park

Jackson

Evanston

Chapter One

Ahead of Lindsay Jordan, the highway seemed to stretch on endlessly. Behind her, she could hear her horse kicking the sides of the trailer. "Easy, lady," she murmured, smiling. "We'll be there soon now."

Lindsay knew how the mare felt. They'd already driven more than a thousand miles. She had to stop every five hours to let her horse out for some exercise and water. They'd been on the road for two and a half days, and Lindsay was just as eager as the mare to reach their destination.

She hoped it wasn't much farther to the dude ranch.

Sighing deeply, she anxiously scanned the highway ahead for the sign that would indicate the turnoff to the ranch. She was so intent on looking for the sign, she scarcely noticed the scenery around her. The Rocky Mountains loomed to her left in all their regal majesty. She had never been this far west before, and the richly colored, snow-topped mountains seemed more like a picture postcard than an actual part of the land. She wished she could just stop and admire them for awhile, yet she knew she didn't dare. Anyway, she'd have plenty of time to appreciate her surroundings in the next few months. After all, she was going to be in Wyoming all summer.

Wyoming—it still seemed more like a dream than reality. When she'd first spotted the ad in a magazine describing the job at a dude ranch over the summer, she hadn't given it a thought. After all, she had a job already, a good, high-paying job, even though working at an insurance company was hardly what she wanted to spend the rest of her life doing. But for days the tiny ad kept haunting her, until she could think of nothing else. A job with horses was what she always longed for but thought she could never have.

She tried to convince herself that she was being a fool, that leaving her job in Chicago was a ridiculous, impetuous thing to do. She knew she wouldn't make anywhere near as much money at the dude ranch, but didn't she already have a sizable savings account at the bank? Financially, she could afford to do this, so her sensible side lost out to the dreamer on that argument.

Words her father had said to her before he died nearly a year ago also kept ringing in her ears. "Don't work yourself into an early grave, like I did," he'd told her earnestly one evening when he felt well enough to talk. "Take time to live a little, honey. Don't make the mistake of waking up one day to find you're old and alone with nothing but a career that, for the life of you, you can't figure out why it seemed so important once. You'll regret it the rest of your days. Believe me, I'm living proof of it."

He'd paused then, and she could still see his misting eyes as clearly as if he were standing in front of her now.

"What I wouldn't give to be young and healthy again like you are," he continued. "Promise me when I'm gone you'll take time to dream, to be happy. You're too much like me for your own good. Money isn't everything, sweetheart.''

She'd bent over and kissed his pale cheek then, promising him she would follow his advice. It had hurt terribly to see him that way, a tired, broken, lonely old man. Not really so old, though, she corrected herself; he had just aged beyond his years since her mother had died seven years before. When Lindsay's mother had passed away, part of her father had gone, too. He worked like a demon after that, and Lindsay watched him fade away slowly, knowing there was absolutely nothing she could do about it.

It wasn't until she was pondering the job in Wyoming that it occurred to her, that in the year since her father had died, she had done exactly what she'd promised him she wouldn't do. She had poured all her energy into her job, not caring whether she dated or went out with her friends. In that flash of self-realization, she firmly decided to at least apply for the summer position at the ranch. What could it hurt to just apply?

So she had carefully prepared her résumé, describing her experience working at a riding stable in Chicago, her years of riding and the fact that she had trained several horses, including her own seven-year-old mare. She'd dropped the résumé into a mailbox and wondered how she was ever going to stand waiting for an answer.

As the days passed, she tried desperately to keep her mind on her job at the insurance company and not on the job at the dude ranch. But with each day that job at the ranch became increasingly important to her, as if her life depended on it.

Finally, the day came when an envelope arrived with a Wyoming postmark. Her fingers were shaking so badly she could hardly open it, and when she did she stared at it in disbelief. It was brief and to the point, barely more than a

form letter, but it informed her that if she were still interested in the job she'd have to come to Wyoming in May for
an interview and a riding test.

When the words sank in, she'd actually danced around
her apartment in jubilation. That very day she sent the ranch
a letter of confirmation, telling them she'd arrive sometime
in the middle of May.

That was near the end of April, and she'd had a lot to do
in the next two weeks. The hardest part had been telling her
boss that she was taking a leave of absence for the summer.
She had built up seniority in the past few years, and her boss
readily agreed to a leave rather than a permanent dis-
charge. Lindsay then made arrangements for a friend to
water her plants and periodically check on her apartment
while she was gone. She cancelled her newspaper, packed
her belongings and readied her horse. By the eighth day of
May, she was on her way.

As she drove along the miles of highway, doubts began to
gnaw at her. What had she done? What if she hated the
ranch? What if her new boss was awful? What if she didn't
like the seclusion of life in the mountains? *What if . . . my
God,* she thought in horror, *what if I don't get the job?*

Lindsay's thoughts were quickly halted as the sign she'd
been searching for appeared. *You idiot,* she scolded herself, *you almost missed it. Keep your mind on your driving.*

She took the proper turnoff, began the twenty-mile as-
cent into the mountains and soon she was pulling into the
Rocky Road Ranch.

It was an impressive setup. Acres and acres of green pastures were partitioned off with white rail fences. Perhaps a
hundred horses were spread out in three fields, and the ones
close enough for Lindsay to see clearly looked very well
cared for. There were three huge red barns that looked like
they had recently been painted. Two long lines of small

redwood cabins, which Lindsay assumed housed the guests, were built on the far right side of the ranch. The main lodge was nearly as large as the barns, and it was neatly painted white with red trim. In the distance, she could see the sparkling blue of a large lake. The whole ranch was nestled in a valley with mountains surrounding it. She felt the knot of apprehension in her stomach ease a bit. The ranch was beautiful.

Lindsay stopped her pickup in front of one of the barns. As she got out of the truck, her mare neighed shrilly and kicked impatiently at the door of the trailer. Lindsay smiled as several horses in the fields answered her mare's call.

"I think you're going to like it here, lady," she said quietly.

Lindsay stood alongside the trailer for several minutes, unaware of just where to go. Several people were wandering around, but none seemed to take any notice of her. Were they guests or employees? she wondered. The letter in her purse said she was supposed to see a Mr. Browning. Well, she was going to have to ask someone. Evidently he wasn't going to be just waiting around to greet her.

"Can I help you?"

Lindsay jumped at the sound of the masculine voice that came from right behind her. She turned quickly. In front of her stood an older man she guessed to be at least fifty. His face had the deeply tanned and prematurely aged look of a man who had spent most of his years outdoors. Judging from his faded flannel shirt, well-worn jeans and dusty cowboy boots, she guessed he was an employee.

She smiled up into his friendly but curious brown eyes. "I'm Lindsay Jordan. I'm supposed to talk to a Mr. Ross Browning. Do you know where I can find him?"

The man returned her smile and nodded slightly. "You just have."

"Oh," Lindsay stammered, her face flushing in embarrassment. This man was no employee; he was the boss! He remained silent, but his eyes were carefully scrutinizing her. She waited, not knowing quite what to say.

After a long moment, he spoke again. "We've been expecting you sometime this week. Glad to see you made it all right. I see you've brought your own horse," he said, patting the side of the trailer.

"Yes, I did," she said anxiously. Why did he seem surprised? "It won't be a problem, will it?"

"No, no," he assured her. He paused, again studying her. "You know, of course, that if you're hired you won't be able to ride your own horse while you're trail guiding. You'll have to use one of our horses."

She had already thought of that, knowing she would have to ride close to the guests and their assigned horses, as well as with the other guides. All the ranch's horses were kept together in a compatible, established herd. Lindsay knew what would happen if a strange horse was ridden among the others. The kicking and biting that could occur would be dangerous not only to her and her horse, but to the guests as well.

She nodded. "I understand."

"Good. I'm glad you've got sense enough not to argue with me on that count. We'll be happy to stable your horse as long as you work here." Taking in Lindsay's disheveled appearance and the circles under her eyes, he continued. "I'm sure you must be pretty tired after the drive from Chicago, so you can have your rider's test in the morning. I'll help you carry your things to Cabin 4A." He pointed to the line of cabins farthest from the main lodge. "It's one of our guest cottages. If you get hired, you'll be assigned to one of our guide cabins. Either way, I suggest you don't get too settled in this cabin for now."

Lindsay was a little surprised at his bluntness. Didn't he think she would get the job? He must have thought she was qualified or he wouldn't have written for her to come out to Wyoming for an interview. And she felt confident she would pass the riding test, as she'd been riding most of her twenty-six years. If she wasn't fairly confident she'd get the job, she surely wouldn't have hauled a good share of her belongings and her horse twelve hundred miles. Well, she consoled herself, this man probably had a lot of people say they were experienced riders, when in fact they hardly knew the first thing about it. After all, he could hardly tell by looking at her that she was an adept horsewoman, so she shouldn't take his comments so personally. She'd have to prove herself in the morning.

"Thanks, but I can take care of unloading everything myself later. I'd like to take care of my mare right now. Do you have an unoccupied corral I could let her loose in to stretch her legs?" Lindsay asked, looking around. She saw several small paddocks near the barn that looked perfect.

"Sure. You can put her in any one of those," he answered, motioning toward the corrals Lindsay had noticed. "When she's had enough, take her into the barn and ask for Jake. He'll give you a stall. Oh, by the way," he called over his shoulder as he headed toward the main lodge, "dinner's usually served around five. Since you missed that, I'm sure the cooks can fix a sandwich or something for you. Breakfast is at seven. Your test will be at nine."

Lindsay nodded and opened the back of the trailer. An eager nicker greeted her. As soon as the mare was out of the trailer, she began prancing and whinnying, trying to take everything in at once. Lindsay kept a tight check on her as she led her into one of the corrals. Unsnapping the lead rope, Lindsay stepped away from her horse and walked toward the corral fence to sit on the top rail.

It only took the mare a moment to realize she was free to run around. Instantly, she dug into the dirt with her hooves. She lunged and ran full speed toward the far side of the corral. Watching her, Lindsay smiled. She knew the horse would either stop at the last moment or turn and follow the fence line.

Turn was what she did, so sharply that her hindquarters brushed the side of the rails. The horse then raced along the whole fence, taking long, leaping strides. She stopped for a moment, snorting and neighing at the distant horses on the hillside, before she ran around the corral again, this time a little slower and with her head held high as she took in her new surroundings.

Lindsay felt the familiar knot of pride well up inside her as she watched her horse. The mare was beautiful in appearance and in movement. Her copper coat was glistening more brightly than usual due to a light layer of sweat. Her long flaxen mane and tail flowed straight out behind her as she ran. The mare made a truly striking picture as she galloped.

"Nice-looking horse. I take it she's yours?"

Lindsay started at the deep voice that came from her left. Did all the men around here sneak up on people? she wondered.

"Yes," she answered, without turning.

"What's her name?"

"Lindsay Jordan," she answered automatically, her eyes still on her mare.

"That's a strange name for a horse," the voice at her side said, amused.

Lindsay frowned, thinking about his words. At last she realized he had asked her what her horse's name was. "Oh, I'm sorry." She smiled as she turned to look at the man. "I thought you asked *my* name. The horse's name is Sun-

dance.'' Her voice trailed off as she stared into the eyes of
the most ruggedly handsome man she had ever seen in her
life.

His eyes were so blue she thought they must be mirrors
reflecting the deep aquamarine of the Wyoming sky. Like
Ross Browning, this man had the look of a person who had
spent his life outdoors. His face was tanned and a bit more
lined than the face of someone who worked inside. He had
dark blond, slightly curly hair almost totally concealed under his worn cowboy hat, and a full, blond mustache. His
lips were turned up into a small smile that failed to reveal his
teeth. He was very tall; his head was even with hers and she
was still perched on the top rail of the corral.

Lindsay couldn't keep her eyes from wandering down his
body, and she took in his powerful build, broad shoulders
and narrow waist and hips. She could see a sprinkling of
blond hair on his massive chest just above the open neck of
his brown plaid flannel shirt. His jeans were worn but clean,
and she didn't miss how perfectly they molded to his muscular thighs.

Lindsay looked back up into his face again, and found
herself transfixed by his gaze. She felt her cheeks grow hot
with color as she realized by the look on his face that he was
only too aware of her studying his anatomy. She quickly
took her eyes off him and returned to watching her horse.

Nick Leighton smiled indulgently. He was used to women
staring at him. His eyes quickly appraised the slender young
woman next to him. Despite her rumpled clothes and the
smudges on her face, she was strangely attractive. For some
reason, that irritated him. ''You must be the little city girl
from Chicago who wants to play cowgirl for a summer,'' he
said flatly.

Lindsay was taken aback by his tone. Why was he so
hostile? His rudeness seemed to snap her out of the trance
he had put her in. ''Do you think a person has to be raised

in a log cabin in the middle of nowhere in order to know how to ride?'' she retorted indignantly.

"Listen, we see a lot of city slickers out here who think they're hot stuff on a horse, when only maybe one in a thousand knows anything about it."

"Well," she replied coldly, "maybe I'm that one in a thousand." She understood what he meant but that didn't give him the right to talk to her like that. He should at least be fair enough to see what she could do before he judged her.

"I doubt it," he replied, his eyes sweeping over her. "You don't look the type." Without another word, he turned and walked away.

As he headed toward the barn, Nick swore silently. He shouldn't have been so harsh to the girl, but if she only knew how many people just like her had wanted to work at the ranch over the years, maybe she wouldn't have been so defensive, either. Hotshot city girls like her were a dime a dozen, and she'd soon find out she belonged in her own element. After tomorrow, when she failed her riding test, she'd go scampering back home and he'd never see her again. With that final though oddly disconcerting thought, he dismissed Lindsay Jordan from his mind.

Lindsay watched his retreating back, noting the long, easy strides he took. She forced herself to stop staring, and again turned to watch Sundance. The man may have good looks, she told herself, but he certainly didn't have good manners.

She was angry at herself for having snapped at him. After all, he was undoubtedly one of the employees here, and it didn't pay to make an enemy when she'd been here less than an hour. Still, he could have been more pleasant himself. She hated to be treated unfairly, especially by some stranger, but she supposed she should have tried to hold her tongue. Unfortunately, her pride and quick temper often took over her good sense. She only hoped all the other people here would give her a fair chance. At any rate, she was more determined than ever to do well at her riding test in the morning.

Lindsay suddenly realized just how tired she was; it had been a very long day. She knew Sundance would like to run around some more, but her horse would have to be content with the exercise she'd had. Lindsay was too exhausted to sit out here any longer, and she still had a lot to do before she could go to bed.

Jumping off the corral rail, she headed toward the barn to find Jake. She only hoped she wouldn't run into that rude blond man again. As she entered through the large overhead door of the barn, Lindsay paused. She took a deep breath and was pleased that the strongest odor she smelled was clean, sweet straw. Evidently the stalls were well kept.

Near the end of the aisle, she saw a man brushing a compact bay quarter horse in cross ties. She walked slowly up to him and hesitated. "Are you Jake?" she asked.

The man straightened up and smiled. "Yes, I am. What can I do for you?"

"I'm Lindsay Jordan, and hopefully I'll be working here starting tomorrow. I brought my mare out here with me, and Mr. Browning said you would tell me where I can keep her tonight."

"Oh, sure. Why don't you put her in the end box stall down there," he said, motioning to the first stall on the left. "I think there's fresh straw in there already."

"Thanks." Lindsay smiled warmly. At least he had been pleasant! She walked over to the stall Jake had indicated and noticed it was indeed full of clean straw. She went out to get Sundance.

She gasped in dismay when she saw the blond man standing a short distance from the corral Sundance was in, talking to Mr. Browning. He was turned to face her horse, and she knew he would be watching her while she attempted to catch the mare. He probably thought she wouldn't be able to catch Sundance because the horse was still enthusiastically galloping around. Well, she would show him her horse was well trained!

With a look of confidence on her face, Lindsay climbed over the top rail of the corral and walked into the center of the paddock. Knowing the man must be watching, along with Mr. Browning, she felt a small pang of anxiety that the horse would pick this moment to be disobedient and make a fool out of her.

Pushing that negative thought from her mind, Lindsay whistled the short notes that her horse knew so well and called her name. She knew Sundance had seen her enter the corral right away, but the mare only stood and watched her from the far side of the corral until Lindsay whistled. Hearing the whistle and her name, the mare seemed to visibly sigh. Knowing her fun was over for now, Sundance trotted straight up to Lindsay, shaking her head a couple of times along the way to let her mistress know she was still feeling frisky. When the horse reached Lindsay, she snorted and pawed the ground with one delicate hoof.

Smiling, Lindsay reached up and took hold of the halter, and then led the mare to the gate. "Thanks, lady," she said quietly to the horse, knowing she couldn't have helped but make a good impression to the two men who had watched the entire scene.

Fifteen minutes later, with Sundance settled into the stall with her grain, hay and fresh water, Lindsay was getting settled in the cabin she had been assigned to. Remembering Ross Browning's caution, she took only her suitcase into the cabin, and left the rest of her belongings locked in the pickup.

Lindsay was immediately impressed with the coziness of the small cabin. It was pleasantly decorated with rustic, western-style furniture. The main room consisted of a stone fireplace, sofa, armchair, a portable TV and two tables that each held a small lamp. Off to the left was a narrow kitchen that contained a tiny refrigerator, a sink, a two-burner heating element and a round wooden table. A doorway from the living room led into a surprisingly large bedroom, complete with a double bed, two dressers, a chair and a night-stand with a lamp. To the right of the bedroom was the bathroom, which had a large vanity and a shower stall. All the rooms were decorated in earth tones, which gave the whole cabin a warm and cheery atmosphere. The furniture was by no means brand new, but everything was very clean and well maintained. Lindsay only hoped the employees' cabins were as nice as this guest cabin.

Taking her robe into the bathroom, Lindsay started the shower. Although she was very tired, she knew she would feel a lot better once the dirt and dust from three days of travel were washed away. While the water was getting hot, she paused to look at herself in the mirror. Lindsay gasped with chagrin as she took in her appearance. Her usually neat and shining brown hair was a tangled, dusty mess. The lit-tle makeup she had applied hastily in the morning had long since worn off, leaving her face looking pale and washed out. Some of her mascara had smudged under her eyes, which exaggerated the already dark circles there. There was a spot of dirt on her nose and another on her cheek, which she must have gotten while unloading Sundance from the trailer.

Lindsay was mortified to think of everyone getting their first impression of her when she was looking like this. Why, oh why, hadn't she stopped before getting to the ranch to freshen up? In her excitement and eagerness, she had completely forgotten how she must look. Well, there was nothing she could do about it now, she told herself, but she was determined to look like a new person in the morning.

After a long, hot shower, Lindsay felt immensely better. The water had also woken her up a little, and she didn't feel nearly so exhausted anymore. She wandered out to the armchair in the living room, which was under a window.

She sank down into the soft comfort of the chair and stared out at her surroundings. For a long time, she watched the horses grazing and playing in the pastures. Everything seemed so peaceful and quiet here; it was about the biggest contrast to the hustle and bustle of Chicago that she could imagine. Well, that was why she had come to Wyoming, to get away from the city, the smog, the impersonality, the traffic. And her job at the insurance company.

Dad, I think you'd be proud of me, she thought.

Feeling sleep threatening, Lindsay went into the bedroom and climbed under the thick, warm comforter on the bed. In the last moments before sleep overcame her, her mind reflected again on the blond man and their brief exchange. He was so sure she would fail at this job. Well, she would show him tomorrow that she was no typical city girl.

When she at last gave in to her fatigue and drifted off to sleep, she had a smile on her face.

Chapter Two

Lindsay was awakened at six o'clock in the morning by a shrill clanging that took her several minutes to identify as her alarm clock. Groaning, she reached over to the night-stand to put an end to the irritating sound. Could it really be morning? It seemed she had just put her head on the pillow. Knowing she had no time to lounge, she dragged herself out of bed and into the shower.

When she was through, Lindsay felt greatly refreshed and no longer tired. Although she was anxious to check on Sundance, she took her time applying her makeup and brushing her long auburn hair until it fell loosely around her shoulders in soft, shining waves. She hadn't forgotten what a mess she'd looked last night and was determined to show everyone that wasn't how she normally looked.

Forty-five minutes later, Lindsay strode from the cabin in clean jeans, a light sweater and a sheepskin-lined jacket. As she walked toward the barn, she was a bit surprised at how cool it was even though it was early May. Maybe it was just that the air was fresh out here, and not really cold, she reflected. Her eyes took in the scenery around her. The Rocky Mountains were indeed a much nicer backdrop to wake up to than the skyscrapers of Chicago.

As she entered the barn, Lindsay heard a loud nicker. She smiled as she saw Sundance's head sticking out above the stall door, watching her. "Now how did you know I was coming?" she asked the mare, affectionately scratching her neck. Lindsay was amazed to see that her horse's stall had already been cleaned, with fresh straw replacing the soiled bedding. Jake certainly was efficient.

As if on cue, Jake emerged from another stall, pitchfork in hand, and walking over to Lindsay. "You're in here early," he said pleasantly.

Lindsay looked him over in the morning light, realizing that she had no more than glanced at him the night before. He was slightly taller than she was, slim in build, and had light brown hair and blue eyes. She couldn't help remembering the sky-blue eyes of the blond man she had met last night as she gazed at Jake's darker blue ones. She was surprised to notice Jake couldn't be older than she was. He seemed young to be in charge of the barns for such a large operation.

"I wanted to check on her," Lindsay finally answered, nodding toward Sundance.

"She had a good night. I looked in on her about three, and she was munching away on her hay, very contentedly."

"Thank you." She smiled warmly. "That was very nice of you."

Jake shrugged. "It's just my job. Besides, she's a beautiful horse."

"Thanks," Lindsay said again. She paused. "How long have you worked here?" she asked casually.

"Oh, practically since I could walk. Ross Browning is my uncle."

Lindsay noticed the tension that had come into his voice. "That's nice," she replied easily. "I wish I knew someone who owned a place like this when I was young. It would have been an ideal childhood."

"Look, I happen to be very good with horses. Just because he's my uncle doesn't mean I'm not qualified for the job," he said defensively.

"No more that I'm not qualified to work here just because I'm from Chicago," she countered with a smile.

Jake stared at her for a moment and then burst out in laughter. "Touché. I guess we both have other people's little prejudices to deal with."

Lindsay joined in his laughter. "Oh, well, I guess it makes us harder workers."

"I suppose you're right. Speaking of work, I better get back to mine. Listen, I hope you get hired today. We could use two new fresh, pretty faces around here. Don't forget breakfast is in about ten minutes," he called over his shoulder as he returned to the stall he had been cleaning.

No, she hadn't forgotten breakfast, but she didn't plan on joining everyone in the main lodge. Lindsay was used to just having a cup of coffee in the morning anyway, and she knew she would feel uncomfortable in a room full of people she didn't know. Besides, she hadn't been officially hired yet. She would feel like an outsider. She preferred Sundance's company to the company of strangers, and the mare needed a good grooming and some exercise anyway.

An hour later, Lindsay was walking aimlessly around the barnyard, unsure where her riding test was to take place. Sundance had been exercised on the longe line and brushed to a brilliant shine and was now back in her stall, finishing her morning hay. Lindsay had gone back to the guest cabin to have a cup of the instant coffee she had brought with her, but it had certainly done nothing to settle her nerves. She fervently wished her test was over, so she would know if she was to work here for the summer or go home to Chicago.

She glanced at her watch again and saw that it was almost nine o'clock. Where was Mr. Browning? It suddenly occurred to her that he may have been waiting for her at breakfast. Maybe he thought she had slept late. That would give him a bad impression. *Oh, just stop it,* she scolded herself. *Everything will be fine.*

Lindsay walked restlessly back into the barn and stood in front of Sundance's stall, watching the mare eat. She certainly seemed at home here, Lindsay thought. Even if she didn't get the job, she would take a couple days to ride around this gorgeous countryside before going back to the city.

"You about ready for the big test?" a voice behind her said teasingly.

Lindsay whirled around and saw Jake standing next to her. "You scared me." She smiled. "It seems to be everyone's habit around here to sneak up on people."

"We don't really sneak. Your ears are probably just bad from living in the city too long. After you're here for awhile, they'll sharpen up again."

"Well, that's something to look forward to, I guess." She laughed. "Have you seen Mr. Browning?"

"Yeah, at breakfast. But I didn't see you. That's another bad city habit, not eating breakfast. We'll have to fix that up, too," Jake replied with mock disapproval. "My uncle should be down here in a couple minutes. Meanwhile, I've got to get the horses ready for your test."

"What's it going to be like?" Lindsay asked anxiously.

Jake winked. "Sorry, but I can't give away company secrets. You'll just have to wait and see."

"Well, well, I see it didn't take you long to warm up to the boss's nephew."

Lindsay jumped at the sound of the deep masculine voice behind her. She didn't need to turn to know it was the blond man delivering the sarcasm. She finally did turn, though, and looked up to meet his gaze squarely. She noticed his eyes widen slightly as he took her in, obviously a little surprised to see her looking a lot better than she had the night before. His brief appraisal made her heart start pounding, and it took her a moment to catch her breath so she could speak.

"I don't need to warm up to anyone to get this job. I happen to be very qualified," she said smoothly.

"Sure," he snorted derisively. "Unfortunately for you, Jake doesn't have all that much influence with Ross. So you're wasting your city charm, and time, on him. Unfortunately for you again, I'm the one who has the pull with Ross. But you don't have to bother trying to sweet-talk me; I've been around a lot more than Jake, and I can see right through it." He touched his hat and dipped his head slightly. "Good luck on your test."

Before Lindsay could answer, he had turned and walked away with that long, confident stride of his. Furious, she turned back to Jake and was amazed to find him grinning broadly. "Who is he, anyway? And what gives him the right to talk to me like that? And what's so funny? It sounded to me like he insulted you, too."

Jake shook his head. "That's just Nick's way. He doesn't mean anything by it, at least not to me, anyway. He is right, though. He's my uncle's right-hand man, and he does have considerably more pull with him than I do."

"But I wasn't, I mean that's not why I was—" Lindsay stumbled over the words, embarrassed and unable to say what she meant.

"I know. Don't worry about him. He's really a nice guy when you get to know him."

"Nice?" she scoffed. "He acts like he hates me for some reason."

"Oh, I doubt that. Nick's got quite an eye for pretty girls," Jake smiled mischievously. "He just needs to get to know you better."

"I sincerely doubt if that would help. Anyway, I plan to stay totally out of his way. He's a very unpleasant man." And very handsome, her mind added. But one certainly didn't make up for the other, she told herself.

Jake smiled and looked at her a bit oddly, as if he could read her thoughts. He appeared to be about to say something, but at the last moment changed his mind. "Oh, here comes my uncle now. I've got to get those horses ready. Good luck," he called as he hurried off.

Lindsay turned to meet Ross Browning and forced herself to smile. She must get that disturbing man out of her mind, and concentrate on the task at hand.

"Lindsay, here you are. I didn't see you at breakfast. Are you feeling all right?" Ross asked as he approached her.

"I'm fine," she assured him quickly. "I had some coffee in my room. I'm not used to eating much in the morning, and anyway I wanted to spend some time with my horse."

He studied her for a moment, considering her words. "Very well. However, if you do get hired, I suggest you learn to eat breakfast. There's a lot of work to do around here, and it's a long time until lunch. I can't have my employees fainting on the trail from lack of food in their bellies."

"I've never fainted in my life. But I promise to eat a hearty breakfast from now on."

"Good. Jake!" he called into the barn. "Have you got Rose and Pepper ready yet?"

"Coming," Jake called back from somewhere in the depths of the barn.

Ross turned back to her. "We always have prospective employees ride two of our horses. One is a real handful, pushy and a touch hardmouthed. The other is very lazy and has to be encouraged to move faster than a shuffle, but is the safest, most trustworthy horse for an inexperienced kid. Both horses are very well trained and behave beautifully with a good rider. But they are also extremely smart, and they know right away just how much they can get away with. I've found that if a person can get both horses to perform well, that person is good enough to work here."

Lindsay nodded. She understood everything he said from working at the trail-riding stable in Chicago. She had ridden both types of horses, and ridden them well. Unless he wasn't telling her something, she felt confident she could pass this test with flying colors.

A moment later Jake appeared, leading two horses down the aisle, one a chestnut and the other a palomino. Here goes nothing, she said to herself as she followed them outside and over to the same corral she had let Sundance out in last night. It was impossible to tell from just looking at the two horses which was the fireball and which was lazy, but she knew she'd find out soon enough.

"Why don't you try the chestnut first," Ross said. "Just take him around the corral a few times and do some trotting and cantering, some figure eights, whatever."

Lindsay walked over to Jake. "Is this Pepper or Rose?" she asked under her breath as she took the reins from him.

"Pepper," he answered quietly and smiled. "But don't let the name fool you."

Frowning, she led the horse into the corral and shut the gate behind her. She walked the horse into the arena and stopped at his side. Without even thinking, she put the stir-

rup over the saddle to get it out of the way and checked the
tightness of the cinch. It was very loose. She probably
wouldn't have made it into the saddle without it sliding back
down with her in it; it certainly wouldn't have stayed in place
for more than a few steps. Lindsay smiled to herself. Although it was a dangerous test, it certainly was a practical
one. Her old, reflexive habit of always checking the cinch,
no matter who had tightened it, had gotten her past their
first test before she was even in the saddle.

As she was pulling the leather tight on the cinch, Lindsay
happened to lift her eyes up over the horse's back. Staring
straight at her were Nick's cool, mocking blue eyes. He was
leaning casually on the other side of the fence, his chin resting on muscular arms crossed over the top rail. She figured
he would be watching her test from somewhere, only she
had hoped he would be out of her sight. His undivided attention made her even more nervous, and she noticed with
dismay her knees felt suddenly weak.

With an effort, Lindsay dropped her eyes back to the
cinch and forced herself to put him out of her mind. He was
so certain she wasn't good enough! Well, she would show
him that a city girl could ride every bit as well as he could.
She took a deep breath and felt her grim determination and
confidence return. With firm movements, she dropped the
stirrup back into place. The force of her actions made it
thump into the horse's side and the gelding gasped in surprise.

"Sorry, old guy," she mumbled, patting his shoulder.
"I'm a little keyed up."

Ready at last, Lindsay climbed nimbly into the saddle and
gathered the reins. The horse stood calmly, waiting for a
signal. Lindsay squeezed him lightly with her legs, but he
still stood there, as if he was asleep. Obviously Pepper was
the lazy one, she realized. She squeezed him a little harder,

and when he still didn't respond she gave a firm kick with both heels. She felt him gasp again, and he moved forward into a walk. "Sorry to wake you up, Pepper," she said quietly.

After walking a couple of times around the corral, she squeezed him again, asking him to trot, but he kept up the same pace as if he hadn't felt anything. Lindsay again kicked him hard with her heels and the horse took off immediately into a ground-covering trot. After that, he seemed to realize he'd be better off to respond to the squeezes and Lindsay never had to kick him again. He trotted, cantered and turned flawlessly at her lightest cues, and after ten minutes Lindsay stopped him by Ross Browning.

"Is that enough for him?" she asked, unable to keep the triumphant smile off her face.

Ross returned her smile. "Yes, you've proven yourself quite well on Pepper. Go ahead and take Rose around."

Lindsay dismounted and led Pepper out of the corral and over to Jake, who was grinning broadly.

"One down, one to go," he said as he handed her Rose's reins.

She took the palomino mare into the corral and checked the cinch. This time it was extremely tight, so tight that it would pinch the horse painfully with the weight of a rider in the saddle, which could possibly cause the horse to buck. As she loosened and smoothed out the cinch, Lindsay knew Nick's eyes were still on her, and try as she might she couldn't keep from looking up at him again. He was indeed still studying her, but his expression wasn't quite so mocking anymore. Lindsay couldn't resist giving him a small, smug smile, and then she looked away. Unless he was a total idiot, he had to have a little more respect for her now.

As she mounted the palomino, the mare skidded sideways nervously. "Okay, fireball, take it easy. You've got to make me look good, too," she said softly and quietly to the mare. Lindsay just touched her legs to the mare's sides and she was off at a brisk trot. Lindsay pulled her back down into a walk, but the horse started prancing instead. Forcing herself to relax in the saddle, for she knew any tenseness on her part would further excite the horse, Lindsay gave the mare a couple of firm checks with the reins, and the horse finally came down into an easy walk. Lindsay only had to check the mare hard twice before Rose behaved nicely and responded obediently to her commands. Again, after about ten minutes, she walked the horse over to Ross and looked at him questioningly.

He smiled broadly. "Yes, that's quite enough. Well, Lindsay, if you still want it, the job is yours."

"Thanks, I'd love it," she answered happily.

"Don't you even want to talk about the salary and the hours?" Ross was clearly amused at her enthusiasm.

Lindsay flushed, knowing she sounded like a horse-crazy teenager. "It doesn't matter," she told him truthfully.

He shrugged. "Suit yourself. We can talk about it later. Take the rest of the day to get settled, and you can start work fresh tomorrow morning." With a nod and a smile, he turned and walked back to the main lodge.

Lindsay was so excited, she nearly floated off Rose. She led the horse back to a grinning Jake.

"Congratulations. I knew you would do it," he said pleasantly.

"No thanks to you," she replied in mock disapproval. "Trying to sabotage me with those cinches."

"Sorry, but that's standard procedure for employee tests around here. I had to do that or I would have caught hell from my uncle."

"I know, I was only kidding. Here, I'll help you put these two away."

As they walked to the barn, Lindsay glanced over her shoulder to where Nick had been standing. But to her surprise, he had already disappeared. *Probably disappointed I've been hired,* she told herself. Oh, well, it didn't matter. The job was hers!

Nick paced restlessly around his cabin, disturbed that he was feeling so ambivalent toward this new female employee. Yes, he had wanted her to fail, or so he'd thought, but now that he knew she was hired he felt strangely glad.

He'd been astonished to see how well she could ride, how confident and adept she was at handling Rose and Pepper. And when he'd first seen her in the barn this morning, he'd been completely taken aback by her change in appearance. She was even more beautiful than he imagined she would be.

It had grated on him to hear her being so friendly to Jake. He chuckled without mirth as he remembered his own cutting words to her. She'd probably never speak to him as pleasantly as she did to Jake. Not that he deserved her to, the way he'd treated her. He smiled as he thought about how her green eyes had flashed in anger, how quickly she'd come to her own defense. She certainly had spunk, that girl.

Nick dropped into the leather easy chair and tossed his Stetson onto the end table. He rubbed callused hands over his face and through his hair. What was the matter with him, anyway? Since when did he let some beautiful city woman get to him like this, taking over his thoughts, making him so damned unsettled? But he knew the answer to that question only too well. It had been a long time ago, but once before he had let a woman get under his skin this way.

And that's what scared the hell out of him now.

Chapter Three

As she lay awake in her "own" bed that night, Lindsay reflected on the happenings of the day, which had passed quickly for her. She'd spent the morning with Jake, helping him clean stalls and care for the horses in the barn. By lunchtime she was ravenous, as Jake had laughingly assured her she would be. They ate together in the main lodge, along with about twenty other employees. Lindsay had scanned the room uneasily for Nick, but he never appeared.

She met the employees who were back for the summer. Jake explained that almost half the employees had yet to return. She found the other guides to be a little reserved at first, but they soon opened up and were quite friendly. In no time at all, she was joining in with their laughter as they retold stories of past summers and the funny things greenhorn guests had done. Everyone had made her feel welcome, and she again realized how much she was looking forward to spending her summer working there.

She took the afternoon to get settled in one of the employee cabins, and was delighted to find it was a little larger and every bit as cozy as the guest cabin had been. By the time she had finished organizing everything, it was six o'clock and time for dinner.

As she sat down across the table from Jake, she was dismayed to find Nick seated at the table directly behind Jake, facing her. Many times during the meal, she looked up to find him openly studying her, and it was all she could do to swallow her food over the tightening in her throat. She continually chastised herself for being so easily stirred by such a man, but it didn't help.

The real blow, however, had come when she was just about through eating. Ross Browning had strode over to her table, and Lindsay could still hear his words just as clearly as if he were in her bedroom repeating them to her.

"Lindsay," he'd said with a smile, "tomorrow after breakfast I want you to ride with Nick Leighton up to the north range to bring down one of our herds of guest horses. He can show you the layout of the land, where some of our trails go and so forth. And it will give you a chance to get used to being in the saddle all day."

Lindsay had nearly choked on the piece of steak in her mouth when she heard him say "Nick Leighton." She'd scanned her memory in a desperate effort to remember all the names of the other employees she'd met at lunch, hoping someone else was named Nick.

But she knew there was no other. As if seeking final confirmation, she'd glanced at the only Nick she knew, and he smiled briefly, a small, gloating smile that seemed to say he couldn't wait to get her out on the trail and make her work her butt off. Lindsay had groaned and looked at Jake, but he only grinned and winked back at her. She'd finished the rest of the meal in a daze, and disappeared from the dining room as soon as she could.

Lindsay turned over again restlessly in her bed. Spend the day with Nick? The thought sent shivers through her. He would make it intolerable, she was sure. Lindsay sighed deeply. Well, she would just have to get used to it, she supposed. After all, she couldn't expect to work here all summer and never see him, could she? Maybe once he got to know her better, and found she was a hard, capable worker, he wouldn't be so rude.

And maybe pigs could fly, she scoffed.

No, there was something about him that disturbed her greatly, but she couldn't quite put her finger on it. It wasn't just that he was rude and egotistical. After all, she'd seen those qualities in men before, and although she'd found those men deplorable, none had ever affected her this way. In fact, she rather enjoyed dealing with chauvinistic men at times because it was such a pleasure to exchange word battles with them and occasionally put them in their place. Her quick wit had often come to her aid. But for some reason, she had the feeling she'd be in for quite a challenge if she tried to match wits with Nick Leighton.

It was early into the morning before Lindsay finally dozed off in a fitful sleep, while cold blue eyes and a taunting smile haunted her mind.

The morning dawned bright and clear. Lindsay awoke restlessly several minutes before the alarm went off. Again she showered and took her time getting herself ready, only too aware that an extremely handsome man, rude or not, would be looking at her for most of the day.

Before she headed out to the barn, Lindsay studied herself carefully in the large mirror that hung over the dresser.

She'd pulled her long hair back with a large barrette at the base of her neck so it wouldn't blow in her eyes while she rode. A few unruly wisps curled stubbornly at the sides of her face, further softening her delicate features. Large green eyes filled with a touch of excitement gazed back at her in the mirror, and then scanned down the rest of her body. Her slender frame was accentuated by the tapered cotton shirt and slightly tight jeans she had chosen to wear.

Lindsay sighed and stuck out her tongue at the reflection in the mirror. "You're not perfect, but I guess you'll have to do," she mumbled to herself. She shrugged into her fleece-lined coat, grabbed her denim jacket for later in the day and headed outside to the barn.

After greeting and grooming Sundance, Lindsay walked slowly to the main lodge for breakfast. A quick glance around the room revealed Nick had not yet arrived, and she sank gratefully into a chair by Jake and one of the other employees, Cindy Thompson.

"Ready for the big day, Lindsay?" Jake teased.

Lindsay threw him a scornful look. "I feel like I'm being sent to a firing squad," she muttered.

Cindy giggled. "Gee, I'll trade places with you. I wouldn't mind spending the day with Nick Leighton. It'd be a lot of fun."

"Fun?" Lindsay snorted.

"Sure," Cindy replied, a light blush rising in her cheeks. "He's a real charmer."

Lindsay glanced at Jake, remembering what he said about Nick having an eye for a pretty girl. Evidently Nick Leighton was discriminating about who he wasted his charm on. Lindsay studied Cindy a moment. She had short blond hair, a pleasant round face and an engaging smile. Yes, Lindsay had to admit Cindy was cute, but not what most men would call beautiful. So why was Nick so nice to Cindy when he wouldn't even speak civilly to her? *Oh, stop it,* she scolded herself, amazed to find her thoughts on such a ridiculous subject.

"Well, look at the bright side," Jake went on, unable to keep the smile off his face. "You'll be surrounded by gorgeous scenery."

"That you will," a deep voice agreed. "The mountains are beautiful in the spring."

Lindsay's fork froze in midair as Nick dropped into the chair opposite her. Her heart leaped immediately into her throat as she stared openly at him for a moment, once more halted by his masculinity. He met her gaze evenly, gave her an amused half smile and then diverted his attention to his food. *Just relax!* Lindsay screamed at herself angrily, knowing that he had once again caught her admiring him. He must have women falling all over him all the time, she told herself, and she would not lower herself to their level. *Where's your pride?*

Her composure regained, she spoke in a surprisingly level voice. "How many horses will we be bringing down?"

"Thirty-two," Nick answered, his eyes meeting hers again.

"How long will this take?"

"Why? Have you got something more important to do? Like doing your nails?"

Lindsay swallowed her angry retort. Why was he taunting her? Well, she wouldn't give him the satisfaction of getting into a battle in front of everyone. She smiled sweetly. "Sorry, but I left my manicure set in Chicago. Actually, I was just curious."

"It'll take most of the day. We'll be packing a light lunch, but it won't be much so I suggest you eat a lot now while you can." He returned his attention to his bacon and eggs, effectively ending the conversation.

Lindsay glanced at Cindy and saw she was staring at Nick like a lost puppy. Disgusted, she looked over at Jake, and he grinned broadly at her, shaking his head in amusement. Lindsay made a face at him and gazed down at her half-eaten scrambled eggs. Thinking of Nick's words, she lost her appetite. Eat a lot now, indeed! Who did he think he was, her mother? Even if she were starving, she wouldn't eat a lot because of his command.

"Suddenly I feel rather full," she announced flatly, rising to her feet. "I'll be in the barn when you're through." Without looking at anyone, she turned and left the room.

Nick chewed his food slowly as he watched Lindsay storm out of the dining room, his gaze drawn uncontrollably to the haughty swing of her narrow hips. He carefully concealed a smile. He was rather looking forward to this.

A few minutes later, a grinning Jake joined Lindsay in the barn. "And what do you find so amusing?" she demanded irritably.

"Oh, I was just thinking how much I'd like to go along with you and Nick and hear all the fireworks that are bound to go off today," Jake replied good-naturedly.

Lindsay ignored his teasing. "What's my horse like?"

"Champ's a real nice old gelding. He's thoroughly used to the mountain trails and he's safe and easy to handle."

"Old? Safe and easy to handle? Who suggested I ride him? He sounds like a beginner horse," Lindsay exclaimed.

"Nick told me to saddle him for you," Jake admitted.

"Just what is his position around here? He seems to rule everybody." Lindsay felt her anger rising again. She could picture it all now: Nick would be galloping around on some young stallion with loads of energy while he yelled at her to hurry up on her broken-down gelding. "Can't I ride a different horse?"

"It's not as bad as all that. Champ is a very good horse. Believe me, he has lots of spunk for his age. And he's a dominant member of the herd, and the other horses you'll be bringing in will drive forward a lot easier with him behind them," Jake reassured her. "As far as Nick's position here, it's hard to say exactly. He doesn't have a regular title, but my uncle does depend on him pretty much to help him run things. I guess you'd say he was second in command. Anyway, we all do what he says, or we'll have hell to pay from my uncle."

"Sounds like he's a dictator to me," Lindsay muttered, then sighed. "Well, where's this wonder horse I'm supposed to ride?"

"Right this way, ma'am," he said dramatically, bowing.

Jake led her outside to two saddled horses. One was a light chestnut with a full blaze, small and compact. The other horse was a huge black and white pinto, much taller than the chestnut, and superbly muscled.

As Lindsay approached the horses, she chuckled sarcastically. "I don't have to bother asking which horse is mine," she said as she patted the small chestnut gelding and wistfully gazed at the beautiful pinto. She knew Champ would have a difficult time keeping up to the leggy black and white horse, who was obviously in the prime of his life.

"Nick's horse is a bit stunning," Jake said, reading her thoughts. "But don't let Champ's looks deceive you. He'll be able to keep up all right. He hates being left behind. Besides, you two aren't going to have a race out there, you know."

"Yes, I know," she said resignedly. "Well, when is Nick going to stop stuffing his face and get out here so we can get going?"

As if in answer, she saw him striding easily in their direction, carrying a pair of saddlebags over his shoulder. He moves like a cat, Lindsay thought as she watched him slowly approach, supremely confident in himself and in no apparent hurry.

When he at last reached them, Nick looked Lindsay over briefly. "Ready for a day's work in the country, city girl?"

"The name is Lindsay. And I've been ready for quite some time," she answered coolly.

"Where's your hat?" he asked, glancing over at her again.

"My what?"

"Your cowboy hat," he said impatiently. "Where's your cowboy hat?"

"I don't have one. I don't like hats."

Nick shook his head, his disbelief of her ignorance clear on his face. "Jake, go get her a spare hat, will you?"

Lindsay bristled at his tone. He was treating her like a child! "That won't be necessary, Jake," she said firmly, stopping him momentarily in his tracks. "I'll be fine without one."

Jake paused, waiting for them to settle their dispute. Nick nodded and waved him on, and he disappeared into the barn to locate a hat.

"Not only will it keep the sun out of your eyes," Nick said flatly, "but it will also shade that pale face of yours so it doesn't get sunburned."

"I don't need it, thanks just the same," she said stubbornly, knowing he had a good point, but hating the way he was ordering her around. Just then, Jake emerged from the barn with a tattered brown cowboy hat in his hand.

Nick's voice was tight with barely controlled anger. "If you don't take it, you don't go. And if you don't go, you're fired." Why did she have to argue with him? And why did he feel the need to tell her what to do?

Lindsay stared furiously at him for a moment, meeting his cold eyes, which had turned steel gray. Knowing she was probably being as unreasonable as he was and that she really had no choice, she reached over and snatched the hat from Jake's hand. Thrusting it heavily on her head, she turned to face Nick again.

"Satisfied?"

His eyes briefly softened, and for a moment Lindsay thought he might laugh at her. *I must look real cute in this damn hat,* she thought sarcastically, *if this pigheaded bully could stop being so bossy for a second and almost smile.*

It took all of Nick's control not to burst into laughter. The hat covered half her head, and he could hardly see those crackling emerald eyes of hers. She looked like a little girl playing dress-up in her mother's oversize clothes. At that moment, she looked very appealing, and he felt a strange stirring deep inside his body.

But he recovered quickly, and his face became hard again. "Let's go," he said curtly. In one quick, easy motion, he mounted the pinto.

Lindsay saluted. "Yes, sir." She tied her light jacket to the back of the saddle and then mounted Champ. "Should I drop in ten paces behind you, master?" she asked in a syrupy voice.

Nick grunted. She wasn't going to make this easy for him. "I have a feeling that would be the best place for you, but it isn't necessary. You can ride next to me until we get farther into the mountains."

If I can get this poor little horse to keep up with you, she thought silently, and urged Champ into a trot until he was even with the pinto. Glancing up at Nick, who towered above her, she was only too aware of the symbolism of his male supremacy on the huge horse in contrast to her far below him on the small one. He probably intentionally picked the smallest horse in the place for her to ride for that very reason, she thought irritably.

"What do you do in Chicago?" Nick asked casually, breaking the silence.

She paused, suspicious of the friendly tone of his voice. "I work for an insurance company," she answered cautiously.

"So why did you come out here? For the money?"

Lindsay let out a short laugh. "No, I make more in one month there than I'll make all season here," she replied without thinking, then realized he must have known that all along, and that he was setting her up for something.

"So you didn't come to work here to get rich. Running away from an old lover?" Where did that question come from? he wondered in amazement. He hadn't meant to say that at all. But now that it was out, he watched her closely, waiting for her reply.

She almost laughed. Nothing could be further from the truth, but she had no intention of letting him know that she hadn't even gone out with a man in ages.

"Of course not. Besides, I never run away from my problems." But that wasn't really true, she realized. Hadn't she run away to Wyoming to escape from a job and a life that were becoming increasingly oppressing?

"So why did you want to work here for the summer?" he persisted.

"Why do you care?" she countered.

"I like to know the motives of all the people I work with."

She shrugged. "I love horses and riding. I've always heard Wyoming is a beautiful state, and I needed a vacation, so—"

"A vacation?" Nick exploded. So she was just a typical city woman after all. "Is that what you think this is going

to be? I've got news for you, little city girl, you'll be working harder here than you've ever worked in your life.''

"You'll see to that, right?" Lindsay cut in mockingly.
"Anyway, you didn't let me finish. If I was out here for a
vacation, I'd have come as a guest. I had some time off
coming from my job, so I decided it would be a good time
to take a break from the city and come out here to work.
And I mean work." She emphasized the last word firmly.

"We'll get an indication of how good you'll be at that
pretty soon," he said, and kicked the pinto into a canter.

Lindsay watched in fascination as he rode away from her.
She'd had the feeling he would be a good rider, but she was
surprised to see just how skilled a horseman he was. As the
pinto took long, ground-covering strides, Nick was truly one
with his horse, his seat never leaving the saddle. His legs remained stationary against the pinto's sides, his hips ab-
sorbing all of the horse's movements, while his shoulders
and head were as motionless as if the horse was standing
still. Although she wished she could find fault with his form,
Lindsay was impressed in spite of herself. She felt an odd
thrill watching him ride, and for a long moment she held
back her own horse as she stared in appreciation. The distance between them quickly increased.

"Are you coming or not?"

Nick's call of irritation jolted her back to reality, and she
urged Champ into a gallop to catch up. As her horse ran, the
too-big cowboy hat bobbed up and down on her head,
threatening to come off at any moment. Feeling defiant and
disgusted at his orders, Lindsay reached up and tipped the
hat off her head, letting it bounce against her back while the
rawhide string tightened against her throat. She soon discovered having if off was almost as bad as having it on. For
two cents she'd just let the whole thing fly, but she didn't
quite feel like facing Nick's full wrath.

As she caught up with him at last and settled into a fast canter to keep up to the pinto's easy one, she noticed him glance down at her and frown when he noticed the hat hanging down her back. She gave him a tight, challenging smile, but he said nothing. Lindsay relaxed a little, glad he wasn't going to press the issue again for now, and focused her attention on the beautiful scenery around her. Already they were out of sight of the ranch, and with all the rugged wilderness on every side of her she felt like she and Nick were the only two people in the world, and for some reason it made her feel strangely close to him.

"We'll walk again for a while now," Nick announced, reining his horse in.

Lindsay followed suit, and they walked side by side for several minutes without talking. Finally, feeling the silence becoming awkward, Lindsay spoke hesitantly. "Have these horses been up here all winter?"

"No, just for a few weeks. We spread out the herds as soon as the weather permits and keep them scattered as long as we can. We get too much snow out here to keep them this high in the mountains all winter. They do have to be fed hay, you know," he finished a touch sarcastically.

Lindsay ignored his sarcasm, determined not to argue. She wished he would at least be civil to her. Everyone else seemed to think he was such a pleasant man, even charming, as Cindy had said, and she couldn't figure out what he could have against her. Just because she was from the city? That didn't seem like a reason to hate her on sight. She wanted to get to know him; for some inexplicable reason he fascinated her, and she knew she was more than a little attracted to him in spite of herself.

"How much farther is it before we get to them?" she asked calmly.

"Why? Are you tired already? We've hardly been out an hour yet," Nick scoffed. He knew he was being unreasonably harsh, but he couldn't seem to help himself.

Lindsay bristled, but again forced herself to keep her temper in check. "I was simply asking a question. No, I am not tired. I have ridden more than an hour at least once or twice," she replied, unable to keep a little sarcasm from her voice.

Nick paused momentarily, studying her. "We've got at least another two hours to ride before we reach them. And it's almost all walking, because these horses aren't in shape to climb much faster than that so early in the year. In a couple of months, we could make it up there in an hour."

Two hours of walking! Lindsay shuddered slightly. It wasn't that she couldn't handle that physically, as she often rode Sundance five or six hours at a time, but she couldn't imagine what she and Nick could possibly find to talk about for two hours. When they were trotting or cantering, conversation wasn't expected, but walking was something else. She glanced up at him, and was disturbed to find his cool blue eyes watching her closely. Feeling suddenly tense and nervous, she looked away.

Nick caught the look of displeasure on her face. For heaven's sake, how did she think she could work here all summer when the thought of spending one day in the saddle bothered her so much?

"What's the matter? Is that more riding than your city bottom can take?" he asked mockingly.

"Hardly," she snapped.

"Then what seems to be the problem?" he probed, his eyes boring into hers.

"You really want to know?" Lindsay exploded, unable to hold her temper any longer. "I can't stand the thought of having to spend all that time just walking along next to you."

Nick threw back his head and laughed. He felt some of the tension leave his body. "Why not? Don't you find me pleasant company?"

"Pleasant company! You? Don't make me laugh. Why, you're the most—"

"The most what?" He chuckled.

"Never mind," Lindsay grumbled. Damn, how could she let him bait her like this? Instead of him being angry, too, he actually seemed to be amused by her outburst, and that fueled her temper even more.

"Well, if you can't stand the thought of walking for two hours next to me, did you have something else you'd prefer doing with me?"

Lindsay gasped and felt the color rise in her cheeks. She looked up at him, furious at his connotation, but was immediately taken aback by the look on his face. His icy blue eyes had softened a bit, and he was smiling pleasantly for the first time since they'd met, revealing a mouthful of straight white teeth. He was teasing, not taunting her now. She was amazed by the transformation in his appearance. Even though he was very attractive with a scowl or a mocking smile on his face, he was exceptionally handsome with a boyish grin lighting up his features. When he looked at her like that, she could easily see why Cindy thought he was charming. Confused, and not liking where her thoughts were taking her, she tore her eyes away from his face.

"Don't flatter yourself," she mumbled, still trying to sound mad, but with that one smile of his, her anger had mysteriously vanished. "I thought you were supposed to be showing me where some of the riding trails are," she said, changing the subject to a safer topic.

"Ah, yes, I'm supposed to be your tour guide, aren't I?" Nick replied easily. "Actually, we're on one of the trails right now, although it's not very well worn yet. By the end of the summer, if you make it that long, this path will look like a road."

Lindsay ignored his little barb, and waited for him to continue. After a moment, he went on to explain about all the different kinds of rides the Rocky Road Ranch offered to its guests: they could go out for as little as two hours; they could ride for several hours in the morning, meet at another camp for lunch, then ride back a different way to the ranch; or they could go out on an overnight ride, making camp and returning to the main ranch the next morning. In addition, there were breakfast rides, steak-dinner rides, moonlight rides and some gaming events for the more experienced riders.

Because of the variety of rides, there were a lot of trails that were used each summer, and Nick explained that one of her duties in the next two weeks would be to ride many of the guest horses over the trails to reacquaint them to working. Even though all the guest horses were gentle and obedient by nature, they still usually had a lot of excess spring energy every year, which the employees had to work out of them before the inexperienced guests could take them out.

Lindsay listened attentively as he told her all about the ranch and its operation and pointed out where some of the trails went. For the most part, his voice remained casual, not extremely friendly but not sarcastic either. The next hour and a half passed quickly, and Lindsay was surprised when Nick stopped his horse and announced they would take their lunch break before they reached the other horses. Her apprehension at talking to him for all that time had proven unfounded.

As Lindsay swung her leg over Champ's back to dismount, she suddenly felt a wave of dizziness sweep over her. She staggered and grabbed the saddle to stabilize herself until her vision cleared.

At once Nick was at her side, and she felt large, firm hands on her shoulders steadying her.

"Lindsay?" he said softly in her ear. "What's the matter?"

"I'm all right," she stammered. In a moment the dizziness had passed and she could see clearly again, but the weakness in her knees persisted. She was conscious only of his touch, and it sent an unexpected shudder through her. His hands gripped her even tighter, sending flames through her whole body. "It must be the altitude," she gasped.

"Altitude my ass," he rumbled. "This is what happens when you don't eat breakfast and ride all morning in the sun with no protection on your stubborn head. If you'd listened to me instead of acting like a spoiled child, this wouldn't have happened," Nick admonished, ushering her over to a large rock.

The momentary spell that had been over her shattered, and Lindsay glared at him. Spoiled child, indeed! "Maybe if you weren't such a bully about telling me things I would listen," she countered angrily.

"And maybe if you had more sense I wouldn't have to tell you such basic things anyway," Nick retorted as he threw a canteen at her.

She caught it and gratefully took a long drink. She still felt a little weak, but whether it was from too much sun and too little food or from Nick's touch she couldn't be sure. Even now, she could still feel where his hands had been as surely as if she'd been burned by a red-hot branding iron.

"Eat these," Nick growled and tossed her two sandwiches enclosed in plastic.

"I'm not hungry," she said stubbornly, although her stomach was arguing otherwise.

Nick stormed up to her, and bent over until his face was only inches away from hers. "I will not have you fainting on me in the middle of a horse herd. Now, do you want me to feed you?"

Lindsay looked up into the cold fury of his face. She had no doubt at that moment that if she refused to eat he would indeed stuff the sandwiches down her throat. Knowing she was being foolish anyway, she looked away and unwrapped one of the sandwiches.

Satisfied, Nick walked over to another rock and sat down to eat his own lunch. He didn't know if he was more angry at her or himself. He wasn't usually so domineering, but dammit, he wasn't used to having someone challenge his every word either. Deep down, though, he knew what really had set him off was the way it had felt when he'd momentarily held her in his arms. It had shaken him down to his boots to feel her tremble beneath his hands. He'd wanted to turn her around and crush his mouth against her obstinate little lips. The thought of it even now had his breath coming too fast.

He had promised himself years ago that never again would he let a woman cause such a weakness in him, and he was furious with himself for allowing such feelings to emerge. Especially for this woman, who was completely wrong for him. *You fool,* he thought in disgust, *won't you ever learn?*

As soon as he was through eating, Nick rose and walked over to the pinto. "Let's go," he said curtly.

Lindsay stuffed half her second sandwich in her pocket. She felt much better now, and she realized it probably was hunger that had made her dizzy before, even though she hated to admit that Nick was right. She felt a little ashamed of herself for acting so childish about the whole thing, and for some reason it bothered her to have Nick angry with her. She should apologize, but she didn't know if she could get the words out. Lindsay sighed. The man certainly did nothing to bring out the best in her.

Nick glanced over his shoulder. "Are you ready?" he asked tightly.

Lindsay nodded, but instead of getting up she sat for another moment on the rock, watching Nick's back as he tightened the girth on the pinto's saddle. He had removed his coat earlier, and she could see the tenseness in his large, hard shoulder muscles through his flannel shirt. She wondered idly how it would feel to run her fingers over his back, caressing and massaging those muscles. Her eyes traveled down to his slim waist and narrow hips, and on down to his bulging, muscular thighs. Lindsay sighed again. Even from the back, this man was beautiful.

"What are you waiting for?" Nick asked impatiently. "You feel all right now, don't you?"

Lindsay stood up hastily. "Yes, I'm fine. Look, I'm sorry for the way I acted before," she said quickly.

"Do you mean your behavior or your dizziness?"

Lindsay shrugged. "Both, I guess."

"If you'll simply follow my orders without arguing, neither will happen again," he said sternly.

"Well, I'm sorry, but I've never been one to blindly follow the orders of anyone, especially when they're put to me the way you do," Lindsay replied flatly. Honestly, did he think she was some spineless female who couldn't think for herself and needed a man to tell her how to make every move?

Nick smiled slightly. He wanted to stay mad at her, to keep up his defenses against the strange way she affected him, but her unexpected apology had disarmed him and he felt the anger seeping away.

"I'll try to remember that in the future. Now, would you please wear that hat for the rest of the day? That is, if it wouldn't be too much trouble," he said in a mock polite voice.

Lindsay frowned. That tone of voice irritated her as much as his strict orders. "It's too big," she protested lamely.

Nick threw up his hands in exasperation. "See? Even when I ask you nice, you still argue."

"All right, all right. I'll try to keep it on, but if it falls off, it's not my fault." Lindsay stuck the worn cowboy hat back on her head.

Nick nodded his head. "Thank you. Now, we better get going or we'll never get those horses back today."

They mounted their horses and rode off in silence. After a few minutes, the trail narrowed and Lindsay had to pull in behind Nick as there was no longer room for two horses to walk side by side. Even though they had been climbing since they'd left the ranch, the trail became so steep that the horses had to strain to keep their footing. Lindsay concentrated only on the path in front of her and did all she could to make the going easier for Champ.

She was leaning as far forward over the gelding's neck as she could so as not to hinder his balance when he suddenly made one powerful lunge and then stopped just as abruptly. Lindsay desperately grabbed his neck, just barely preventing herself from being pitched right over his head.

Shaken and upset with Nick for the extremely steep trail he had probably deliberately taken just to test her, she settled herself back in the saddle and looked up, an angry remark on the tip of her tongue. But at the magnificent sight that lay before her, all her anger instantly dissipated and she could only stare open-mouthed.

"Oh, Nick, this is gorgeous," she breathed in awe. Glancing over at him, she saw he was again watching her closely, but she dismissed this and returned her attention to the valley.

Dark azure mountains, their peaks dotted with snow, filled every horizon as far as she could see. Thousands of tall, deep green pine trees lined the steep walls of the cliffs on every side, while only a few were scattered in the valley itself. In the center of the meadow was an expansive pond, its sparkling waters reflecting the sunlight like a large mirror. What completed the picture and made it truly breathtaking was the herd of horses grazing peacefully in the lush grass.

"I take it this is the herd we're supposed to bring in," Lindsay stated quietly.

"That's them all right. I had a feeling they'd be in this valley. The grass is always the best here, and there's a pond handy so they don't have to travel far for water. There is an easier way to see into the valley than the way we took, but I think the view from here is worth the climb," Nick said amiably, pleased at her reaction.

Lindsay smiled at him. "It certainly is. Although I almost went headfirst down there in the process."

"So I noticed." Nick chuckled. "From now on you'll know to keep your head up and let the horse concentrate on the trail himself. They're all used to this terrain, you know."

"So I noticed," Lindsay admitted, reflecting on how adeptly Champ had climbed the rocky incline. She turned to look at the herd below her and sighed. The horses looked so content, and she thought she could easily sit there with Nick and watch them all day. "It's a shame we have to disturb them. It seems like they belong here."

As she spoke, Champ neighed shrilly at the other horses, loudly announcing their presence. Instantly every horse in the herd looked in their direction. A few whinnied back, and several began to move around restlessly.

"It's too late to worry about disturbing them now." Nick grinned. "They know we're coming. We better get going before they decide to take off."

"Ah, how are we going to get down there?" Lindsay asked, anxiously peering over the side of the ledge they were on.

Nick laughed. "Don't worry, we're not going that way. The horses aren't quite that good on mountain trails."

Lindsay breathed a sigh of relief and turned Champ to follow Nick as he headed back the way they had come. Going down was even more difficult than going up, and the horses slid and stumbled often, yet always managed to keep their feet. Lindsay tried to do as Nick had suggested and not worry about the path Champ took, but there was only one thing her mind was more willing to think about, and that was Nick.

She watched him now, instead of the trail, her eyes taking in his masculine form as he leaned far back over his horse's hindquarters, his body moving in perfect rhythm with the pinto. So transfixed was she in staring at him that before she knew it they were down from the worst of the steep decline and on almost level ground again.

Nick headed down a trail through the pines. Within minutes, the trail suddenly opened up into the meadow where thirty-odd horses were watching them from a distance. One of the horses neighed at them and Champ instantly returned the greeting.

"You can tell he knows all these guys, can't you?" Nick commented. "We'll get a little closer so I can count them and make sure they're all here."

As they walked into the valley, Lindsay made her own count and came up with thirty-one. She was sure Nick had said at breakfast that there were thirty-two horses in the herd, which obviously meant one was missing. She kept silent, however, waiting to hear what total Nick arrived at.

"Good, they're all here," he said at last.

"How many did you say there's supposed to be?" she asked hesitantly.

"Thirty-two."

Lindsay paused. "I only counted thirty-one."

"Did you now? Well, I counted them three times and got thirty-two. They're all here," he repeated tensely.

Lindsay frowned and rechecked her count. Thirty-one. "I still only see thirty-one," she told him, shifting uncomfortably in her saddle.

"You better get your eyes checked. Or else learn how to count."

Lindsay could tell he was having a difficult time controlling his irritation. Why should he get mad just because she didn't agree with his count? she fumed silently. She was sure there was one horse missing, but if her lord and master was sure there wasn't, then there wasn't. Oh, well, maybe he could see a horse somewhere she couldn't, she told herself, trying to calm down. She had made him angry again, and that bothered her. It was so much nicer when he was pleasant, as he had been since lunch.

"Have you ever driven a herd before, by any chance?" Nick asked sardonically.

"As a matter of fact, I have," she answered confidently. But only twice, she added silently. And once it was cattle.

"Well, do me a favor, and just give Champ his head and let him do the work. He knows what to do. I don't need you screwing things up trying to play cowgirl," Nick ordered roughly.

"Why don't you for once just give me a chance to prove myself before you decide I'm totally incompetent?" she exploded.

"I don't have the time to give you a tryout just now, thank you. One mistake out here and these horses could scatter and run to God knows where and then we'd have one hell of a mess. I can handle this alone, you're just along for the ride. Just do as you're told and don't interfere with Champ," Nick said. Then he cantered off to the left side of the herd.

Fuming, Lindsay kicked Champ into a canter to the right. It took only a moment for her to realize the gelding was indeed very experienced in herding animals. He would cut and dodge around any horse that broke from the herd and drive it back with the rest of the horses. There were times when he needed guidance, and Lindsay directed him when she felt it would help. Several times she noticed Nick watching her, but she did not meet his gaze or give him the chance to criticize her.

It didn't take them long to get the herd out of the valley and on the broad trail that led back to the ranch. The horses knew where they were headed, and they all walked along easily in formation. As the horses spread out in a long line, Lindsay moved slightly to the side of them and recounted heads. She was certain now there were only thirty-one horses. She wondered if Nick had checked his count since they'd left the valley. She refused to ask him again, though, and they rode along slowly on opposite sides of the herd without exchanging any words the rest of the way back.

It was long after supper when they at last drove the horses into a large paddock at the ranch. Exhausted and famished, Lindsay gratefully handed Champ over to Jake and went to the main lodge to get something to eat. One of the cooks fixed Lindsay a plate of leftovers, which she downed in minutes. She then went to her cabin, stumbled into bed and fell into a deep, dreamless sleep.

Chapter Four

Lindsay groaned and put her pillow over her head as the alarm loudly announced it was time for her to get up. Could it really be morning? She rose slowly, and was pleased to find her muscles weren't very stiff from the long ride the day before. But to her surprise, she found her face sported a light sunburn. It hadn't seemed that warm out yesterday, but evidently Nick had been right in saying she should have some protection from the sun.

Well, even though he had been right about that, she wondered which one of them was right about the number of horses in the herd. Lindsay sighed deeply. For some strange reason, she almost hoped she had been wrong, knowing Nick would be angry if it turned out that she had counted right. Men and their egos, she thought and sighed again.

Lindsay froze for a moment as she started to get in the shower. Was this Lindsay Jordan wishing a man turned out to be right in an argument? Wasn't she the one who just two nights before had been thinking about how fun it was to put a chauvinistic man in his place once in a while? She shook her head, puzzled. After the way Nick had continually put her down, she should feel triumphant about catching him being dead wrong about something.

As she let the stinging hot spray cleanse her body, she pushed the confusing thoughts out of her mind. It was a bit premature to think about how she was going to react when she heard Nick was wrong—she didn't know if he was.

A half hour later she was grooming Sundance when Jake suddenly appeared outside the stall. He was grinning from ear to ear as he watched her for a moment without speaking.

With a feeling of dread, Lindsay finally broke the silence. "What's the matter with you?"

Jake chuckled. "I'd sure hate to be you today."

Lindsay's heart jumped into her throat. "What do you mean by that?" she asked, even though she knew what was coming.

"It seems you and Nick left one horse up in the mountains somewhere. You only brought in thirty-one."

Lindsay closed her eyes briefly. Even now that she knew for sure Nick had been wrong, she still didn't feel very excited about it, just as she had known she wouldn't. "So why don't you want to be me today?"

Jake raised an eyebrow, surprised at her reaction. "I thought you'd be ecstatic to find out you were right about there being a horse missing."

Lindsay stared at him. "How did you know I thought that?"

"Well, right after you two brought them in, Nick was telling me all about how you were so sure there were thirty-one horses in the herd, you know, joking about it, when all of a sudden my uncle stormed into the barn and asked Nick why he left one horse up there." Jake chuckled again. "You should have seen his face. I've never seen Nick so mad. He ran out in the paddock and spent ten minutes recounting the horses, but he had to admit in the end there were only thirty-one there."

Lindsay groaned, afraid to ask the next question. She took a deep breath. "So what happens now?"

"You two have to go back up there today and find Candy, the mare that's missing."

"What!"

"That's right." Jake laughed. "That's why I'm glad I'm not you today. Nick's fit to be tied."

"Some friend you are, enjoying my agony," she grumbled. "Why do I have to go along anyway? I don't know the area at all. Nick can find that horse easier without me along."

"That's what he said, too. But my uncle said as long as the two of you screwed up together, the two of you can go back and find her together."

"Wonderful," Lindsay muttered.

"Oh, it won't be that bad." Jake winked. "Come on, it's time for breakfast."

Lindsay walked up to the main lodge with Jake, hoping she wouldn't see Nick, even though she knew she couldn't avoid him for very long if they were going to be riding together all day again. She shuddered to think about how this day would go, knowing Nick would be in a foul mood and would probably make her miserable because of it.

As they entered the dining room, Lindsay quickly scanned the room for him, but to her vast relief, he was nowhere around. She bolted down her food without tasting it and returned to the solace of Sundance's stall without waiting for Jake. Try as she might, she couldn't stop her hands from shaking as she ran her fingers over Sundance's sleek sides. Hearing footsteps approaching, she froze in panic.

"You can't hide in here forever, you know," Jake's pleasant voice called over the stall door.

Lindsay breathed a sigh of relief. "I know. Where is he, anyway?" she asked nervously. "Ross made it clear to me at breakfast that we were supposed to get started right away."

"He'll be here in a minute. He's getting lunch packed in the saddlebags."

Lunch. How well she remembered their lunch from yesterday. Just thinking about Nick's arms around her after she'd dizzily dismounted brought a heated flush to her cheeks. She had to stop thinking about such things!

She cleared her throat. "Do I have to ride Champ again?"

Jake shook his head. "He wasn't that bad though, was he?"

"No, I guess he really wasn't," she admitted, reflecting on how the little gelding had gamely kept up to the large pinto all day. "So who am I riding today, then?"

"A gelding by the name of Thundercloud." Jake frowned. "Actually, I'm a little surprised Nick picked him for you. He's only four years old, and really only green broke. Nick's been training him, but he's still pretty unpredictable, and he's not that accomplished on the mountain trails yet."

Lindsay shrugged. "Maybe he hopes the horse will dump me out there and I'll break my neck," she said lightly, but she couldn't shake the feeling that there might be some truth to that.

"Jake! Is she ready?"

Lindsay shuddered at the booming voice. "Where's that cowboy hat I gave you back last night?" she whispered hurriedly.

Jake laughed out loud. "I don't believe you. Where's the spunky girl from yesterday who told Nick she wasn't about to wear a hat?"

"Never mind. I just don't want to add any more fuel to his fire. I'm sure he's going to find plenty of other things to yell at me about today, anyway. Will you please just get me that hat?" she pleaded.

Jake returned with it.

"Thanks," she mumbled as she put it on her head. Taking a deep breath, she walked quickly outside and over to where Nick sat on his pinto. A tall gray horse stood tied next to him, impatiently tossing his head.

"This is Thundercloud?" she asked in a surprisingly steady voice. Nick nodded curtly, his face blank. Lindsay mounted quickly, and the gelding danced beneath her.

"Be careful with him," Nick warned flatly as he turned and cantered off, "he's still a little green."

No kidding, Lindsay thought after she touched her heels to Thundercloud's sides and felt the young horse bolt like a shot. The horse immediately caught up to the pinto and then pushed his nose out, trying to get enough rein to dash past the older horse. Lindsay pulled hard on the reins, bringing him back in line, but not calming him much.

"My compliments to the trainer of this horse," she said sarcastically, disgusted at him for sticking her with a hot-headed youngster that would take all her attention and skill throughout the day. "He's really well trained."

Nick looked down at her coldly. "If he's too much for you, say so now. I'm sure I can find some placid old horse for you to ride."

Lindsay glared back at him. "That's quite all right. I've had experience with young horses before. What I can't figure out is why you honored me so much by letting me ride him."

He shrugged noncommittally. "He needs the exercise. You're so sure you can do anything, I thought I'd see how you handle a green horse."

Lindsay looked up at him, but he refused to meet her glance. They were silent for several miles before Nick finally spoke up again.

"You might as well say it now and get it over with," he said tensely.

"What?"

"You know what," he answered impatiently.

Lindsay thought she knew what he meant, but she kept silent, studying his hard, chiseled features. He was angry all right, that much was clear. His normally full lips were drawn tightly together in a pinched scowl, his brows were furrowed and his eyes were the color of dark storm clouds.

When he didn't continue, she spoke at last. "What is it you expect me to say?"

"I told you so." His voice was deceptively calm. "I've never known a woman yet who could resist saying it."

"I don't imagine you've given too many women the opportunity to say it," she replied quietly.

"As few as possible. However, when the opportunity did arise, they've always jumped to meet it. I'm sure you're no different."

Lindsay felt a small prick of anger growing inside her. "Look, this conversation is ridiculous. So I was right and you were wrong. So what? Mistakes happen sometimes, at least they do to me. It doesn't throw me into a rage to be wrong. Maybe if you were more of a man, it wouldn't throw you into one either."

Without waiting for a response from him, she kicked Thundercloud into a gallop. The gelding eagerly took off, stretching out farther with every stride. Lindsay could hear Nick galloping behind her, yelling at her to stop. It was the last thing she felt like doing, but she knew she shouldn't let the young horse run like this. She began pulling back on the reins, but Thundercloud refused to slow down. Feeling a little anxious at the prospect of having an uncontrollable runaway on her hands, Lindsay jerked back hard on the reins. To her relief, she felt the horse reluctantly respond; he finally began to slow his pace.

In a matter of seconds, Nick drew alongside her. One glance was enough to tell her he was absolutely livid.

"You crazy fool!" he exploded. "You could have both been killed. That horse has never been run full out over this terrain before. I thought you had more sense."

Lindsay bit off the retort she had been about to make. She forced herself to smile. "You're completely right, Nick. I was wrong, and I admit it," she said in a voice that was calmer than she felt. "You see how easy it is to say that?"

Nick stared at her for a moment in total disbelief. "You didn't have to go to such an extreme to make a point."

"I didn't really plan it," Lindsay admitted quietly. "But it was a stupid thing to do with a young horse, I know."

His eyes narrowed as he studied her closely. She had taken him totally off guard with this turn of events. "Well, at least you're smart enough to realize how dangerous it was," he said begrudgingly. "I see you wore a hat today. And I also see you got a little sunburned yesterday."

"So you were right about that, too. But a little sunburn never hurt anyone."

"Maybe not, but why get sunburned if you can prevent it by wearing a hat, at least until you're used to the sun out here? And your dizzy spell yesterday?" he prompted.

"It was probably from hunger and too much sun, just as you so eagerly pointed out." She paused for a moment and looked him right in the eye. "And what about the number of horses in that herd?"

Nick met her challenging smile with an easy one of his own. "You must have been right about there being only thirty-one."

"There. Was that so painful? And all without one 'I told you so' from me." Lindsay smiled brightly again, glad he seemed to be over his dark mood at last. He had to be right about three things to her one to be cheerful. She chuckled to herself.

As they rode in companionable silence, Nick kept watching Lindsay out of the corner of his eye. He was still amazed at her. When he'd found out they had really left one horse in the mountains, he'd been furious at himself. Why hadn't he been more careful when he counted the herd? Still, he'd have sworn there were thirty-two horses in that valley. But no, Lindsay had counted thirty-one. That was the real blow, of course.

He'd tried his darnedest to talk Ross into letting him go alone to look for Candy today. The thought of spending the day with a haughty, smug city female was more than he could stand. He'd fully expected Lindsay to make it hell for him today, constantly reminding him how right she'd been. And the way he had been so hard on her the past couple of days, he really couldn't have blamed her if she had taken that attitude.

But no, she hadn't been that way at all. She'd shown him she wasn't going to rub it in that he was wrong. He shook his head as he glanced over at her again. She had a little smile on her lovely face, but it wasn't smug, just pleasant. She appeared to be relaxed and enjoying herself. Dammit, she sure had him baffled.

They rode for several more miles until they came to a fork in the trail. Nick glanced up the steep trail that led to the small ledge overlooking the valley, then frowned at Lindsay. A twinge of guilt tugged at him. He regretted choosing Thundercloud as a mount for her. It had really been a childish thing to do, he chastised himself. He had deliberately picked a horse he hoped would give her problems.

Lindsay noticed his hesitancy and the conflicting emotions that were playing across his face. "What's wrong?" she asked finally.

"That ledge up there gives the best view there is, and it would save us a lot of time, but I'm not so sure Thundercloud is up to a climb like this," he said at last.

"You mean you're not so sure he can handle it with me aboard instead of you?"

He shook his head impatiently. "That's not what I said."

"But if you were on him, would you try it?" she pressed.

Nick hesitated for a moment, then shrugged. "Probably."

"Then let's go."

"All right. It's your neck," he grumbled, and turned his horse up the steep path.

Lindsay took a deep breath and urged Thundercloud to follow the pinto. She had her doubts about attempting this, too, but she'd be darned if she'd let Nick know that. She only hoped her uncertainty wouldn't be conveyed to Thundercloud, who might become nervous and then stumble.

Her fears proved unjustified, however. They reached the ledge without any problems other than a few slips and slides. Just how much it actually took out of Thundercloud, however, was evident by the way his sides were heaving and the amount of froth that was on his neck as the young horse fought to catch his breath on the ledge.

Lindsay patted the gelding. "See? That wasn't too bad. He hardly stumbled at all, but he is a little tired."

Nick's glance took in the horse as he reached in his saddlebags for a pair of binoculars. "Yes, I'd say he's tired. But don't get too cocky. You're not back down yet. Going up is the easy part."

Lindsay smiled confidently at him, but inwardly she groaned. She'd forgotten about getting back down. Oh, well, she told herself cheerfully, after a little rest she was sure Thundercloud would be just fine. She lifted her eyes out to the valley below, and was once more spellbound by its sheer beauty. It didn't seem quite the same without the horses in it, but it was still breathtaking. She searched the whole valley floor carefully, but saw no sign of the mare.

"I don't see her," Nick said resignedly. "I was hoping she'd be right here so we wouldn't have to travel much. There are a number of other places she could be."

"You don't think anything's happened to her, do you?" Lindsay asked anxiously.

He shook his head. "I doubt it. Candy was born and raised in these mountains. I can't imagine her hurting herself out here. Still, you never know." He looked over at Thundercloud again briefly. "We'll give him a few more minutes, and then we'd better get moving. We've got a lot of territory to cover."

Lindsay nodded and returned her attention to her horse. His breathing was just about back to normal, and some of his energy had returned as he was starting to shift his weight around nervously and paw at the rocky ledge beneath his hooves.

"Relax, boy," she said soothingly and patted his damp neck.

Thundercloud would not be easily calmed, however, and with each passing minute the young gelding became more restless. Still pawing the ground with one front hoof, he snorted and then neighed loudly. A bird's distant chirping was all that answered the anxious horse's call.

"Thanks for the confirmation that there's no horse in that valley, Thundercloud. If Candy was down there, she'd have answered that call for sure." Nick turned and put his binoculars back into the saddlebags. "Well, we better get moving."

Lindsay nodded and steadied herself for the long trip down. The pinto led the way slowly and carefully, and she was sure Nick was being cautious on her account, and she was grateful. Thundercloud wasn't handling the trail as well going down, and he stumbled and slid frequently. Lindsay tried to help him but the horse was getting more upset with each step he took. She was thankful that there was another horse barring Thundercloud's way, or she was sure he would have panicked and tried to bolt down the steep decline. Good rider or not, Lindsay knew there would be little she could do if the horse did something like that.

The trip seemed to take forever, and Lindsay rarely took her eyes off of the trail in front of her to see how much farther they had to go. Finally, she heard the change in the sound of the pinto's steps as he made his way back onto the dirt trail from the rock.

Whew, we made it, she thought. *Just a few more feet to go, and we'll be back on the regular trail.*

In that instant, Thundercloud felt his rider relax her hold on the reins, and he lunged for the end of the rocky trail to the dirt where the pinto stood waiting.

"No!" Lindsay cried out, but it was too late. The young gray horse had slipped as he jumped, and he fell forward and down on his knees. The jolt of the sudden forward motion threw Lindsay out of the saddle and over the gelding's neck. She landed heavily in the grass, her hands just barely breaking her fall before her face hit the ground.

Shaken but unhurt, she looked up just in time to see Thundercloud jump to his feet and take off at a dead run in the direction of the ranch. With a groan, she let her head drop back on her arms.

"Lindsay? Lindsay!"

She could hear Nick's anxious voice, but she didn't want to get up and face him. She laid there with her eyes closed, wishing she could melt right into the ground and disappear.

"Lindsay! Are you all right?"

This time his voice was very near, and a second later she felt his hands on her arms. Carefully, he rolled her over.

Lindsay sighed, opened her eyes and smiled faintly. "I'm okay."

"God, you scared me to death! Why didn't you answer me?" he demanded.

Lindsay carefully searched his face, looking for anger and sarcasm, but instead she saw only genuine concern. Their faces were only inches apart as he continued to support her with one arm. With the other hand, he gently brushed some dirt off of her cheek. Lindsay felt her heart pounding dreadfully loud in her chest, whether from the fall or from being in such close contact with him she couldn't be sure. His light touch on her face sent shivers up and down her spine, and it was all she could do to keep from reaching up and touching those full, sensuous lips with her trembling fingers.

For a moment she thought he was going to bend down and kiss her, but suddenly she was being pushed forward to a sitting position and then he released his hold on her. A bit confused, she searched his face again, but his eyes were now carefully veiled and impersonal.

"I'm sorry, Nick," she stammered at last, feeling he was waiting for her to say something. "It happened so fast, I didn't have a chance to react."

"It's not your fault. I knew better than to have you ride him. He wasn't trained well enough for this kind of ride," he said lightly.

"Well, he's got to get experience some time," she pointed out somewhat dubiously.

Nick shook his head. "Not with you on him." He continued quickly as he saw her start to protest. "That doesn't mean you're not a capable rider. I hate to admit it, but you do know how to ride pretty well. But there was no reason for you to risk getting hurt by riding that horse."

"So why did you want me to ride him in the first place?" she asked quietly.

Nick looked away, refusing to meet her eyes. "I'm sorry. It was a stupid thing for me to do." He paused a moment, but still wouldn't look at her. He wasn't sure why, but he felt he owed her the truth. "You're just so damn sure of yourself, I guess I wanted to put you in your place by having you ride Thundercloud. It's not that I wanted you to get hurt or anything, I just wanted to take a little of that cockiness out of you."

Lindsay stared at him, amazed at his honesty. She wasn't surprised at his motives, but for him to humbly admit them was something else.

"You're sure you're not hurt?" he asked again anxiously.

Lindsay stood up slowly and dusted herself off. "I'm fine, really." She looked up just in time to see Thundercloud's tail disappear. "Some loyalty that horse has. He dumps me and heads for home without a look back."

Nick chuckled. "He didn't look a bit guilty, did he?"

"How are we going to find that mare and get back again now?" Lindsay moaned as she finally realized their situation.

"We'll have to forget about Candy for today, and I guess you'll just have to ride back double with me."

"I can't ride all that way behind the saddle on your horse's kidneys," she protested. "His back will get sore for sure."

The look Nick gave her was one of surprise and respect. "You're right about that. We'll leave the saddle here and ride bareback so we can keep our weight closer to where it's supposed to be on his back."

Lindsay felt a light blush rise in her cheeks. Ride all those miles sitting so close to him? She couldn't do that, she told herself.

Yet what alternative did she have? She certainly couldn't walk all the way back, nor would Nick want to when he could ride. Although the thought of having his body that close to hers for such a long time sent shudders of excitement through her.

She watched nervously as Nick removed the saddle and blankets from the pinto's back and sat them carefully under a tree. He led the horse over to where she was standing.

"I'll get on first and then help you up," he told her, and with one swift motion he jumped up effortlessly on the large horse's back.

"Maybe it would be easier if I stood on a rock or something," she suggested, doubtfully looking up at the pinto.

Nick smiled. "Just give me your hand and jump a little bit. I can swing you up."

Frowning, Lindsay held up her hand and Nick grasped it firmly. She braced her other hand on the horse's rump, and jumped. She would never have made it up alone, but with

Nick's strong pull she landed easily behind him. He let go of her hand and reined the pinto back toward the ranch.

Lindsay sat stiffly behind him, aware of their closeness. She didn't know what to do with her hands. If they only walked, she didn't need to hang on to him, but what if he decided to trot or canter? She'd be eternally mortified if she fell off while riding with him, which meant she had no choice but to hang on.

Suddenly, she felt the pinto turn sharply to the right. She desperately grabbed Nick's waist to keep from falling. She felt him shaking, and it was a few seconds before she realized he was laughing.

"You'd better hang on," he said, turning his head around to glance at her. "You never know when this horse might make a sudden move."

"You turned him on purpose!" she accused.

"This time, but only to prove a point." He chuckled again. "I won't break, you know. You don't have to be afraid to hold on."

Feeling extremely self-conscious, she maintained a light grasp on his narrow waist. There's not an ounce of excess fat here, she thought. She could feel his tight stomach muscles through the flannel just as easily as if he'd had no shirt on at all. She tried to keep her thighs back and away from his, but sitting back forced her upper body too far forward. Her breasts brushed against his back. That was worse than allowing their thighs to touch occasionally. She was keeping her whole body very stiff, and Nick felt her rigidness.

"Just relax, city girl. Don't you ever ride bareback where you come from?" The mocking tone had returned to his voice.

"I've ridden bareback a lot, thank you, but mostly by myself. It's different back here," she explained lamely. She paused for a moment. "What have you really got against city girls anyway?" she asked quietly.

She felt him tense noticeably, and she was instantly sorry she'd asked the question.

"I've known too many phony, hotshot snobs," he replied curtly.

"Meaning me?" The words were out before she could stop them.

"I didn't say that," he said after a moment.

"Why do you work here when all summer you have to cater to city people?"

"Guests are usually all right. They don't try to put on airs with the employees. It's when a city girl tries to pretend she's a born cowgirl and decides to work here that the problems begin."

Lindsay was stung by his cold voice. Still, he hadn't explained his prejudice adequately. "You must have had a pretty bad experience with one city girl to hate all of us on sight," she pressed him.

"You're right about that," he admitted drily. "I was married to one for two years."

Lindsay was glad he couldn't see her face because she knew her mouth was wide open in surprise. She never thought of him being married.

It was several moments before she again found her tongue. "You're divorced?" she finally asked, holding her breath though she wasn't sure why.

"Very much so. But I consider all of that past history and a closed subject. So let's drop it, okay?" His voice left no room for argument.

"Sure." Nick married and divorced? To a woman from the city? It hardly seemed possible. Yet it did explain his aversion to city girls. He must not have had a good marriage. There were so many things she wanted to ask him, but she knew any more questions would only anger him. Even now, little of the tension had left his body. She couldn't be sorry, though, because she had learned something about him, and for some reason she wanted to get to know him better.

Time passed slowly for Lindsay. Nick relaxed again, and Lindsay gradually loosened up. She'd even given up trying to keep her thighs from touching his.

Although she fought it, Lindsay felt herself beginning to doze off. Her back had started to ache, whether from sitting stiff on the pinto for so long or from her earlier fall she didn't know. What she did know was that the combination of sleepiness and her sore back made her gradually lean more and more against Nick.

Her mind drifted around lazily until she was almost in a trance. Before she knew it, her head had dropped against Nick's shoulder and she closed her eyes drowsily. It felt so good to just rest against his strong form with her arms around him, so sensuous to move along in time to the horse's swinging gait with him so close to her.

The next thing she knew, she was dreaming, at least she thought it must be a dream, for she was laying on the grass with Nick sprawled out next to her. He was stroking and caressing her whole body, kissing her lips with searing passion. She answered his every touch and kiss with equal rapture, until soon they were leisurely shedding their clothes. He was whispering words of love and desire to her as he slowly moved on top of her, and she moaned with a yearning she had never known was possible. . . .

Lindsay awoke with a start at the sudden movement of the horse beneath her. It took her a full minute to realize where she was, but only a second more to remember her vivid dream. Her face flushed a deep crimson, and she abruptly dropped her hands from Nick's waist and shifted her body back away from him. She held herself stiffly once more to keep from touching him, her hands resting on her own thighs.

Her whole body was still tingling from the dream, and she chastised herself angrily. How could she possibly have dreamt such a thing? What if she had called out his name while she slept, or moaned, or, worse yet, caressed him like she had done in her dream?

Nick looked at her briefly over his shoulder, but his face gave away nothing. "You're awake?" he commented and stretched as much as he could on the horse. "I'm glad. With you resting on me like that I was beginning to get a little stiff from leaning forward all the time."

"I—I'm sorry," she stammered awkwardly. "I didn't mean to drop off. You shouldn't have let me."

"You were so peaceful it seemed a shame to wake you," he said easily. "Pleasant dreams?" he asked, turning to look at her again.

Lindsay felt renewed color rush into her face, and she looked at the ground, refusing to meet his eyes. She must have given something away while she slept! But what? "Why do you ask?" she dodged his question.

"Just curious. I looked at you once, and you had quite a smile on your face."

Could that be all? she wondered. "Actually, I don't think I was dreaming. At least I can't remember what it was about if I was," she lied. He dropped the subject then, and she breathed a sigh of relief.

"How about a short lope to get our blood circulating again? I could use a change, and this is a good stretch for it."

"Sure," Lindsay agreed readily. Anything to take her mind off that dream.

"Ah, you better hang on again. But not too hard. If you get out of balance and you've got a death grip on me, you're liable to pull me right off with you," he warned. "If you feel like you're going to fall or something, just tell me to stop. Understand?"

Lindsay giggled. "Yes, I certainly do. I remember once when I was trail guiding at the stable in Chicago with Sundance, I had to take a little boy bareback with me because he was afraid to ride alone. Everyone else wanted to trot, so I told the boy to hang on tight, and we started to trot a little. Well, that little kid held on as tight as he could and then some, and after about two strides he was bouncing up and down. Even though he wasn't real big he pulled me off my horse. Luckily neither one of us got hurt, and when we got back on he wanted to trot again because it was so much fun! But I'd had enough of that." She laughed at the memory.

Nick chuckled. "Some people have to learn the hard way. Well, we'll just be loping so we shouldn't have any problems. Ready?"

Lindsay nodded and put her arms lightly around his waist. Before she had time to think about anything, they were off in a long-strided, easy canter. She smiled in pleasure at the wonderful feel of the rocking-horse gait of the pinto beneath her and Nick's firm body in front of her. She had never felt more alive.

They had cantered about a mile when the trail started a gradual incline. Lindsay soon found herself sliding back until she was almost on the pinto's hindquarters. Because of the powerful thrust the horse gave with his hind legs at each stride, the ride became considerably rougher the farther back Lindsay slid. Nick's warning about hanging on too tight rang in her ears, and she was reluctant to increase her hold on him.

Nick must have noticed her bouncing. She felt him start to rein the pinto back into a walk. However, in making the transition, the horse broke into a trot instead of a walk. The jolt was too much for Lindsay, and she started to bounce hard, uncontrollably out of sync with the horse. Still she refused to hang on any tighter to Nick, and after a couple more strides she felt herself getting precariously close to falling off.

"Nick—" she cried out.

He turned slightly and reached back with his right arm to grab onto her. He reined back sharply and yelled "whoa" to his horse, but the pinto stopped one stride too late. Even with Nick's firm grasp around her arm, Lindsay could keep herself on the horse no longer, and with one last mighty bounce she was off. Nick was pulled off right along with her.

They hit the ground with a thump almost simultaneously. The pinto stopped a second later and stood quietly gazing at the two humans with an expression of surprise in his large brown eyes.

Nick had landed half on top of her, and as soon as she caught her breath, Lindsay struggled to disentangle herself from him. After a moment of futile effort on her part, she realized Nick wasn't cooperating; in fact, he hadn't moved at all. She sat up as best as she could and tried to look at him, but his head was turned away from her.

"Nick?" she called anxiously, but still he did not stir. "Nick!" she repeated, panic rising in her voice.

Suddenly, he rolled over and smiled. "I'm okay," he said in a tone that mocked hers from earlier in the day when she'd fallen off Thundercloud.

"Oh, you—!" Lindsay exclaimed as she slapped his arm. "That wasn't very nice of you to scare me like that."

"Just giving you a taste of your own medicine," he replied. His face was very close to hers, and he was staring intently in her eyes.

Lindsay squirmed under his scrutiny. "You're sort of squishing me," she said lamely, looking pointedly down at his lower body, which was pinning her down.

With one quick movement, he had shifted himself so he was next to her. With his head propped up on one elbow and his other hand draped casually across her waist, he smiled warmly. "Better?"

No, she thought, *you're still too close.*

But she nodded in agreement, and met his gaze for a moment. It was so easy to get lost in those swimming blue eyes of his. Her heart was in her throat again, and even though she wanted desperately to get up and run away from his close contact, she was powerless to move her body.

"Now there's a good horse," she said at last, trying to break the spell that was slowly overcoming her. "He stayed right here instead of running back to the ranch."

"Um-hm," he mumbled agreement, and reached out to lightly stroke her hair. "Your hair has come loose. I like it better down," he told her quietly as he toyed with the soft auburn curls.

"You know, maybe I'm not cut out for this job after all. I've fallen off a horse twice in one day. That's pretty embarrassing." Lindsay looked up at Nick again, hoping he would take the bait and give her a pitch on how she wasn't qualified to work at the ranch. But she saw no sarcasm or mocking look in his eyes. What she did see was unmistakable desire.

"I'm sure there's certain things you're qualified for," he whispered, and bent his head slowly down to hers.

At the touch of his lips to hers, Lindsay felt immediate flames of passion burn through her entire body. His lips moved over hers tantalizingly slowly, and she responded instinctively. As his mouth opened hers enough for his tongue to begin a leisurely exploration, she reached up and put both her arms around his neck, drawing him closer to her. Gradually his kiss changed from slow and gentle to bruising and demanding, until she was left gasping for air. She turned her head to the side in order to break contact from his mouth for a moment so that she could catch her breath, and he in turn kissed and nibbled her ear.

"You really are beautiful," he told her quietly, his own breathing impaired.

Lindsay heard a low moan escape from her lips, and she brought her mouth back under his. She couldn't believe the feelings he was bringing out in her, feelings she'd never thought existed. Her whole body was on fire, and she ached with desire for him in a way she'd never experienced before. His mouth was still hard and crushing, his tongue pursuing hers with a purpose seemingly all its own. His hand moved slowly from her hair to her neck, then her shoulder, and down to her small, round breasts. His touch was gentle and teasing at first, but soon increased to firm, demanding caresses. Lindsay moaned again and arched her body against him, in such pleasure that it was almost torture.

This was even more wonderful than her dream had been, she thought to herself in amazement.

Her dream! This was just like her dream had been, she realized suddenly. But no, she couldn't let it turn out the same way her dream had. Why, she hardly knew this man, and he had never given her much indication that he liked her at all.

It took every ounce of her strength and willpower to grab Nick's hand and move it away. Then, she used both hands to push against his shoulders to break contact from his mouth. When his lips were at last inches away from hers, she ducked under his arm and pulled herself into a sitting position.

"Nick, I, uh, think we should be going," she said shakily.

"Right now?" His voice held a touch of irritation.

"Yes." She glanced at him but looked away again quickly, unable to bear the look he gave her. His expression changed from desire, to disbelief, and then to disgust.

Nick stood up and walked over to the patient pinto. In one deft motion, he was on the horse's back. Without looking at her, he spoke sharply. "Well, let's go."

As Lindsay rose on shaking legs, she heard the sound of galloping hooves in the distance. She looked in the direction of the ranch, and to her surprise saw a lone horse and rider approaching. She stood where she was, waiting for the person to reach them. In a few minutes, the rider was close enough for her to recognize. It was Jake.

"What the hell?" Nick muttered as Jake stopped in front of them.

"Are you two all right?" Jake asked quickly.

"We're fine," Nick answered before Lindsay could speak. "What are you doing out here?"

"Thundercloud came in at a dead run by himself, and you ask what I'm doing out here?" Jake asked incredulously. "Don't you think we all got a little worried when he came in without Lindsay? What happened?"

Lindsay quickly but briefly explained what happened.

"How is Thundercloud?" she questioned Jake anxiously.

"He seems all right, but I imagine he'll be pretty stiff in the morning."

"So will I," Lindsay mumbled under her breath.

Jake turned to Nick. "How far back is your saddle?"

"Quite a ways. I'll get it tomorrow when I look for Candy again."

"You don't have to worry about that. She came in herself about an hour after you two went out."

"What?" Lindsay cried. "You mean we came out here and wasted the day for nothing?" Although she tried to avoid Nick's glance, she couldn't help but see the infuriated look he gave her. She wondered vaguely why he wasn't upset about wasted time. He only seemed upset at her.

"Well, we still have three people and two horses to get back to the ranch," Jake pointed out. "How should we work this?"

"I'll ride back with you," Lindsay said quickly. She couldn't bear riding so close to Nick any more today. She needed time to think and regain her wits.

Nick threw her a questioning, sarcastic look. "Behind the saddle on that poor horse's kidneys?"

"It's not that far back to the ranch from here, I'm sure it won't bother him much. Besides, your horse could probably use a break for the rest of the way," she said, hoping it sounded plausible to them both.

Nick shrugged. "If you're going to do that, I'm going back for my saddle today. See you later," he stated coldly. He turned the pinto sharply and rode off at a gallop, his blood boiling.

He didn't know whether to be more angry at Lindsay for stopping him or himself for allowing such feelings to emerge. How could he let her get to him like that? She was beautiful, she was intelligent and she liked to keep him guessing, but she was city born and raised, and she was only here for a summer of amusement.

But never had any woman made him ache the way she did. And never had he wanted a woman as much as he had wanted her back there in the grass. In the grass! Hell, what was the matter with him? He was acting like a star-struck, hot-blooded teenager.

His stomach tightened as her flippant words to Jake came back to him. *You mean we came out here and wasted the day for nothing?* Wasted, hell. If she hadn't suddenly gotten flighty on him and if Jake hadn't shown up, it sure wouldn't have been a wasted day. But if that's all it was to her, he would make damn sure he never "wasted" her time again. He was through with Lindsay Jordan.

Lindsay watched Nick ride away, knowing he was angry at her. She sighed and turned to Jake. He gave her a questioning look, but she ignored it. She didn't feel like talking about it, even though she could tell Jake suspected something had gone on between her and Nick.

Wordlessly she walked up to him, put her foot in the stirrup and swung up behind the saddle. They walked all the way back to the ranch without once mentioning what else had happened during the day.

Chapter Five

Lindsay spent the next three days riding various trail horses she and Nick had brought in from the mountain valley. Not once in those three days did she see Nick. She knew he must be avoiding her, but why he found it necessary was beyond her. Her mind had gone over the events of the day they'd been looking for the lost mare. In fact, she'd been able to think of little else other than Nick and the incredible way it had felt when he'd kissed and touched her. The only conclusion she could come to was that he was angry with her for stopping him before he'd gone as far as he'd wanted to go. And that could only mean he'd just used her that day as an outlet for some sexual feelings he must have for her.

It was funny that idea should upset her as much as it did. After all, she'd had men lusting after her before, and although she'd never given in to a man who wanted only a one-night stand, it had never bothered her a great deal when a man had propositioned her. She merely let him know she wasn't interested, and that was that. She'd never given any of them a second thought.

But it tore at her terribly that Nick didn't care about her one bit, actually disliked her, yet was willing, even eager to make love to her. When she was totally honest with herself, she knew she had been very close to letting Nick have his way that afternoon. That he could arouse such feelings in her was beyond her comprehension.

She had tried to reason with herself and rationalize the situation. He was handsome, yes. He had a fantastic body, yes. And when he wanted to, he could be pleasant and charming. But he was also arrogant, chauvinistic, domineering and patronizing—qualities she'd always detested in a man. So why could she think of nothing but him these past three days? Why did she long for him to touch her, to feel his lips on hers again? Why did the mere mention of his name send her pulse into triple time? Lindsay had given up trying to understand it all.

For the past three days she'd tried to catch Jake alone to ask him about Nick's ex-wife, but she'd been unsuccessful. Finally, on the fourth night after she and Nick had looked for Candy in the mountains, she found Jake by himself oiling tack in the barn.

But now that she was at last alone with him, she couldn't think of a tactful way to bring up the subject.

"I haven't seen Nick for a few days," she began after a few minutes, trying to keep her voice casual.

Jake didn't look up from the bridle he was oiling, and remained silent.

"Have you?" she asked after a moment.

He looked up at her briefly before he spoke. "Have I seen Nick?" he repeated. "Not much since the day Thundercloud threw you." He paused, eyeing her carefully. "I told him what I thought of his decision to have you ride Thundercloud when he came in that night, and we sort of had an argument. He's been in a foul mood ever since, and I'm just as glad he's making himself scarce lately.''

Lindsay swallowed nervously. She wished Jake would stop looking at her so knowingly. ''I didn't have to ride Thundercloud, and he didn't want me to take him up that steep trail,'' she pointed out quietly.

Jake shook his head. ''Nick was in a bad mood when I found you two. I know there's more to it than either one of you will admit. Just what happened that day?''

''Nothing, really.'' Her voice didn't sound convincing, even to her. ''We actually got along pretty well most of the time. We did some talking, and that's about all.''

''What did you talk about?''

''Well, he did mention he was married before. To a city girl.''

Jake raised one eyebrow in surprise. ''He told you about Julie?''

''Not really. He didn't even tell me her name. Just that he was married for two years to a city girl and then got divorced.'' She paused and took a deep, shaky breath. ''What happened?''

Jake returned his attention to rubbing oil into the leather bridle. His voice took on a slightly bitter tone. ''Julie was a beautiful woman; long blond hair, blue eyes and quite a figure. She came out here as a guest at the beginning of the season and set her hooks into Nick right away. Two weeks after she went home again, she came back and begged for a job. Nick talked my uncle into hiring her, even though she couldn't ride and didn't have any experience. She was quite the manipulator. They got married the next spring.''

Nick had been charmed by a city woman? It hardly seemed possible. She waited anxiously for Jake to continue.

"At first, Nick seemed very happy, and so did Julie. But she flirted, and they were always fighting about some guest Nick had caught her flirting with. That season she got really lazy, too, and tried to get out of every bit of work she could. She missed the city and spent most of her time going into town. Nick took it only so long and then he called her on that, too. They got in a horrendous fight one night, and she took off in a huff on Spy, one of our best stallions." Jake frowned at the memory. "She couldn't handle a gentle gelding, let alone a stallion. Of course Spy bolted on her, and she couldn't do a thing to stop him. They finally got back two hours later, Spy on three legs. He'd stepped in a hole while he was running and broke his leg."

"You mean she rode him all the way in on a broken leg?" Lindsay asked incredulously.

"That girl didn't have an ounce of sense. Even if she had known better, she probably would have ridden him in anyway so she wouldn't have to walk." His voice caught a little as he continued. "We had to put Spy down. He was only five years old and had fathered two fillies, both of them gorgeous. It was such a waste. I don't think Nick ever forgave her for killing that horse, and neither did the rest of us.

"Their marriage went steadily downhill after that, but Nick still tried to make it work. The next season he caught her in bed with one of the guests. That was the last straw, of course. Nick was in such a rage I thought he was going to kill them both. If there's one thing Nick can't take, it's infidelity. Loyalty means everything to him. Anyway, that was that. They got a divorce as soon as Nick could arrange it."

Lindsay stared at Jake, her eyes wide in disbelief and wonder. She was so astounded by the story that she couldn't think of a single thing to say.

Jake flashed her a grin. "Anyway, that was quite a few years ago, but I guess it's safe to say that Nick never really got over it. He's avoided getting involved with any woman since then. Oh, it's not like he's been celibate or anything, and he does seem to always have some beautiful woman, single or married, chasing after him. He wouldn't be human if he didn't take advantage of some of them. He just doesn't get close to them. Well, at least not emotionally." Jake chuckled and winked.

Lindsay felt her cheeks grow crimson as she understood Jake's meaning. So Nick liked to love 'em and leave 'em. He liked to have his fun and then toss them aside. She had guessed as much already, so why did Jake's confirmation bring such a sinking feeling?

"Oh, by the way, I wouldn't mention to Nick that I told you all of that. He's a very private person, and he wouldn't take too kindly to the fact that I confided in you."

"Why did you tell me?" she asked, suddenly curious.

Jake rested the bridle on his lap and looked up at her for several moments before he finally answered her.

"I have a feeling that you may be the one person who could bring Nick around again. And I know something happened between you two the other day. I haven't seen him react to a woman so strongly as he does to you in a very long time." Jake shrugged and picked up the bridle again. "Anyway, I just thought you should know."

Lindsay shifted her weight restlessly. Nick reacted strongly to her all right, but in a negative way. Bring Nick around? That was a joke.

"Thanks for telling me, whatever the reason." She stretched her arms high above her head and groaned. "You know, even though I've spent almost every waking minute in the saddle since I got here, I've terribly neglected riding Sundance. I think I'll take her out for awhile now. See you later."

Jake waved, and as she headed to her horse's stall she heard him whistling as he worked. He certainly was a nice person, she thought. It was always so easy to talk to him. And he was nice-looking, too. Still, when her thoughts turned to romantic, there was only one person who came to mind. And it wasn't Jake.

Lindsay frowned as she quickly saddled Sundance. Why couldn't she get Nick Leighton off her brain? She'd just found out for certain that he would never get involved with her at the level she wanted, so why couldn't that be that? Besides, she was only going to be here for one glorious, wonderful summer, and then it was back to the drudge of everyday life in Chicago. Back to a high-paying but tedious job. Back to an empty apartment. Back to reality.

As Sundance trotted slowly out of the barnyard, a deep feeling of melancholy overtook Lindsay, a feeling she just couldn't shake. She sighed and pulled Sundance down to a walk and gave her a loose rein. What was the matter with her anyway? How could she let a man affect her like this? Especially a man like Nick. She'd come to Wyoming to breathe some new life into her existence, not to get involved with a man.

If she had any sense she'd pack up and go home now and forget about this foolishness entirely. After all, what was she really going to accomplish out here anyway? Her true life was unequivocally in Chicago, that much she couldn't change. Coming out here was just a silly, irresponsible, childish thing to do.

Take time to live a little, honey.

Her father's words came back to her, and with them, her promise to him that she wouldn't follow in his tragic footsteps. She sighed. For better or worse, she would stick it out at the ranch until fall. Besides, she couldn't just up and quit now after Ross had given her the job and counted on her to work there the whole summer. She was simply going to have to keep a very tight check on her emotions, or better yet forget about Nick entirely.

Lindsay looked up with a start as she felt Sundance stop. She was amazed to find herself in front of the small lake that was three miles from the ranch. She patted the mare and sighed again. "At least you brought me to a pretty place," she mumbled.

She'd been down by this lake several times before, although it was well away from the main trail. It was a secluded spot, with trees surrounding the water. There was only one break in the dense foliage, where the trail from the ranch could come through.

Lindsay gazed longingly at the water. It was dusk now, and without the sun warming it she knew the lake would be very cold. Even the air was getting pretty chilly already. But still the calm, sparkling water beckoned to her.

She dismounted and tied Sundance to a nearby tree and walked up to the edge of the lake. She looked all around nervously, but she was sure no one would possibly come out to this particular spot so late.

"I'll probably get pneumonia, but what the hell," she mumbled.

She shed her clothes quickly, before she could change her mind, and dumped them in a pile under a tree. Taking a deep breath, she ran and made a clean dive into the water. An instant later she was at the surface, gasping and crying out in spite of herself. The water was freezing! Her teeth began chattering immediately from the cold, but she made no move to get out. It was immensely refreshing and invigorating, and she was determined not to get out unless she started to get numb.

In an effort to warm herself up, she swam several laps around the lake as fast as she could. Breathless from the exertion, she stopped in the middle of the small lake and floated lazily on her back. She felt remarkably warm now; her teeth had stopped chattering and her goose bumps had disappeared.

This is just what I needed, she told herself. Her body and mind felt clean and alive.

As she floated on top of the water, the waves lapped gently at her sides, her mind drifted unconsciously back to Nick, even though only minutes before she had vowed to forget about him. An impossible task indeed, she realized, and let her thoughts wander to that afternoon in the grass when he had kissed and touched her. How could he raise such desire, such a need in her so easily? Never had a man aroused such feelings in her.

Could it be she was falling in love with Nick?

No, no, no! her mind argued back instantly. She couldn't possibly be in love with Nick. He was all wrong for her, he had qualities she hated, and besides, he didn't even like her. That wasn't all true, her heart argued. Nick had a lot of good qualities, and when he was being nice he made her feel everything was right between them. And he must like her a little. Surely he couldn't have wanted to make love to her if he really hated her, could he? Of course he could, her mind answered smugly. Lindsay sighed. Never had she felt more confused.

"Great night for a swim, don't you think?"

At the sound of the deep voice from the shore, Lindsay started. She suddenly found herself below the surface of the water. She popped her head up, sputtering and coughing up the water she had inadvertently swallowed. She blinked the water out of her eyes, trying to focus on the lone figure on horseback at the edge of the lake. Even before her eyes confirmed it, she knew it was Nick.

"What are you doing here?" she yelled back at him. Suddenly she remembered she'd been floating on her back for several minutes. She blushed furiously, glad he was too far to see her face clearly. "And how long have you been spying on me? How dare you sneak up on me like this!"

"I didn't sneak up on you," he replied innocently. That much was close to being true, anyway. He'd seen Lindsay ride off just as he himself was preparing to go for a ride, and he'd been inexplicably drawn to follow her. He'd done his best to avoid her these past few days, and he felt completely in control of himself again, so what harm would it do to ride sort of in the same direction she went?

Until he saw her hurriedly strip and dive naked into the lake. Then he didn't feel so much in control anymore. A deep stirring in his loins told him what he really wanted to be doing just then. But he ignored that as best he could and decided to have a little chat with her instead. The fact that she was completely nude would only add enjoyment to the conversation.

"I was out for a ride myself, and I happened to come this way. I had no idea you were here, or I would have made more noise." He paused and chuckled, thinking about how exquisite and unself-conscious she looked with just the water and the moonlight for clothing. "Maybe."

Lindsay felt renewed color rush into her cheeks. "Well, I prefer being alone, so could you please leave now?"

"I'm in no hurry," he said easily. "Besides, my horse needs a rest."

Even from this distance, she could see the pinto was breathing quietly and appeared to be falling asleep. Rest, indeed! She watched him for a moment, sitting relaxed in the saddle, his arms crossed casually over the saddle horn, his ever-present Stetson tipped back on his head. He certainly didn't appear to be in any hurry.

"I'm starting to get a little cold," she told him finally. Her teeth were beginning to chatter a little and her body had started to shiver. Simply treading water did not keep her warm enough in the icy water. "I'd like to get out now."

He shrugged, and one corner of his mouth was twitched up in a smile. "So who's stopping you?"

"You are!" Her voice was slightly edged in panic.

"I'm just sitting here minding my own business. How am I preventing you from getting out?"

Damn him, he was obviously enjoying this. And she was freezing! "Nick, please."

"Please, what?"

"If you won't leave, then at least have the decency to turn around."

He tipped his hat. "Certainly, ma'am." He turned the pinto in one complete revolution, ending up facing her again.

"Nick!"

Laughing, he dismounted and tied his horse next to Sundance. He walked slowly to the edge of the lake and peered out at her. "Perhaps I'll join you," he ventured.

"No!" she yelled quickly. She knew she wouldn't be able to handle that, wouldn't be able to keep control of the situation.

"It does look a little cold in there," he commented, noticing her rattling teeth even though she was still pretty far away from him. "All right, you win. I won't look."

She watched him walk over to a large rock and sit behind it, his back to her. Suspiciously, she dog-paddled slowly toward the shore, her eyes never leaving him. But he seemed to be ignoring her, and with one mad dash she was out of the water and behind the tree where she'd left her clothes. She threw on her jeans, shirt and boots in record time. She jogged soundlessly over to Sundance, her mind bent on escaping from him while she had the chance.

As she untied Sundance, she glanced at the pinto standing patiently next to her. A totally devilish idea popped into her head, and impulsively she decided to act on it. She freed the pinto's reins from the tree and vaulted up on Sundance, keeping Nick's horse's reins in her other hand.

"What the hell..." Nick jumped up from the ground, hearing the saddle creak as Lindsay mounted.

"Great night for a walk, don't you think?" she called over her shoulder, mocking his earlier words to her.

She kicked Sundance and clucked to the pinto, praying he wouldn't balk. For one awful moment the gelding held back, nearly pulling her out of the saddle. But then he gave in to the pressure from the reins and trotted out easily at the mare's side.

She heard Nick curse again and start to run toward her, so she urged both horses into a canter. Within seconds, Nick gave up and stood there, his hands on his hips in disbelief.

Between the pounding of her heart and the noise of the gravel scattering beneath the two horses' hooves, Lindsay did not hear Nick's sudden hearty laughter from far behind her.

Chapter Six

Lindsay paced nervously around the living room, her stomach in knots. What had ever possessed her to do such a thing?

She checked for the hundredth time out the window that overlooked the trail from the lake, but there was still no sign of Nick. It had been an hour since she'd left him. Maybe something had happened to him. No, what could happen? She knew what would happen once he got back, though. He would be absolutely furious with her. She shivered involuntarily. She hated to even consider what he might do to her in retaliation.

Well, he never should have put her in such a humiliating situation. He deserved a long walk. She had shown him she wasn't someone he could trifle with and get away with it. She took a deep breath and let it out slowly, trying to calm her nerves. She wondered idly whether all this anguish she was going through now was worth getting even with him.

She pulled back the curtain and peered outside into the darkness again. Nothing. Why didn't he come back so she could relax, go to bed and sleep in relative peace? She began pacing again, frowning at the floor. If Nick didn't show up soon, she was going to wear a hole right through this poor rug.

A quiet knock on her door made her jump. She whirled to face the door, her heart pounding. What if it were Nick? No, it couldn't be. She couldn't have missed seeing him walk back. Still, her lights were out, and it was late. Who else could it be?

She snapped on a lamp and stepped softly over to the door. Out of habit, she looked around for the peephole so she could see who was outside. *You idiot,* she chastised herself, *they don't have peepholes here.*

"Who is it?" she called out tentatively, her shaking hand on the knob.

"Jake," a muffled voice answered.

Relief surged through her, and she quickly opened the door. But the man who stood there with a slight mocking smile on his face was not Jake.

It was Nick.

She gasped and slammed the door, but he was quicker and stopped it easily before it could close. He pushed his way in and shut the door behind him.

"I, uh, see you made it back," Lindsay stammered, backing away from him.

"Yes, I did." He stepped slowly toward her. "And my horse?"

He didn't even check on his horse yet! She was really in trouble. "He's in his stall."

"That was some little trick you pulled," he said flatly, his voice betraying no emotion. For some ridiculous reason, she felt he wasn't really angry with her.

"I—I'm sorry, Nick, but you asked for it. You shouldn't have spied on me like that."

"I told you I didn't plan on it, but once I saw you I couldn't resist." He gave her a devilish smile.

She flushed and continued to back away from him. She didn't like the warm look that had suddenly come into his eyes as he boldly scanned her body. Involuntarily, she drew the belt on her bathrobe tighter around her waist and crossed her arms over her chest. She wished fervently she hadn't changed into her short cotton nightie and robe when she'd gotten back to the cabin. She backed up another step and felt the couch against her legs.

"Why did you try to slam the door in my face?" he asked lazily. He took two long strides and closed the distance between them.

"I thought you would be mad at me," she answered breathlessly. His nearness sent little tremors through her. "Why did you lie and say you were Jake?"

"I didn't think you would open the door if you knew it was me," he told her softly, and reached up to lightly stroke her cheek. "Do you know how beautiful you looked out there, with the moonlight and water sparkling on your body?"

Lindsay trembled under his light touch, flames of raw desire spreading through every inch of her body. His hand reached down to caress her shoulder, and then he moved it suddenly to the small of her back and brought her body tightly against his. He bent his head to plant small kisses along her neck. Lindsay's breath was coming in gasps, and she felt dizzy with longing. *How can he affect me like this?* she wondered wildly. She had to stop him, had to...

Before she could open her mouth to protest, he had covered it with his own. His lips moved over hers gently in a long, tender kiss that left her weak. She couldn't help but respond. Her body betrayed her need for him. Her arms went around his neck for support, and her fingers toyed with his thick blond hair.

"Do you seduce all the new employees?" she whispered brokenly, finally breaking contact with his mouth.

He took to kissing and nibbling her neck again. "Not all," he mumbled.

"Then why me?"

"Why not?" He brought his lips to hers and kissed her briefly before moving his mouth to the other side of her neck.

Why not indeed, she thought. She wanted to be silent and let him make love to her, but a part of her had to say more. "You don't even like me."

"At the moment I don't think you're too bad," he said huskily, and roughly covered her mouth in a hard, demanding kiss.

At the moment. Damn him, he didn't even have the decency to lie about it so she wouldn't feel so cheap. Maybe she could have given herself to him if he had said he liked her, but him liking her just "at the moment" wasn't good enough. She pulled away.

"I want you to leave now." She tried to sound firm, but her voice was unsteady.

Grabbing her arm, he whirled her around to face him. "What kind of game are you playing?"

"I'm not playing any game."

"Oh, no? I know you want me. Your body says that pretty clearly."

"Wanting and doing are two different things. Will you please just go?"

He shook his head in disbelief and confusion. "I don't understand you."

Lindsay boldly met his angry gaze. "Do you think all city women are loose?" she blurted out coldly. "Hasn't one ever said no to you?"

"Not after leading me on like you just did," he growled.

"Well, I'm sorry if you got the wrong idea. But I'm not that kind—"

"That kind of girl?" he interrupted, laughing mockingly.

She looked down at the floor uncomfortably. This wasn't going very well. She raised her eyes bravely to meet his icy blue ones again. "That's right. I don't care for one-night stands. No matter how attractive the man." She walked quickly over to the door and opened it. "Goodbye."

Nick stared at her for a moment, then as he walked toward the door, he stopped and grabbed her in a strong embrace. His lips crushed hers in a hard, bruising kiss. He pried her mouth open and his tongue boldly took possession of her mouth. Lindsay struggled briefly, but then weakly submitted, and finally was swept away into responding hungrily. He stopped abruptly then, and released her so suddenly she stumbled forward.

Nick touched one finger to her swollen lips. "Have it your way—this time. But I'm not through with you yet," he promised, smiling jauntily. He turned swiftly on one booted heel and walked out into the darkness.

Lindsay shut the door softly and sank to the floor, her whole body weak and shaking. She rested her head against the door and hugged her knees to her chest. It was several minutes before her heart stopped pounding and her breathing was normal. She rose slowly then, and went to bed. It was more than an hour before she finally dropped off in an exhausted, troubled sleep.

Sleep was not so easy for Nick, either. He never should have gone to her cabin, he knew that. But somehow, his legs had carried him right to her door without any hesitation.

Strangely enough, he hadn't been at all angry with her for running off with his horse. In fact, he found it rather amusing. But he wasn't about to let that little vixen have the last word. He'd really had no choice but to go to see her as soon as he got back to the ranch.

He cursed loudly as he paced around his cabin. She'd been so close to making love to him. He didn't really understand why she froze up so suddenly again. Maybe it was his remark about him liking her pretty well at the moment. He'd felt her stiffen as soon as the words were out. He'd meant it to be a light remark, but she must've taken him literally.

The funny thing was, he thought she might've reacted that way before he even said that. And he still said it anyway. Had he wanted her to draw away from him, to put a stop to his advances?

Hell, that was nonsense. A very demanding part of him wanted nothing better than to make long, passionate love to her. But then what? What would happen after that?

Nick suddenly stopped his pacing and shook his head. Since when did he ever think about the aftereffects of an affair? He was always the one to keep things cool and casual. His loins were starting to rule over his common sense.

No, there was only one way to solve this crazy situation he'd gotten himself into with Lindsay. And that was to make love to her. Then he'd be able to get her out of his system, once and for all. For some odd reason, she'd started to get to him, but he could get over this strange fascination he had for her. Dammit, he had to.

Although he felt he'd resolved his problems, he was still too tense to go to sleep. After trying unsuccessfully for half an hour, he got out of bed and put his jeans on. A moment later he was outside, trying to lose his restlessness in the dark night. It was a long walk.

Lindsay awoke the next morning feeling tired and irritable. She hadn't gotten much sleep, and what she had gotten had been filled once more with dreams of Nick. She was angry and confused. Never in her life had she felt less in control of herself than she did when she was around him. And when he was kissing her, touching her, well... She shivered uncontrollably, remembering his parting words from the night before. *I'm not through with you yet.*

She really should just forget about him entirely while she still could, she told herself as she walked slowly to the barn to see Sundance. Getting involved with Nick would be a sure mistake. She would be going back to Chicago at the end of the summer anyway.

Yet she knew deep down that she already was involved with him. Her feelings for him were too strong to turn on and off as easily as a faucet. All she could hope to do now was keep a tight rein on her emotions and never let him know how much he affected her. But she sighed as she entered the barn. If Nick decided to try to charm his way into her bed, she'd be helpless.

When she'd asked him to leave last night, she'd hoped he would be angry and forget about her, but instead he'd become more determined. Chances were that his battle plan was to be nice to her until he got what he wanted, then he'd go right back to being his old sarcastic, distrustful, disliking self. And that would be too painful a blow to handle. No matter how wonderful their times together might be, it wouldn't make up for the awful day when he'd surely turn on her again.

As she neared Sundance's stall, Lindsay frowned. The mare was always waiting for her, with her head propped over her stall door. But today her horse's face was not visible, nor did a welcoming whinny greet her.

Lindsay hurried the last few steps to the stall. Her worst fears were realized as she stared aghast at her mare, who was rolling and pitching around in the straw in obvious pain. The symptoms were unmistakable. The mare was colic.

"Jake!" she shrieked and threw open the stall door.

She rushed to Sundance, grabbing her halter and urged the mare to her feet. Reluctantly, the horse scrambled up, but tried immediately to lie down again. Lindsay yelled and pulled hard on the halter, holding the mare up. She led Sundance out into the aisle and snapped on her lead rope. Just then, she saw Jake come running.

"What's wrong?" he asked anxiously, out of breath.

"She's got colic," Lindsay told him, trying to keep her panic under control. "I'm going to walk her. Get the vet out here right away."

Jake looked uncomfortable. "That may take awhile."

"What do you mean? Don't you have a vet on the staff?"

"Well, we do, but he doesn't come out here permanently until the guests start coming. We usually don't need him in the off-season."

"You mean you're out here in the middle of nowhere, and there's no vet around?" she asked incredulously.

"I'm sorry, Lindsay. I'll call the closest one. He should be able to get out here in a couple of hours."

"A couple of hours! She might not make it that long!"

"She'll be fine," Jake tried to reassure her. "I'll go call."

Lindsay led her horse slowly outside. She had walked the mare for a few minutes when a glum-faced Jake approached her.

"The answering service said they'd get him out here as soon as they could," he told her.

"I don't understand how this happened," she said, her voice quivering. "She was fine last night."

Jake cleared his throat nervously. "The only thing I can think of is that last night was the first time she had our hay and grain by itself. I've been mixing what you brought along with our stuff to get her used to the change, but maybe it was still too much of a change," he finished remorsefully.

Lindsay smiled weakly at him. "It's not your fault, Jake, if that is what caused her to get sick. You had to feed her something; she had to have Wyoming feed sooner or later. It probably isn't anything serious." Her voice was dubious.

"Well, call if you need me for anything. I've got to get back to work." He patted her arm comfortingly. "I'm sure she'll be fine."

She nodded and continued to walk the mare, knowing that keeping the horse moving and not letting her lie down and roll was the best thing to do until the vet got there.

For about the first hour, it wasn't difficult. Several times the horse stopped and tried to lie down, but with a sharp command from Lindsay and a tug on the lead line the mare would obediently but reluctantly continue walking. However, after an hour and a half of walking, the horse began stopping every few minutes, and it became increasingly difficult for Lindsay to keep her moving.

A half hour later, Lindsay was close to giving up. The two hours she'd spent walking Sundance felt more like two days. She was feeling weak herself from not eating breakfast, and the exertion of keeping the mare on her feet was fast wearing her out. The fact that she'd had only a couple of good hours of sleep the night before didn't help either.

When Sundance balked and pawed the dirt restlessly, wanting to lie down yet another time, Lindsay felt her own strength almost gone.

"Please, lady, just keep going a little while longer," she begged the mare with tears of worry and frustration in her eyes. But the horse decided to obey no longer, and started to lower herself to her knees despite Lindsay's feeble pulls on the halter.

"Hyaaah, get up there!"

Lindsay and Sundance both jumped at the sound of a deep, commanding voice and a hand clap that came from right behind them. The horse, the more startled of the two, jumped back up on her feet immediately and sidestepped to see what loud monster had suddenly appeared behind her. Lindsay had no need to look to identify the voice, however. She turned and smiled gratefully at Nick as she once more pulled the mare on in a slow walk. He fell in step beside her.

"Jake told me what happened. How's she doing?"

Lindsay shrugged helplessly and shook her head. "You just saw for yourself she isn't any better yet. I was hoping by now whatever it is that's giving her a stomachache would've worked itself out. But she seems to be getting worse."

"The vet should be here soon," he said quietly.

"You can say what you like about the city, but at least in Chicago a vet never took more than a half hour to get to you in an emergency." Her voice broke as she continued. "By the time this one gets here, it'll probably be too late. I can't keep her on her feet much longer."

Nick put his arm around her shoulders. "She'll be all right, you'll see."

His comforting touch and soothing words were too much for her. Unable to hold them back any longer, the tears finally spilled down her cheeks.

"Nick, this horse means everything to me. I've been with her from the time she was born. She's been my best friend for eight years. I know it sounds silly, but I honestly don't know what I'd do if she . . ." Her throat constricted tightly.

"It doesn't sound silly at all. I have my own horse, too, you know. I know how much they can be a part of your life, how much you grow to depend on them. And unlike most people, your horse never lets you down." He shook her gently. "Come on, stop crying. She's going to be just fine."

His tenderness and understanding moved her immensely. Never had she met a man who not only understood her attachment to her mare, but also had similar feelings for his own horse. She looked up at him, unable to say anything or stop her tears. His eyes were filled with compassion and concern. And it wasn't an act, she was sure. That look was genuine. Could it be he did feel something for her after all?

She had no time to ponder that question, though, as Sundance stopped yet again. She pulled on the lead rope and spoke harshly, but it took Nick to once more jolt the horse into moving. Lindsay sighed deeply with fatigue and kept walking.

"You're exhausted," Nick exclaimed, just noticing.

"I didn't get much sleep last night," she admitted, glancing meaningfully at him.

He ignored her remark. "I bet you haven't had anything to eat today either, have you?"

She shook her head. "No, but I'm not hungry."

"I've heard that before," he groaned. "You're not going to be any good to this horse if you collapse out here. Why don't you go get some breakfast and rest for about an hour? I'll walk her for you."

Once more, Lindsay was touched by his concern and kindness. "Thanks, but I couldn't leave her. She might not keep going for you."

"She would have gone down twice now if it hadn't been for me," he pointed out. "She needs a little urging from a stranger. She'll walk for me."

"But if something happens, I have to be here. I just can't leave her."

"I'd say at this point, you have no choice," he reasoned. "At least run to the kitchen and get something and bring it back. You can sit over there under a tree and watch while you eat, if it'll make you feel better."

Lindsay hesitated. She could use a break and a little food. But she couldn't bear to be out of Sundance's sight. "Well, how about if you go get me a plate and then I'll sit for a while and eat?"

"All right, I'll settle for that. I'll be right back." He smiled briefly at her and then turned and strode quickly off in the direction of the main lodge.

Lindsay watched him until he disappeared through the front door of the lodge. It suddenly struck her what she had just done. She had asked Nick to wait on her, to help her, and he'd agreed! It seemed unbelievable. She remembered her earlier thought that Nick would probably dazzle her with charm now until he got what he wanted. But either he was a very good actor or she was a very big fool. She just didn't think all of this was an act. She shook her head in confusion. She'd have to give it some thought once she got through this crisis with Sundance. Right now all her efforts had to go into making her mare well again.

It seemed like only two minutes before Nick was back, carrying a plate heaped with steaming scrambled eggs, toast, bacon and hash browns. In his other hand was a large glass of milk.

"You must be a good friend of the cook," Lindsay quipped as she stared down in wonder at all the food. She giggled in spite of herself. "Are you sure you didn't bring that out here for yourself? I can't eat all that."

"Sure you can. If I know you, this'll be your lunch, too." He handed her the plate and took the lead rope from her other hand. "Go on and eat before it gets cold."

Lindsay reached for the glass of milk. As she took it from him, their hands touched. She kept her hand over his for a moment, not taking the glass from him right away. She looked up into his warm, sky-blue eyes.

"Thank you, Nick. I really appreciate all you're doing for me. And me, a mere city girl." She couldn't resist adding the last sentence with a slightly mocking smile.

He narrowed his eyes teasingly. "Well, I can't hold that against a good horse. She can't help who she has for an owner."

Chuckling, Lindsay finally took the milk away from his grasp. She walked wearily over to the nearest tree and gratefully sat down against it. In minutes she had devoured half the food and all the milk. She rose then, unable to eat any more.

"Just sit there and rest for a while," Nick called, noticing her stand. "She's walking better for me than for you anyway."

Lindsay stood still for a moment watching closely. She did have to admit Nick was having more luck keeping Sundance going than she had been having. Whether it was from Nick's superior strength or because he was a stranger to the wary horse, she didn't know. Finally convinced Sundance was in good hands for the time being, she sat back down again.

She stared at the two of them walking. They were the two most important beings in her life right now. Suddenly she felt renewed tears sting her eyes. She might lose her beloved Sundance, and Nick, well, she didn't even have him to lose.

Even though he was being very kind now, she knew he would never feel the things for her that she did for him. In fact, his tenderness today was almost more than she could take, for she knew it wouldn't last forever.

Forever. That's what she wanted with Nick. A forever relationship. Lindsay exhaled a long, shaky breath. Never had she felt more alone.

Pushing the disconcerting thoughts of Nick and Sundance from her mind, she sat for a few more minutes blankly observing her horse. She hoped it wasn't just her imagination that made it seem like the mare was walking more steadily now and attempting to stop much less. Finally unable to just sit still any longer, she walked back over to Nick.

"I'll walk her now," she said quietly, holding out her hand to take the rope from him. "Thanks for relieving me. I feel a lot better."

Nick continued to walk, not handing over the lead line, and studied her closely. She felt his eyes on her, but she refused to meet his gaze. Instead she kept her attention on Sundance's beautiful sorrel face.

"You still look pretty tired. Why don't you rest some more?" Nick suggested at last.

She shook her head. "I'm fine, really. I'd like to walk her myself now."

"You're sure? I don't mind, you know."

She smiled lightly and brought her eyes up to meet his. There was warmth and caring reflected in his eyes, and she looked away quickly. It actually hurt to look at him.

With a tremendous effort, she kept her voice steady. "Really, I want to do it myself. I feel better being close to her."

"All right," he conceded. "But call me if you need me, okay?" He handed her the rope.

"I will. And thanks again." Lindsay took the rope from him, being careful not to touch his hand in the process. She stepped away from him quickly, and was pleased to see that Sundance kept right up to her. Maybe she was getting better.

Lindsay made a large circle, and didn't look for Nick until she was facing the direction she had left him. She quickly scanned the area then, but he was gone. Simultaneously, she felt relief and regret. "Oh, Sundance," she murmured brokenly. "Please don't leave me, too."

She kept walking, her mind carefully blank, for another hour before a brown pickup truck finally rolled slowly up to the barn. She had seen enough vehicles driven by vets to know at once who must be driving this truck. She turned and pulled Sundance quickly back to the barn.

They reached the vet just as he was getting out of the truck. Jake had heard him pull up and was already there talking and motioning in her direction. A pleasant looking middle-aged man dressed in clean navy coveralls turned experienced eyes to look briefly at her before moving on to study Sundance.

"Let's take her in the barn," the vet spoke up authoritatively. "Jake, why don't you tell me what happened."

Jake briefly explained the situation while they walked into the barn. The vet nodded occasionally, his gaze never leaving the horse.

"Oh, by the way," Jake added, "Lindsay, this is Dr. Bishop; Dr. Bishop, this is Lindsay Jordan, the owner of the mare and one of our new employees."

"Nice to meet you, young lady. Lovely mare you have here."

"Thanks. I'd like to keep her that way. What do you think?" Lindsay asked anxiously.

After a brief examination, the vet straightened and faced Lindsay squarely. "Her temperature and pulse are near normal, which is a very good sign. I think the problem may be just an impaction. I'm going to give her a tranquilizer and then pump some oil into her stomach. Hopefully, that should do the trick."

Lindsay breathed a small sigh of relief. The vet sounded optimistic. As she held Sundance while Dr. Bishop continued the treatment, she wished Nick were there. No sooner was the thought in her mind than she felt a firm hand on her shoulder. She turned quickly to see him standing next to her, a worried frown on his face.

"Well?" he asked quietly.

She smiled brightly at him. "I think she's going to be okay. Dr. Bishop thinks it's just an impaction."

Nick gave her a warm smile. "That's great. I told you she'd be fine." He winked a bit mischievously and squeezed her shoulder. "You should listen to me more often."

Lindsay felt the heat rise in her cheeks as she realized what he seemed to be referring to. "Maybe I will next time," she returned with a challenging grin.

A few minutes later the vet was through. Lindsay put Sundance back in her stall on his recommendation and then followed him out to his truck.

"I'll go get you a check," she told him as he began making out a bill and hurried off to her cabin.

When she returned a couple of minutes later, the vet was already gone. She walked up to Nick in disbelief and confusion.

"Where did he go?"

"To see another patient somewhere else."

"But I didn't pay him yet," she protested.

"I took care of it," Nick stated matter-of-factly.

"You what?"

"Well, actually the Rocky Road Ranch took care of it. I had Dr. Bishop charge it to our account."

"Why? Sundance is my responsibility, not the ranch's."

"As long as you're working here, we pay not only for your horse's feed but also any accumulated vet bills. Consider it a fringe benefit."

Lindsay frowned. "Ross Browning didn't say anything about that."

Nick shrugged. "He probably forgot. Anyway, what's the big deal? I should think you'd be happy about it, not defensive."

He had a point there. Why was she being so defensive? Perhaps she was just suspicious of some ulterior motive when Nick did something nice. "Well, I just like to take care of my own responsibilities," she explained lamely. "But it is nice of Ross to do that."

He put his arm carelessly around her shoulders. "Let's go see how she's doing."

Lindsay walked with him into the barn, her heart thumping loudly from the intimate contact. Now that her mind was almost free from worry about Sundance, her senses had taken over immediately in reacting to Nick.

They reached the mare's stall and stood there for a moment watching her. The horse appeared to be resting peacefully.

"She seems pretty good," Lindsay commented softly. "Although we won't know for sure until the tranquilizer completely wears off."

Nick pulled her into his arms and gently kissed the top of her head. "You've had a long, rough morning. Why don't you go take a nap? Jake and I will keep an eye on your horse."

Lindsay felt a tremor run through her body and noticed her knees had suddenly gone weak. With her head resting on his broad chest she could hear his heart beating unnaturally fast. She smiled to herself and clung to him a moment. *At least I affect him physically,* she told herself. That was better than nothing.

She lifted her head to look into the two sparkling pieces of sky that were his eyes and was momentarily held by the look of hungry desire she saw in his eyes.

"I...wouldn't be able to sleep anyway." She stumbled over the words, unable to tear her eyes away from his.

"Why not?" he whispered as he lowered his head to within inches of hers.

She licked her lips unconsciously, remembering all too vividly the pleasure his mouth gave. "I'd be too worried about Sundance."

"Oh, I see." He smiled wickedly. "I thought maybe it was because you'd be thinking about this." He closed the slight distance between their mouths and kissed her very delicately.

Lindsay dug her fingers into his arms, giddy with longing for him. How could he do this to her with one kiss? How could she possibly expect to resist him? Yet resist him she must, starting right now, she told herself firmly. After all, they were in the barn, where anybody could see them.

"Nick, please, not here," she said nervously, pushing him away a little.

He raised one eyebrow. "Where, then?" he asked with a jaunty smile.

"Nowhere. I...we have work to do." She tried to keep her voice steady and firm, but failed miserably.

Nick chuckled and released her at last. "A company girl, are you?" he teased. "You're right, anyway. I'll see you later, though." He flashed her another lecherous grin before he disappeared outside.

Damn him, Lindsay swore to herself as she clutched Sundance's stall for support until her heart returned to its normal slow, steady rate. She entered the stall then and buried her head in the horse's silky flaxen mane. Her body ached with longing for his touch, and her heart ached with longing for his love.

"What am I going to do, lady?" she whispered miserably to the horse, whose only answer was the flick of an ear and a deep, contented sigh.

Chapter Seven

Lindsay was dreaming she was in Chicago, literally chained to her desk at the insurance company and morosely unhappy, when the sound of a stallion screaming broke into her nightmare. She was grateful to be pulled out of the bad dream, but it took her several minutes to comprehend that the horse's shrieks were real and coming from outside.

She became instantly alert and glanced at her clock. Two-thirty. She jumped out of bed as she realized with a feeling of dread that one of the stallions must be loose. In seconds she was dressed and out the door.

There were several overhead lights around the barns, but the stallion sounded like he was in one of the pastures and Lindsay could only make out vague shadows of horses out there. As her eyes strained to locate the stallion, she saw Jake running out of the barn with a lead rope and halter over his arm. She sprinted to his side.

"What happened?" she asked breathlessly. "Who's loose?"

"Tramp," Jake informed her as they headed toward the south pasture.

"Tramp!" Lindsay repeated, her eyes wide. Tramp was a huge bay stallion, and the primary breeding stud on the ranch. "But how did he get out?"

"I don't know." His voice was taut. "What I do know is that he's in a pasture with several good trail mares who just happen to be in heat. Not to mention the geldings out there who might get kicked to smithereens."

By the time they reached the gate to the pasture, a few other employees along with Ross Browning were running toward them. Lindsay made out Nick's unmistakable form leading the group. He hadn't taken the time to put on a shirt, and despite the emergency situation at hand, Lindsay couldn't keep from staring at his tightly muscled chest as he neared.

"Who is it, Jake?" Nick asked immediately when he reached them.

"Tramp. He must have jumped the fence to get in here because the gate is still latched solid."

Lindsay could hear the stallion's screams and several other horses' squeals from over the hill. A chill ran through her at the sound. There was nothing as eerie as a stallion's call in the darkness.

"Jake!" Ross barked out as he finally caught up to them. "What the hell is going on out here? What stallion got out?"

"Tramp," Nick and Jake told him in unison.

Ross threw up his hands in exasperation. "He's probably bred half the mares out there already! Do you know what that'll mean to the size of our trail herd next year? We'll lose a lot of our best mares while they have foals."

Jake nodded grimly. "Yes, I realize that, Uncle Ross. Right now all we can do is catch him before he does any more damage."

"Or before another horse does some damage to him," Nick added. He followed Jake through the gate. "Jake and I will try to get him calm enough to get hold of him. Everyone else better stay back here. Too many people chasing after him will just get him more excited."

The half dozen other employees who'd joined them nodded in agreement. As Lindsay watched the two men jog up the hill, she wished she could go with them to help. She'd spent quite a bit of time with the big stallion lately, admiring his gentle and good-natured disposition. She'd been feeding him the past few days, as part of her chores in the main barn. In fact, she'd fed him tonight.

Lindsay's mouth dropped open in sudden horror. What if she hadn't latched his door tight when she left his stall? What if it were her fault he was loose?

She shook her head in the darkness, replaying the evening feeding in her mind. No, she was absolutely sure she'd secured the bolt on his stall. She always double-checked it before she went up to the lodge to eat supper, and she specifically remembered slipping Tramp a sugar cube as she patted his nose good-night. And the latch had been closed properly then. She was sure of it.

After what seemed eons, Nick and Jake finally returned over the hill, leading a prancing Tramp beside them.

"Thank God," Ross muttered when he saw Tramp was under control and appeared to be walking all right.

"He wasn't real thrilled with us interrupting his fun, but he let us catch him pretty easily," Jake said as he led the stallion through the gate.

Nick chuckled. "Yeah, I think he wore himself out before we got to him. He probably had more exercise tonight than he's had in months."

Lindsay reached out to pat Tramp. "At least he isn't hurt. Did all the horses in the pasture seem okay?"

Nick shrugged. "It was too hard to tell in the dark. We didn't see any of them walking on three legs, though. We'll have to give them all a thorough check in the morning."

Lindsay trailed after Nick, Jake and Ross as they led the stallion back to the barn. When they finally had Tramp safely in his stall, Ross cleared his throat.

"I want to know how this could happen. Who fed this horse tonight?"

Lindsay drew in a sharp breath. Even though she knew Tramp's escape hadn't been her fault, she wondered if the others would believe her. But before she could open her mouth, Jake spoke up.

"Lindsay and I did the evening chores," he said awkwardly. "But I really don't remember which one of us fed Tramp tonight."

"Jake, you've been feeding the horses here for years," Nick broke in with a touch of irritation. "I hardly think you would be so careless."

Lindsay met his gaze squarely, her anger rising. Nick obviously blamed her for this. She shouldn't be surprised, but she was a little hurt at his immediate accusation.

"Jake, you don't have to try to protect me," she said evenly, her eyes never leaving Nick's face. "I was the one to feed Tramp tonight."

"It's big of you to admit it, Lindsay," Ross said stiffly. "But perhaps in the future you should leave the feeding of the studs to Jake. Just as a precautionary measure, you understand."

Lindsay turned away from Nick and faced Ross in shock. "Now just a minute, here. I know for sure that when I left Tramp, his stall was tightly latched. I remember double-checking it. Someone else must have been in there after I fed him."

"Lindsay's always been extremely careful and conscientious in feeding all the horses, Uncle Ross," Jake put in. "I really don't think she would have left his stall open."

"Such chivalry is admirable, Jake," Nick spoke up coldly. "However, let me remind you she is new to this type of work. I'm sure she didn't do it intentionally, but accidents can happen when you're new on the job. Handling of stallions is best left to experienced men."

Lindsay stared at him in disbelief. How could he talk as if she wasn't here listening? And how could he say such cruel things about her?

"I'm every bit as competent as you in handling that stallion," she told him indignantly, her fury barely suppressed. "And if you're looking for someone to blame for this happening, you better look elsewhere. I know I had nothing to do with it." With that, she turned swiftly and left the three men standing there staring after her.

"You were a little hard on her, weren't you, Nick?" Ross commented as soon as Lindsay was out of earshot. He eyed the younger man, who stood stiffly beside him, his face unreadable. "After all, we don't really know she left the stall unlatched."

"You sure accused her of it quick enough," Jake pointed out to his uncle. "Why the sudden turnaround?"

"I like the girl, and she does seem pretty responsible," Ross explained uneasily. "I suppose I did jump to conclusions, but she did act pretty sure that she didn't do it."

"I'm sure she didn't do it, too," Jake said stubbornly.

Nick threw him an exasperated glance. "She's got you swooning, Jake, my boy. You'd believe anything she said."

"I don't think I'm the only one she has swooning, my friend," Jake said shrewdly. "The only difference is that I'm fair to her, and you're going out of your way not to be."

Ross cleared his throat and put a hand on each man's arm. "It's late and we've had a busy night. Why don't we all turn in now? Things will look a lot clearer in the morning."

"You're right, Ross," Nick said, his eyes still on Jake. "Good night." He nodded at the two men and then slowly made his way back to his cabin.

An hour later Nick was still awake, tossing and turning in his bed. He wondered if Lindsay was asleep. Probably not, after all that had happened and the nasty things he'd said to her. Jake was right, he was being unfair to her. He had to admit she seemed very certain she'd left Tramp's stall bolted tightly. And maybe she had. Why did he find that so hard to accept? Why did he always want to think the worst of her?

Well, tomorrow was another day, and he'd make it up to her. After all, a person was innocent until proven guilty. He'd apologize to her, even though it would be damn hard to do it. But after the way he had jumped all over her, she deserved an apology. Hell, she deserved a lot more than that.

Although he felt better, it was still another hour before Nick's guilty conscience eased enough to let him sleep.

Despite Lindsay's efforts to relax and calm down, sleep had evaded her the rest of the night. Finally, at six in the morning she rose and showered. This was her first day off, and she was glad of it. In the next twenty-four hours, she hoped she would cool off, along with Nick and Ross. She was sure it would be all around the ranch by noon that she was responsible for Tramp's escapades last night, so she was further relieved she could make herself scarce. It was a perfect day to do some shopping in town. There was one item in particular she just had to buy.

It just wasn't fair, she thought in frustration. Just because she was a new employee, everyone assumed she must be responsible for leaving Tramp's stall unlatched. For heaven's sake, she'd been around horses her whole life and had raised Sundance from a foal. She certainly knew better than to do something like that.

What hurt the most was the way Nick had turned on her so quickly. At times he seemed like a total stranger to her, and it was as if they had never gotten to know each other at all the past few days. And for him to say only men should handle stallions, well, that had been the last straw. Who did he think she was, his ex-wife?

Suddenly Nick's accusations made a little sense to her. She remembered Jake telling her about how irresponsible Nick's wife had been with that stallion, riding him when she shouldn't and crippling him to the point of having to destroy him.

Still, that didn't give him the right to treat her like he had last night. She sighed again. At least Jake had been quick to defend her. She smiled as she realized that Jake's standing up for her had seemed to really irritate Nick. Served him right, she thought with satisfaction.

Not wanting to face everyone in the dining room at breakfast, Lindsay decided to grab something to eat in town. She headed first, though, to visit Sundance for a while. She was relieved to get all the way to the barn without running into anyone. After brushing her horse until she gleamed, Lindsay hastened back to her cabin. Soon everyone else would be coming out from breakfast, and she wanted to be gone before that happened.

Lindsay was just climbing into the driver's seat of her pickup when a large tanned hand stopped the door before it could close. She looked up in surprise at Nick.

"I missed you at breakfast," he said quietly, his unreadable eyes boring into hers.

"Sorry, but I wasn't hungry," she murmured, looking straight ahead and not at his penetrating eyes.

"Where are you off to so early in the morning?"

"This is my day off, and I have a few things to get in town." She was proud of herself for keeping her voice level and cool. But inside, she was a fluttering mess.

"Your first day off, and you have to spend the whole day in town?" he said tensely. "Do you miss the city that much already?"

His cutting remark infuriated her. She tossed her long hair over her shoulder and faced him at last. "I didn't realize it was a crime to need to buy a few things. I don't see a general store out here, do you?" she retorted icily.

The corner of his mouth twitched as he tried to control his own anger. "When will you be back?"

"What do you care?"

He shrugged and broke contact with her flashing emerald eyes. He took a deep breath. *Calm down, man,* he ordered himself. *You're doing it again.* He came over here to apologize, and here he was fighting with her.

"I thought maybe we could go for a ride later this afternoon," he said lightly.

That seemed to surprise her. Her eyes softened but remained guarded. She waited in silence for him to continue.

"Lindsay, look, I'm sorry about last night. I don't know what got into me. I didn't mean those things." He turned to stare into her wide, suspicious eyes.

"It wasn't my fault," she whispered, feeling suddenly tired and vulnerable. "I double-checked his stall, and I know it was latched."

He smiled, his gaze coming to rest on her quivering lips. He had the almost irresistible urge to kiss her. "I believe you. A dozen other people could have gone in his stall for some reason."

Lindsay didn't think he sounded very convinced, but she accepted his words anyway. "I should be back around one. I planned on taking Sundance out when I got back, so if you want to go along it's fine with me."

He nodded. "Okay." He carefully shut the door of the truck. "Drive safely."

She smiled. "See you later."

She waved as she pulled away from him, her heart in her throat. Was he really the same man who said such awful things to her last night? she wondered. When she was around Nick, she felt like she was constantly on a roller coaster, one minute flying high and carefree and the next dropping down into the depths of despair. But right now she was on the upswing, soaring to an altitude that might be unlimited.

She didn't care to guess how long it would be before she fell again.

As it turned out, it didn't take Lindsay as long as she had expected in town. She was able to purchase the one special item she wanted at the first store she tried, and the rest of her shopping took an hour. So, at ten minutes after twelve, she was pulling into the ranch.

It seemed Nick must have been watching for her to return, for she was scarcely out of her truck when he appeared out of nowhere.

"Well, well, well, what have we here?" he teased, looking at her with sparkling eyes. "A new cowboy hat?"

Lindsay flushed. It sure hadn't taken him long to notice. "Do you like it?" she asked anxiously. Why his approval mattered so much she couldn't fathom, but she knew she had purchased the hat partly because of him. Just as she knew she looked a lot more attractive in it than in the old, tattered one.

"Mmmm." He smiled, his gaze sweeping her from the Stetson on her head to the boots on her feet. "Yes, I certainly do like what I see."

Lindsay felt color rush to her cheeks. "I just have to put these things away," she told him as she headed for her cabin with her arms full of packages. "Then I'll be ready for that ride. If you still want to go with me," she added self-consciously.

Nick crossed his arms over his chest and leaned lazily against the side of her pickup. "I'm ready any time you are."

"Is your horse ready?"

"No, but he will be by the time you get those things in your cabin and get your horse ready."

She felt his appraising stare on her as she swept past him. She stopped then, and turned around to face him. "You know, a real gentleman would offer to help me with these," she said, flustered by the look he was giving her. It was a hungry look, and it made her body tingle all over.

He raised one eyebrow curiously. "You're right. But who ever said I was a real gentleman?"

Her eyes narrowed. "That's true," she replied in mock seriousness. "I doubt if anyone ever did make that mistake about you."

Nick sighed dramatically. "Well, just to show you that not everyone is right about me, I will help you carry your trusty bags to your cabin.'' He walked over to her and plucked every package but one from her arms.

"Thank you, kind sir," she said, bowing her head.

"You're not fooling me any," he told her in a conspiratorial voice. "You just didn't want me staring at your back end while you walked all the way to your cabin by yourself."

"I won't even dignify that with an answer," she retorted with as much hautiness as she could muster, her face crimson. How could he read her so easily? That's exactly what had been on her mind.

Nick laughed good-naturedly and shook his head. "Methinks the lady doth protest too much. If you've got it, flaunt it, I always say. And there's no harm in looking."

Lindsay kept silent, unwilling to continue the conversation on its present course. The truth was, though, that she was thrilled with the idea that Nick liked to look at her. Just as she loved to look at him. She glanced sideways at him, taking in his strong, masculine profile. She could never get tired of looking at him.

When they reached her cabin, Lindsay simply thrust the bags inside the door and went right back outside again. Nick looked at her with surprise.

"That's it? You're not going to put them away?"

She shook her head. "I'll do it later."

"Well, then, let's get going on that ride. I'll race you to the barn," Nick called over his shoulder, already running ahead of her.

Laughing at his boyish behavior, Lindsay ran after him. "No fair, you got a head start!" she yelled.

Not that it mattered. Win or lose their little race, she had the feeling it was going to be a wonderful afternoon.

* * *

"How long have you worked here?" Lindsay asked curiously.

They were sitting side by side under the shade of a huge oak tree several miles south of the ranch. Their horses were tied securely to stout branches, and both animals swished their tails absently at annoying flies.

Nick grunted and stretched his long frame out until he was laying on his back, his arms crossed behind his head. "It seems like forever."

"Yes, but how long?"

"Oh, I guess I didn't start working at the ranch full time until I was nineteen. But I worked here summers since I was about twelve. Ross has been like a father to me."

"What about your real father? Where is he?"

Nick squinted up at her. "What is this, twenty questions?"

"I'd just like to know more about you, that's all," she replied casually. "What's so awful about that?" *Don't pull away,* she begged him silently. *Not this time. Let me find out more about the real Nick.*

He plucked a long piece of grass and absently started to chew on it. "My real father ran out on my mother and me when I was eight," he told her flatly.

"I'm sorry," she began, but he cut her off.

"Don't be. It was probably the best thing for everybody. He was just a bum anyway." He sighed and tipped his Stetson over his eyes. The pain was still there, even after twenty-five years, and he didn't want Lindsay's probing eyes to see it.

"Were you born in Wyoming?" she asked after a moment when he didn't offer any more information.

"Born and raised," he confirmed, his voice carefully level. "My mother used to own a big ranch about seventy miles from here. Not as big as the Rocky Road, but it was still a good working size, five thousand acres.''

"What happened to it?'' She knew she should stop pressing him. Even now, she could feel he was tensing up and retreating from her. Still, as long as she could draw anything out of him, she knew she had to go on.

Nick pulled the stem of grass out of his mouth and tossed it away from him. "That ranch had been in my mother's family for generations. Unfortunately, when my father took off on her she didn't have the strength or money to run a ranch that size alone. And an eight-year-old boy isn't a lot of help." He sat up suddenly and stared out at the distant mountains that dominated the horizon. "She sold it two years later. But not before it almost killed her."

Lindsay wanted to reach out and touch him, to comfort him some way, but she knew he would only resent it. She picked a small wildflower and toyed with it to keep her hands occupied.

"Where is your mother now?'' she asked softly.

Nick didn't answer for a long moment. "She died fifteen years ago,'' he told her at last.

She kept silent, idly pulling the tiny petals off the flower in her hand.

Nick nudged her with his elbow. "Let's cut this morose conversation, okay? It's too nice a day to bring up unhappy memories. Besides, if we don't lighten up, every wildflower in the area will be bald."

Lindsay laughed and threw the petalless flower at him. She pulled off her new hat and ran slender fingers through her long hair. "You're right. It is a lovely day. But I do have one more question for you."

Nick groaned and dropped his chin to his chest. "What is it?''

"What does the future hold in store for Nick Leighton? Do you plan on spending the rest of your life working on this ranch?" She didn't know exactly why, but this question was particularly important to her.

"That's kind of a strange question." He lifted his head and turned to look at her, only to find her carefully avoiding his gaze. He stared at her delicate profile for a moment, enjoying the way the gentle breeze played with the silky auburn waves that framed her face. She was so damn beautiful.

"Does that mean I don't get an answer?" She dared a glance at him and was immediately disturbed at the intense way he was studying her.

"No, the answer is pretty simple, and not really a secret. I'm saving up to buy back my mother's ranch. One of our neighbors owns it now, and he swore that if the day ever came when I had enough money and I wanted it, he would sell the land back to me."

"You mean he just bought it to hold it for you?" Lindsay couldn't keep the doubt and surprise out of her voice.

"Well, not really. I mean, he's using the land for his cattle, of course, but the house is empty."

"How old were you when he told you he'd let you buy it back?" It seemed incredulous to her that anyone would be so kind-hearted.

Nick took a deep breath, and when he spoke, his voice was tight. "I know what you're thinking, but you're wrong. You don't understand country people. They're entirely different from city people, who only try to screw you any way they can. George Parker is as honest a man as I've ever known, and if he told me I could buy my place back, then that's the way it is."

"Okay, okay." Lindsay held up her hands in defeat. "You don't have to get angry with me. But it does seem pretty incredible, you have to admit. I'd just hate to see you get hurt by working for a dream all your life only to have it fall apart someday.''

"What about you, Lindsay?" he asked suddenly. "What do you dream about?"

You, she thought, and felt her cheeks turn crimson. "That's a pretty good attempt to change the subject," she protested to cover up her true thoughts.

"The third degree about my life is over. Now you have to return me the favor."

Lindsay picked up her cowboy hat and put it back on her head. She stood and brushed the grass and dirt off her jeans.

"I don't have any dreams," she said simply.

Nick sprang up from the ground and grabbing her arm, he turned her around to face him. "I don't buy that for a minute."

"I don't," she insisted. How could she possibly tell him her real dreams were coming true right now, working on this ranch and being with him? She didn't even understand it herself. A few weeks ago she would have answered his question a lot differently than she could now. Now her whole life had turned upside down.

Nick's grip on her arm tightened. "You mean this summer is only a mild distraction for you, and when it's over, you're going back to Chicago to get rich working at some insurance company for the rest of your life? And that's it? That's all you want?" he demanded impatiently.

Lindsay stared into his cool sapphire eyes and wondered why he was so angry at her all of a sudden. What did he want her to say? He didn't really want to hear the truth, of that she was certain.

"I don't really know anymore," she whispered at last. That was almost true anyway.

He waited for her to say more, but after a minute when it became clear she wasn't going to tell him anything else, he released her arm. "It's getting late," he grumbled disgustedly. "We'd better be getting back."

Lindsay watched him stride over to his horse and untie it in crisp motions. She couldn't let the conversation end this way. She walked over to Nick and hesitantly put her hand on his shoulder.

"Just what is it you want from me, Nick?"

He turned to meet emerald eyes that were now very vulnerable and confused. It stirred him, and most of his anger instantly dissipated. He pulled her into his arms and brought his lips down to hers.

"This," he murmured, kissing her deeply and seductively. "This is what I want from you."

Lindsay's blood began to smolder and she felt an intense yearning spread through her every fiber. Hungrily she responded to his lips, his tongue. But as the true meaning of his words sunk in, she pulled away indignantly.

"This is all you want from me, isn't it?" she said, unable to keep the resentment and hurt out of her voice.

"Dammit, Lindsay," he began, and then stopped. What did he want from her anyway? It was a fair enough question, but not an easy one to answer. He wanted her body, that was obvious to him, but now he wasn't so sure that he didn't want more. Much more.

"Look," he went on gently. "I don't think either one of us knows just what they want right now. Why don't we just go easy and take things one day at a time for awhile?"

Lindsay bit her bottom lip to keep it from quivering. She was disconcerted at his sudden change of attitude. Would he never stop throwing her off guard?

She gave him a small smile and held out one trembling hand. "It's a deal."

Chapter Eight

Okay, ladies and gentlemen,'' Ross Browning announced loudly with a clap of his hands, "tomorrow's the big day. Our first group of guests will be arriving in the afternoon." He paused a moment to allow everyone to quiet down before he continued. "You've all been great the last few weeks, and I see no reason why everything shouldn't go very smoothly. The cabins are ready, the horses are ready and I think all of you are ready, too."

Lindsay smiled. She certainly was ready for the guest season to begin. Although the other employees had assured her it was an extremely busy time, they also told her how much fun it was. She looked around the dining room at all the pleasant faces of her coworkers. She'd gotten to know most of them quite well, and there was no one here she didn't like. She found the days had flown past, and never had she enjoyed working anywhere as much as she did here.

She glanced over at Nick, who was in his usual place beside her, and felt a warm feeling wash over her. Of course, he was one of the main reasons she found it so wonderful working at the ranch, she knew.

It had been two weeks since their ride together. And since that day, when they'd called a truce, Nick was like a different man in the way he treated her. Gone was the sarcastic, mocking, chauvinistic man, and in his place was a considerate, kind, amiable man. For a few days, Lindsay had been wary of this sudden turnaround in character, waiting for the old "real" Nick to emerge without a moment's notice, but he was always pleasant and charming. They still argued from time to time, but there was little ferocity in those disagreements. And before long, Lindsay was completely lost in the spell he seemed to have cast over her.

They spent nearly every day together, Nick always making sure she was working on something either with or around him. All their meals were eaten at the same time, at the same table. On their days off, which always seemed to coincide, they went riding together or drove into town for miscellaneous supplies.

And although they were alone together many times, Nick had kept his desire for her under control and the contact between them limited to a quick kiss, an arm around her, or holding her hand.

For that Lindsay was grateful although she guessed it was only a matter of time before his advances would become demanding again. And she knew she would have great difficulty putting him off if that happened. Yet as much as she yearned for him, she was still uneasy about his true feelings for her. A tiny, nagging voice inside her kept insisting Nick would soon tire of her when he got her in his bed. Deep down, she felt the longer she could put him off, the more time he'd have to get to know her and maybe fall in love with her. Her sensible side told her that was preposterous, that Nick could never feel for her what she felt for him. For she had long ago stopped deluding herself—she had to admit that she was in love with him. Her feelings were just too strong and too deep to deny any longer.

Not that she hadn't tried to banish those feelings from her heart. After all, she would be going back to Chicago, back to reality. And she knew Nick would never ask her to stay here with him. If he did, she wouldn't hesitate to say yes. She could easily adapt to life out here with him, but could he ever love her enough to want her to stay? No, she had to be honest with herself, and that meant facing facts. In September she would go home, and try her darnedest to forget about him.

Lindsay jumped as she felt her knee being lightly squeezed. She pushed the sad thoughts out of her mind so she could concentrate on the present; thinking of the future was just too depressing. She looked up into Nick's questioning eyes.

"Are you all right?" he leaned close and whispered. "You look like you're a million miles away."

Lindsay stared at him for a moment, memorizing every tiny detail of his face, from his bushy, unruly blond eyebrows to his strong, angular chin to his fathomless blue eyes. God, how she loved him! How could she possibly ever feel any happiness again in her life without him in it?

She smiled slightly and put her hand over his, which was still on her knee. "I'm fine," she answered softly at last.

Nick shifted his hand to grasp hers firmly. He gave her a warm smile before returning his attention to Ross Browning's words, and Lindsay tried to do the same.

"As most of you are aware by now, your daily work schedule will be posted at seven a.m. on the bulletin board in the kitchen," Ross droned on. "Nick and I try to vary everyone's duties so you are all versatile and don't get bored with always performing one specific assignment. However, if you ever have any beefs about anything, please feel free to come to me about it. I've been doing this long enough to know that satisfied employees are a big key to a successful business.

"Well, I guess I've gone over everything I need to for now. So let's make this season our best ever at the Rocky Road Ranch," Ross finished up with a flourish. A loud round of applause from all the employees shook the dining room as he sat down looking slightly embarrassed. "Aw, go on and finish eating," he said over the noise.

"Good old Ross." Nick chuckled affectionately. "He makes the same speech every year." He pushed his plate aside and smiled at Lindsay. "Well, I'm all through. What do you say we go play with the little ones?"

"Sure," she answered, warmly returning his smile. The "little ones" were the three foals that had been born in the past four weeks. Lindsay and Nick tried to visit and handle the youngsters as often as possible, and to Lindsay it was one of the most special things they did together.

They walked in a companionable silence out to the brood mares' pasture where the three mothers and their babies were. They ducked under the rails and walked into the field. Nick whistled loudly and in minutes the mares were trotting toward them, their respective foals close behind.

Lindsay laughed with glee watching the two young colts and the one young filly bouncing along beside their mothers. The three babies were all legs, and it never failed to amaze her how limbs that fragile and spindly could support any weight at all, let alone run without collapsing.

"See, my filly's beating your colts again," she teased Nick, hitting him playfully on the arm. The filly was the youngest of the three, but she had the longest legs, and almost unbelievably had better control of them than her two pasture mates.

"Only because her mother's the biggest pig, and she has to hurry to keep up with her," Nick protested good-naturedly. "My colts could beat that straggly filly any day."

"Ha!" Lindsay disagreed as the horses at last reached them. The three mares nuzzled the humans' pockets expectantly, and soon received their customary apples. In a few minutes they lost interest in the two people and moved a few feet away to graze. It was then that the foals finally were able to approach their new human friends and were instantly rewarded with the usual scratching that so delighted them.

As had become their habit, the filly soon sought out Lindsay while the two colts fought over Nick's attention. Lindsay gazed down affectionately at the creamy colored buckskin filly beneath her scratching fingers and smiled wistfully.

"I wish you really were mine," she whispered to the tiny, flicking ears.

Nick, a few feet from her, caught her eye for a moment. "If you were going to stick around here a while, maybe that wouldn't be impossible," he replied carefully.

Lindsay's heart jumped into double time. Was that an invitation or was he merely baiting her? She decided it was safest to make light of his comment. "You weren't supposed to hear that," she chastised him mockingly. "That remark was for my filly's ears only."

"Why?" Nick asked casually.

She glanced over at him and was surprised to see how serious he had suddenly become. She quickly returned her eyes to the foal. How was she going to get out of this one? She desperately wanted to tell him how much she wanted to stay at the ranch forever, but somehow she just couldn't voice that to him. He would have to ask her to stay; she wouldn't offer.

"She and I have lots of secrets, don't we, girl?" she finally answered in a lame explanation that was really no explanation at all. "So you and your two colts just keep your male ears to yourself and leave us girls alone."

Lindsay breathed a small sigh of relief when Nick didn't press her any further. Yet she was also somewhat disappointed that he didn't want to continue the discussion.

A few minutes later she risked a sidelong glance at him and found he was completely engrossed in scratching the two colts. She watched him then, out of the corner of her eye, and at once became entranced by his gentle and affectionate handling of the young horses.

"It doesn't seem possible that Sundance was once as tiny as this little filly," she said breaking the long silence.

Nick nodded. "They do grow fast."

Lindsay waited, but he didn't say any more. She had the uneasy feeling he was upset with her but she had no idea why. Would she ever know the real Nick? Shrugging, she gave up trying to figure him out, and concentrated on scratching and rubbing the friendly young filly.

Ten minutes later, Lindsay groaned and stretched into a standing position. "Well, little girl, that's about all I can do today," she told the filly. Her back and shoulders ached from the awkward bent-over stance she was forced to take to scratch the small horse. Giving the filly a final goodbye pat, she walked over to Nick.

"Ready to head back?" she asked him pleasantly.

"I guess so." Nick rose to stand beside her. "But it doesn't look like your little friend is ready for you to leave yet."

Lindsay just started to turn around when she felt a tiny nose thrust hard into her back. Taken off guard, she stumbled forward right into Nick's chest. Strong, sure arms instantly reached around her waist to hold her breathlessly close.

"Did you conspire with your filly to pull this little trick?" Nick asked huskily, his eyes boring into hers. "If so, I heartily approve."

Lindsay felt her face flushing. "She has a mind of her own," she smiled, trying to keep her voice steady. This was closer than she had been to Nick in a long time, and her body at once told her it had been too long.

"So do you," Nick commented quietly as he lowered his mouth ever so slowly to hers.

She wondered fleetingly what he meant by that, but as soon as his lips touched hers, her mind went deliriously blank as her mouth and body responded to his. Her arms curled up around his neck, pulling him tightly to her. They devoured each other's lips hungrily, the passion blazing between them as quickly as a flame ignites dry timber.

Unable to keep her hands still, Lindsay reached up to caress the back of his head, searching under the cowboy hat for his thick, wavy hair. As she reached, she tipped the hat off his head, and it tumbled to the ground. Neither took any notice until a moment later when their mouths gaspingly broke contact. Lindsay's eyes were closed as she clung to him, her head resting against his massive chest, trying to catch her breath. Suddenly Nick released her so abruptly she nearly fell to the ground. Her eyes flew open in confusion as she stumbled to regain her balance.

"Nick, what's the—" she began.

"My hat! Get off my hat!" he yelled, waving his arms.

Lindsay stared at him, thinking he must have lost his mind. Still shaken from the passion of their kiss, her numb brain seemed to be working in slow motion. It took several moments for his words and actions to sink in and finally she looked to the ground, searching for Nick's hat. It was then that it hit her, and she burst into laughter. For there, not three feet away from them, was Nick's beloved Stetson being pawed and smashed unceremoniously into the dirt beneath one delicate hoof of the curious young filly.

Nick threw her an exasperated glance. "Get out of here, you little—" he yelled again at the filly and moved quickly toward her.

But before Nick could get a swat at her, the young horse wheeled and galloped off to join her mother, shaking her tiny head rebelliously as she ran.

Lindsay had tried to curb her laughter, but as Nick slowly picked his hat up off the ground with a crestfallen look on his handsome face, fresh peals of glee burst from her.

"You really are a true-blue cowboy, aren't you? You think of your hat before your woman. You toss me aside to rescue your precious cowboy hat from certain doom," she teased, her emerald eyes dancing in merriment.

Nick raised his eyes from his crumbled hat to Lindsay. The look of irritation that was on his face suddenly changed to a silly grin as he digested her words.

"You're all right, aren't you?" he asked a little sheepishly.

She nodded, her face still lit up in a large smile. Then she sobered her features dramatically. "Do you think it will live?"

Nick jumped forward and grabbed her forearms in one easy motion and shook her gently. "You! You probably put her up to that, didn't you?" he demanded, one eyebrow raised thoughtfully.

"I see it all now," he continued grandly, releasing her and gesturing with the hand that still held his hat. "First you had her push you into me, because you knew I wouldn't be able to resist kissing those luscious lips of yours." He eyed her wickedly. "Then, when my guard was down, you pushed my hat off, and she took it from there. Lucky for you two, I noticed your little plot before she could completely ruin the hat!"

Lindsay was laughing so hard, tears began to stream down her cheeks. She shook her head and tried to speak, but she couldn't get any words out.

"What are you laughing at?" he demanded with mock gruffness. Then he reached up and plucked Lindsay's cowboy hat off her head. "I'll teach you a lesson," he threatened, turning away from her. "Where'd my colts go?"

"Nick!" she burst out, running after him. She grabbed his arm and tried to wrestle her hat away from his firm grasp. "Give that back! You know it cost me an arm and a leg to get an authentic cowboy hat you would approve of."

Nick stopped and squinted down at her. "Tried to impress me, huh?"

Lindsay flushed. She glanced up at Nick, aware that he was expecting some kind of answer. She was sorry their lighthearted playfulness had taken this sudden serious turn.

She shrugged and looked away from his intense gaze. "You didn't like me much back then," she replied quietly, her heart suddenly and unreasonably heavy. "I didn't want to give you any reason to find fault with me. Besides, I hated that other hat."

Nick chuckled and reached out to smooth a stray strand of hair away from Lindsay's face. "You did look pretty foolish in that old hat. Every time you moved, it would fall over your eyes." He paused and sobered. "I guess I was a little rough on you in the beginning."

Lindsay smiled at the reluctant admittance. It was as close as she was going to get to an apology, she knew. But it didn't matter anyway. Those early days on the ranch seemed like a lifetime ago.

She lifted her gaze to meet Nick's again, and a tide of love and emotion surged through her as she stared into those blue, suddenly fiery eyes. She watched him lower his face to hers and felt him brush her lips ever so lightly. Then he straightened.

"We better be getting back," he said in a tightly controlled, almost choked voice. He threw one arm casually around her shoulders, and she reached up with her hand to grasp his fingers in her own.

They walked back to the ranch in silence. Lindsay didn't question him when he kept going right by her cabin and didn't stop until they stood on the doorstep of his own cabin. They often had a nightcap together in his cabin or just talked or watched TV.

But tonight Nick hesitated before opening the door. Lindsay turned to look at him, waiting for him to speak. For some reason, she noticed her pulse had suddenly started racing and her mouth had gone dry.

"Lindsay," he whispered huskily, pulling her into his arms. "Will you stay with me tonight?"

She'd known what the words were going to be before her ears confirmed them, so she was somehow prepared for the question. What she wasn't prepared for, however, was the depth of desire she saw as she met Nick's eyes. She trembled as she realized instinctively that no man had ever wanted her as much as Nick did now. Nor had she ever wanted anything as much in her life as she wanted him, needed him, to make love to her. And yet . . .

She kept remembering his words the night she turned him down before. *I'm not through with you yet.* Was she just a pursuit, a game, a challenge to him? He had never voiced any feelings of any kind for her, so how was she to know how he really felt?

At least he hadn't lied, either, which was some comfort, she supposed. She truly believed he at least liked her now, and there was certainly a great deal of chemistry and magnetism between them. But did he respect her as a woman, a friend, a *person*? He knew of her plans to return to Chicago after the summer, so he surely wouldn't be thinking of getting involved in a relationship with her. So why did he bother at all?

Lindsay sighed and felt Nick stiffen against her. He wanted an answer, she knew. It seemed he always wanted answers from her, but when did she ever get an answer from him? she thought with a touch of irritation. She wished fervently that they could just be totally honest with each other, but at the same time she was afraid to ask him a direct question because she knew he probably would tell her the truth. And negative honesty was more than she could take. The only thing that kept her going now was the clinging hope that someday Nick would love her as much as she loved him.

"Lindsay?" Nick broke softly into her troubled thoughts, his hand lifting her chin so she had to look at him. "It shouldn't take you that long to think about it. Listen to your body; you want me as much as I want you. I've wanted you since the first time I saw you." He lowered his head to lay gentle kisses on the side of her throat. "I've tried to be patient, to give you the time you seem to need, but, honey, I don't know how many more cold showers I can take."

Lindsay closed her eyes and tried to quiet her trembling body. He was just too close for her to think rationally. "Nick," she began in an unsteady voice.

"Why are you fighting me, fighting making love to me? I can't believe you're an innocent—saving yourself for your wedding night." The words were spoken softly, but there was also an undercurrent of sarcasm there that Lindsay didn't miss.

His words were as effective as one of his cold showers. She pulled away from him, and when she spoke, her voice was deadly calm.

"Sometimes I wonder if I even know you at all. Or if you know me. When are you going to stop insulting me? Is that a cowboy's way to seduce a lady?"

"Honey, you ain't no lady." Nick's voice had also become low and cold. "But thank you for reminding me of how different we are. Sometimes, with your little games, I seem to forget that for awhile."

It was so strange, Lindsay thought silently, how we can be ready to fall passionately into bed one minute and be taking off each other's heads like hated enemies the next.

She gave him a bittersweet smile. "Why do you assume I'm playing some sort of game whenever I do something that you don't happen to agree with?" she demanded, her anger starting to rise.

"Because I know you better than you think I do. I know when you're being honest and when you're not."

"And just because I won't jump into bed with you I'm not being honest?"

"That's part of it." Nick grabbed her roughly by the wrists, forcing her to look into his eyes. "Why don't you really tell me why you won't make love to me?"

Lindsay struggled to get away from him, but it was futile. There was no way she could break loose until he let go of her. "What's the difference, anyway?" She spat the words out. "You don't care about any truth from me. All you want is one thing. Well, maybe I want something more."

"What do you want, moonlight and roses?" he scoffed. "Do you want to be courted, serenaded, seduced by candlelight? Do you want me to whisper false promises to you, to tell you I love you just so you'll sleep with me?''

Something like that, her mind answered, even though in her heart she knew that empty, insincere words would be worse than none at all. She did not look at him as he continued.

''The reality is that I find you wildly attractive, that I want very much to make love to you, and you want it too. Don't you?''

Lindsay was staring at the third button of his shirt, and refused to answer. He shook her again, this time more gently.

''Don't you?'' he repeated.

Boldly, angrily, she raised her eyes to meet his. ''I did a few minutes ago. But I sure as hell don't want to now.''

''Oh, no?'' The words were barely out of his mouth before he had taken possession of her mouth in a crushing, punishing kiss.

She fought determinedly against responding; she wouldn't give him the satisfaction. But he wouldn't give up until she did, and he kept up his bruising attack on her lips until at last, despite her best intentions, Lindsay was kissing him back, matching his fierceness with a desire so strong she thought she would explode.

As abruptly as the kiss had began, it was suddenly over, leaving Lindsay so weak she had to hang onto Nick's arms to keep from falling.

''I rest my case.''

He had meant to say it unemotionally, but there was a tremor in his voice that betrayed he was as shaken as she was by the furor of their desire.

Lindsay shook her head. ''How can you say those awful things to me and then kiss me like that?'' Her confused voice was barely audible. *And how can I respond after he talks to me like that?* her mind finished.

"Go back to your own cabin, Lindsay." He released her and turned to the door.

Before he could get inside, she pulled him around to face her. "Why me, Nick? You could have any woman you want and you know it. So why are you wasting your time on a city girl like me?" The words were out before she knew it, and she instantly regretted them.

His hard features softened for a moment, then returned to their usual unreadable mask. "Is it a waste of time?"

"You tell me," she countered.

"I really don't know," he answered quietly. Then he bent down and lightly kissed her cheek. "Good night, Lindsay. Sleep well."

She watched him walk into his cabin and close the door. It was a full two minutes before she at last turned and walked slowly back to her own cabin.

When she finally reached the sanctuary of her bedroom, she laid down on top of the bed, hugging her pillow to her chest. Gradually her anger and hurt gave way to a numbing emptiness that left her feeling so restless she had to get up and move around. Not knowing where else to go, her legs carried her automatically to Sundance's stall.

It was almost dark in the barn, but it suited Lindsay's mood so she did not turn any lights on. As she entered the mare's stall, she stood quietly waiting for her eyes to adjust to the shadows. It was several minutes before she could make out the figure of her horse laying down in the corner of the stall. Lindsay knelt so as not to startle the mare and crawled through the fresh straw to sit beside her.

"How you doing, lady?" she whispered, stroking the mare's velvety nose. Sundance merely sniffed at her in answer.

Lindsay sighed deeply and waited for the serenity that usually enveloped her when she was with her horse. But tonight it seemed she could not find peace no matter what she did. Rising again after about twenty minutes, she was about to return to her cabin when she noticed a light on in the tack room at the other end of the barn. Aimlessly, she headed toward it.

"You're working late," she commented idly, leaning her lithe frame against the doorway.

Jake looked up from the leather bridle he was repairing and flashed her a grin. "I usually am the night before the first guests arrive. It gets so hectic around here starting tomorrow that I always think of a thousand things to do at the last minute." He paused and gave her a long, hard look. "What about you?"

She shrugged. "I don't know. I just couldn't sleep. Maybe I'm excited about tomorrow, too."

Jake nodded but seemed unconvinced. Lindsay decided she'd better change the subject. "I haven't seen much of you lately," she said conversationally.

Jake didn't look up. "That's no surprise. Nick's been keeping pretty close tabs on you." He paused for a moment and raised his dark, questioning eyes to her. "How are things going between you two?"

"I wish I knew," she told him truthfully. "Sometimes it seems like we get along great, and other times it's like we're distrustful strangers."

"I told you once before that Nick was a hard man to get to know. After Julie betrayed him, he was bitter toward all the married women guests who threw themselves at him. Considering his past experience, I guess I can't blame him for not trusting women much anymore. Anyway, since his divorce he hasn't let any woman get close to him."

"Well, he's still batting a thousand," she muttered, more to herself than to him.

Jake returned his attention to the bridle he was stitching. "So now that you've been here a while, how do you like it?"

She smiled with genuine pleasure. "I love it, I really do. Wyoming is so beautiful and everyone here is so nice. It seems like years since I've been in Chicago, not just a few weeks."

"I know it's early in the season and all, but are you thinking about maybe staying here?" he asked casually.

The question startled her, and she wasn't sure just how she should respond. "I haven't really thought about it, I guess," she said hesitantly. Oh, but she had thought about it, thought about being with Nick for the rest of her life. If only....

"Besides," she rushed on, hoping Jake's knowing eyes wouldn't see her true thoughts, "I was under the impression that not many people were kept on through the winter."

"That's true," he agreed. "But my uncle is always looking for a few good people to work here year-round. And I know so far he's pretty happy with the job you're doing."

"Even though he blames me for Tramp getting out that night?" she asked with raised eyebrows.

Jake didn't look up. "Oh, I think I've convinced him that you weren't the one who did it."

"Now if only you could convince Nick," she grumbled. Even though he hadn't brought it up again, she still had the feeling that Nick wasn't entirely sure she really wasn't to blame.

Jake glanced up at her and smiled warmly. "I'm not always too successful at reasoning with Nick. But anyway, just give some thought to maybe staying on here. Then you won't be surprised if Uncle Ross asks you."

"All right, I'll think about it." Think about it! She'd probably be able to think about nothing else! If Ross offered her a job, then surely Nick would come to love her as much as she loved him. And what better place to be with him than here, in the gorgeous, glittering, glorious mountains? The thought sent shivers through her.

Her spirits lifted, she gave Jake a bright smile. "I guess I'm going to turn in now. Don't you work too hard."

"I won't," he promised. "See you in the morning."

After bidding Jake a final good-night, Lindsay headed toward her cabin. As she walked, she tried to calm herself down a little bit. After all, she reasoned, Ross hadn't offered her anything yet. And it would probably be a couple of weeks before he would be sure enough of her work that he would ask her to stay on for the winter. She shouldn't get her hopes up over something that was still up in the air. She vowed, though, to work harder than ever the rest of the summer.

As she reached out to open her front door, Lindsay jumped back at the sound of movement to her left. It took her straining eyes a full five seconds to identify the figure that stood there, but it only took her pulses a mere two seconds to tell her it was Nick who was waiting in the shadows.

"Nick!" she scolded nervously. "You scared me."

"Sorry," he replied quietly. "I couldn't sleep, and I thought maybe you couldn't either."

"No, I couldn't," she said simply.

"Lindsay, I . . ." He paused for a moment, then held out open arms to her. "Come here," he ordered huskily.

She hesitated just long enough to let his words sink in, and then rushed into his arms. She buried her nose in the front of his brawny chest and wrapped her arms tightly around his waist. It was several minutes before either one spoke.

"I sat in my cabin thinking about what a nice day we'd had together today, and I wondered why we had to end it the way we did." Nick's voice was quiet and thoughtful in her ear. He pulled her away from him just enough so he could peer earnestly into her face. "I'm sorry, Lindsay. I guess sometimes I want you so badly it just about makes me crazy, and I don't stop to think of what I'm saying."

"I know you don't understand, but—" she started, but Nick interrupted her.

"That doesn't matter. You have your reasons for holding back, and you're right, I don't understand them, but I've never forced a woman into my bed before and I don't intend to start with you."

"I don't imagine you've ever had to force a woman to sleep with you before," Lindsay mumbled, not meeting his eyes.

Nick ignored that. "Will you tell me what's bothering you?"

She pushed away from him and stood staring out into the night. How could she possibly explain any of it to him?

"Earlier, I said I couldn't believe you were an innocent. Is that it? *Are* you a virgin?"

Lindsay didn't miss the slight catch in his voice. "You should have asked me that before you started making nasty accusations," she snapped.

He was so close behind her that she could feel his breath on her hair. But he did not touch her. "You're right. But you didn't answer my question."

How she wished she could fling it in his face that she really was untried, and she even momentarily considered lying to him, but she realized this was something she had to be honest about.

"I'm not," she said quietly. She heard him exhale sharply. Angrily, she turned back to face him with her emerald eyes flashing. "That doesn't make me loose, either. For your information, I've slept with exactly one man in my entire life. And that was quite some time ago. And I'm not even that sure I enjoyed it."

He reached out and stroked her cheek gently. "It doesn't matter, anyway," he told her, but he was unable to keep a trace of disappointment out of his voice. He'd really hoped he could be the one to show her about the wonders of making love, even though he'd figured he couldn't possibly be the first. "I just thought maybe that was why you were holding back."

No, that wasn't really why. Instinctively she knew just how special and wonderful it would be to make love to him. Lindsay sighed. Actually, she pretty much considered herself an innocent. She was a freshman in college when she'd slept exactly three times with her steady boyfriend, Jeff, who was a senior. Her new friends had made her feel different because they were all experienced while she wasn't. So she'd pretended to herself that she was in love with Jeff and had eventually given in to his pressuring her to sleep with him. She had never told him the first time they did was really her first time, and she'd been more hurt than happy after their lovemaking.

At least Jeff had realized the truth afterward when she'd been unable to keep back her tears. Promising he would be gentler the next time and that she would enjoy it, Lindsay had almost felt obligated to try again. But even after the third time, all she'd felt was empty and unaroused. A few days later, she'd broken up with him.

She'd dated men on occasion after that, but had never felt any desire to be intimate with any of them. She even had wondered if she was somehow unable to be truly aroused by a man. But meeting Nick had changed all those doubts. It was still hard for her to believe how fully passion and desire overtook her when she was around him.

Nick pulled her into his arms again, which effectively pushed away all her thoughts of the past. Her body responded instantly to the here and now, and to the hungry, overpowering need she had for him.

Nick read the confusion and doubts in her face and sighed. It was obvious she wasn't ready to accept him yet. And dammit, no matter how much other parts of him argued otherwise, he was just going to have to be patient and wait. He wouldn't force her. For some reason, it had become important to him for her to be sure about sleeping with him. He didn't want her to have any regrets.

"Okay, my sweet little city girl," he murmured as he gently caressed her back. "Have it your way. But someday you're going to stop listening to your head and start listening to your body."

He bent over to kiss her deeply, passionately, his tongue doing erotic dances with hers. She melted in his arms, her heart pounding so loudly it shook her whole being.

Just when she thought she could take it no longer, his mouth pulled away. "Get some sleep," he ordered brokenly. "We've got a big day tomorrow."

Giving her one final light brush with his lips, he turned and strode off into the night. Lindsay stared after him as long as she could make out his powerful frame, but within seconds the darkness seemed to swallow him up. Exhaling deeply, she went shakily into her cabin and got ready for bed. She had a feeling this was going to be a long night.

Chapter Nine

As the orange Wyoming sun was first lighting up the new day, Lindsay was sitting in the window watching it illuminate the ranch. She'd spent a restless night. She knew that her relationship with Nick would change soon; either she would give in to the desperate need of her body or she would have to break off with him entirely. She didn't think she could handle these feelings of restlessness and unfulfillment much longer.

She rose and walked into the bathroom to take a shower. Resolutely, she decided that the next time Nick started to pressure her, she would give in and the consequences be damned. The decision was oddly thrilling, and she suddenly felt as if a heavy burden was lifted off of her mind. Whistling cheerfully, she quickly showered and dressed for what she knew would be a big day, perhaps in more ways than one.

As she entered the dining room for breakfast, her eyes searched for Nick. In moments she located him, and as was uncannily the case every morning, his dark blue eyes had noticed her first. Smiling briefly, she went over to get her food and then joined him. She was somewhat surprised to see Jake and Cindy Thompson at the table with him. Usually they sat alone.

"Good morning, everyone," she said as she sat down in the empty chair next to Nick.

Jake and Cindy chorused their greetings, but Nick just gave her that special smile that was hers alone. He was watching her so intently she suddenly had the uneasy feeling that he had read her mind and was aware of her new decision to make love to him. Chiding herself for being silly, she broke away from his gaze and looked down at her breakfast.

"Well, Lindsay," Jake spoke up pleasantly, "about two o'clock the first group of guests should be arriving. Then you'll see what this ranch is all about, and the work will really begin."

She smiled easily at Jake. "Speaking of work, I hope you didn't stay up too late working last night."

Lindsay immediately caught the surprised and somewhat suspicious look Nick gave her. She realized that he didn't know where she'd been last night before he found her back at her cabin. She was secretly pleased at his jealous reaction.

"I couldn't sleep last night, and after I visited Sundance, I found Jake working away into the wee hours of the night in the tack room," she explained carefully to Nick.

"Yeah, but she didn't offer to help me. When I mentioned working late, she took off back to her cabin," Jake added lightly, also not missing the possessive way Nick was looking at Lindsay.

Lindsay relaxed as Nick's tension eased and he returned to eating. *If he didn't care about me, why would he get upset the minute he found out I had seen Jake last night?* her optimistic side quickly thought. But her pessimistic side just as quickly had an answer: *Maybe his ego doesn't want anyone else to get to me first.*

"Any regulars coming in this week?" Cindy directed her question at Nick.

He shrugged. "The usual. The Martinsons, the Thorps and the Babcocks. The rest are newcomers, I think."

"Lindsay, wait until you see Michael Babcock." Cindy giggled. "He's just gorgeous. He comes here every year with his daughter. He's divorced. Or at least he was last year."

Nick threw Cindy an irritated glance. "I'm sure Lindsay didn't come to work at this ranch just to see every gorgeous man that vacations here for a few days." He gave Lindsay a pointed stare before looking back at Cindy. "And Babcock hasn't given you the time of day since the first year he came here."

"I know, but a girl can always hope." Cindy sighed. "Besides, there's nothing wrong with enjoying *all* the scenery around here, is there?" She winked at Lindsay. "And I haven't seen many beautiful women go by that have escaped your notice."

Lindsay chuckled as Nick momentarily looked decisively uncomfortable. Then he suddenly grinned.

"It's part of the job to be nice to all the guests." He paused and again looked directly at Lindsay. "But not too nice."

She understood what he meant, but she had no desire to even look at another man now. All other men paled in comparison to Nick. Yes, Nick's ex-wife had indeed been a fool.

She smiled warmly at Nick. "I'm sure that after awhile I'll get the feel of just how nicely to treat everyone by following your example."

Nick nodded once, his cobalt eyes burning into hers. "Touché, love," he whispered so quietly she barely heard him.

The morning passed quickly in a rush of last-minute activity. Ross, in his anxiety to have every detail perfect, yelled for Nick so often that at last Nick gave up trying to get anything else done and stayed by his boss's side while together they triple-checked everything.

With Nick's time being monopolized, Lindsay hardly saw him all morning. This was the first time in more than two weeks that she and Nick had not spent the entire day together. And she realized ruefully just how much she missed him.

At precisely two-fifteen the first car was spotted driving up the long road to the ranch.

"For God's sake, at least you all could look busy instead of standing here gawking!" Ross yelled as he noticed almost every one of the employees was standing by the main lodge doing absolutely nothing.

"Come on, we'll hide in the kitchen," Cindy whispered to Lindsay. "Then we'll still be able to see who it is."

Lindsay giggled and followed her into the kitchen, where the two of them peered out at the registration desk from behind the window in the kitchen door. A few minutes later a family of five came in through the front door. Lindsay quickly assessed the parents, about fortyish, and their three teenagers. They were all impeccably dressed, the man in a three-piece suit and the woman in a silk dress with high-heeled sandals. She would have expected their children at least to be dressed more suitably for a ranch, but they were also done up in their Sunday best.

Definite greenhorns, Lindsay thought to herself. And then she almost burst into laughter. Here she was, judging the guests, when only a few weeks ago she was angry about everyone judging her without first seeing what she could do.

"Those are the Thorps," Cindy explained quietly. "They've been coming here for three years now, but they still hardly know which end of the horse is which."

Lindsay chuckled. At least her assessment of them had been accurate.

"They're sort of prissy, but they're pretty nice." Cindy pulled her away from the doorway. "Come on, we'll go out the back door. If Ross catches us in here, we'll be on shoveling duty for a month."

Shoveling duty, Lindsay knew, was helping clean manure out of all the stalls. Not the most pleasant job in the world, it was assigned to those employees who grumbled about being told to do a certain task or who didn't do their jobs as they should. Shoveling duty was more of a threat than an actual occurrence, but it kept all the employees happily doing whatever they were told to do, and doing it well.

As the afternoon progressed, eight more carloads of people arrived. Dinner was served at seven that night to accommodate later guests, and as Lindsay walked into the dining room, she was amazed at how crowded the large room appeared with the addition of the guests. Her eyes scanned the room eagerly for Nick, as she hadn't seen him in hours. She found him at last at a table in one corner. She was pleased to see he was sitting at one of the smaller tables that only sat two people.

She hurried and got her meal and then made her way across the room to him. After weaving through the maze of tables, she at last sat breathlessly beside him.

"Whew," she said, smiling at him. "It's harder to get around in here with all these extra people."

"There's still about twenty more guests who won't get here until tomorrow. Then we'll be at maximum capacity for a while."

He paused and Lindsay felt his hand on her knee beneath the table.

"I missed you today," he told her gruffly.

Her heart jumped into double time, and her knee tingled under his touch. "I missed you, too," she told him honestly.

"Did you see Cindy's 'gorgeous' Michael Babcock yet?" he asked curiously with one raised eyebrow.

Lindsay flushed. Actually, Cindy had pointed him out to her. He was slender and blond, and he was handsome in a male-model sort of way.

But he's nothing compared to you, she wanted to tell Nick. He looks like a strong wind could blow him away, while I think you could even stand through a tornado. It was like comparing a twig to a giant redwood. Lindsay sighed. She used to enjoy looking at attractive men, but now there was only one man she cared to look at. And she was looking at him right now.

Realizing Nick was waiting for some kind of answer, she wrinkled up her nose. "Cindy can have him. He's not my type."

"Oh? And just what is your type?"

You are, she thought. You and only you.

"I sort of prefer the obstinate cowboy type," she finally said lightly, gazing into the aquamarine depths of his eyes. She waited for some sort of comment from him or some reaction in his eyes, but as usual his face gave away nothing. Damn him anyway, she thought with a touch of anger, why can't he ever give some sort of clue as to how he feels?

She looked away from him and stared at her plate. The roast beef and mashed potatoes had looked enticing, but suddenly she couldn't taste a thing. It was several minutes before Nick spoke again.

"Why are you picking at your food?"

Lindsay jumped and stirred uncomfortably. "I guess in all the excitement of the guests finally arriving, I'm not that hungry," she offered lamely.

Nick seemed to accept that. "Just don't make a habit of it. You need to eat."

"You must have been a grandmother in another life." She laughed, shaking her head. "If I ate as much as you think I should, I'd weigh two hundred pounds."

"If you ate as much as I think you should, I could work you harder," he countered with a chuckle.

She slapped him indignantly on the arm. "As if you don't work me hard enough as it is!"

"It just seems hard because you're used to easy work in the city."

"In some ways, the work was harder at the insurance company." Lindsay pointed to her head. "It was taxing on my mind, not my body. And I would be almost as tired at the end of the day as I am here."

Nick pushed his empty plate into the middle of the table. "Well, my soft little city girl, are you done eating?"

She nodded, even though she'd left almost half of her dinner.

"Come on, let's get out of here before Ross makes his big speech to the guests. It's pretty boring."

She followed him out of the dining room, noticing the appreciative glances several of the women guests gave him as he walked by. Nor did she miss the looks of envy they gave her.

"What's Ross going to talk about?" she asked Nick when they got outside.

"Oh, just about the general procedure around here, the different rides they can take and how to sign up the day before for what they want to do."

"Will there be a ride tomorrow?"

"Probably." He reached out to put his arm around her waist as they walked. "If you check the assignment sheet in the kitchen like a good little employee, you'll see that you and I will be among the guides for the afternoon trail ride tomorrow, if enough people sign up for it."

"Oh," she said simply. But she was glad Nick had still evidently chosen to assign her to the same jobs he had.

She hadn't been paying particular attention to where they were walking, so she was surprised a minute later to see Nick had stopped in front of her cabin. He pulled her into his arms and briefly kissed her.

"I've got to talk to Jake about some things," he told her. "I'll see you tomorrow."

He kissed her again, but was careful to stop before it got too passionate. Then he smiled at her confused expression, turned and strode away.

She watched him head toward the barn, too astonished to even say good-night. When he was out of sight she went into her cabin and irritably slammed the door. She immediately felt a sense of disappointment and emptiness so strong that she didn't want to dwell on the meaning of it. She only knew that somehow Nick had turned the tables on her again. Would he be unpredictable forever?

For the next three days, Lindsay didn't have a chance to be alone with Nick. The ranch was bursting with guests and activities, and she was so exhausted by evening that she went to bed soon after she and Nick had supper. He seemed glad to have it that way, and she was just too tired to be perturbed by his behavior. During the days, though, he was as attentive as he could be considering how busy they were.

On the fourth day of the guest season, Lindsay was helping several other employees saddle the horses that would be used on that day's breakfast ride. The group would be riding several miles before stopping high in the mountains for a steak-and-egg breakfast, and Lindsay was ravenous already. She laughed to herself as she realized how little time it had taken for her stomach to get used to eating a hearty meal early every morning.

"You don't look quite so tired this morning," Nick commented to her as he led a saddled horse past her.

"I think I'm finally getting used to the pace," she said cheerfully. "But I hope it doesn't take long to reach that chuck wagon. I'm starving!"

Nick chuckled and winked at her. "We might get you converted to this way of life yet."

Lindsay took a deep, shaky breath as she watched him walk over to the corral and tie up the horse he had been leading. How she wished he would stop making little references like that about her maybe staying on and instead just openly give her some encouragement.

In a few minutes all the trail horses were ready, and the guides started the lengthy process of getting the guests up on the horses, adjusting stirrups and giving instructions on how to handle the horses.

Lindsay was aiding a particularly hefty woman up in the saddle when suddenly something snapped. The saddle slipped to the side of the horse and the woman, totally off balance, toppled against Lindsay, landing the two of them on the ground in a heap.

"Oh, dear," the woman gasped as she gingerly got up. "What in the world happened, young lady?"

Lindsay jumped up as soon as the heavy woman was out of her way. "I'm not sure. Something broke on the saddle. Are you all right?"

Several people rushed over, including Nick. "Lindsay, what happened?" he asked anxiously.

She straightened the saddle on the calm horse's back and began to examine the tack. In a moment she discovered that the leather latigo strap on the off side of the horse had split in two. When the woman's weight had been put into the stirrup, the stress had caused the strap to break and the saddle then slipped to the side of the horse.

"I don't understand," she said quietly to Nick, shaking her head.

He frowned. "That strap must have been partially torn before. There's no way it could have split in two all at once."

"I know. But yesterday I helped Jake clean and check all the tack. We certainly couldn't have missed something like this," Lindsay said in puzzlement.

"At least Jake couldn't have missed it."

Lindsay turned to stare in disbelief at him. "How can you say that?" she began angrily.

"I've been coming to this ranch for three years now, and nothing like this has ever happened before," the heavy-set woman interrupted, her voice starting to rise. "I want to see Ross Browning. He must be getting mighty careless about hiring his help nowadays."

"Now, ma'am, take it easy," Nick said to her in his most charming voice. He flashed her a forced smile. "Accidents do happen. At least you weren't hurt, right?"

"Well," she huffed, "I guess not. But I could have been! And I still want to see Ross. Where is he?"

Nick motioned towards the lodge. "You can probably find him in his office in the main lodge. But wouldn't you rather just take another horse and go out on that breakfast ride?''

"I should say not. I'm much too upset about this whole matter to ride today, or maybe ever again at this place," the woman stormed, and marched off to the lodge.

"She certainly wasn't very understanding," Lindsay grumbled when the woman was out of earshot.

"She has a right to be concerned. Something like this should never have happened," Nick whispered sternly. Then he turned away from her and smiled into the worried faces of the guests. "Just to ease everybody's minds, we'll go over all the tack on your horses again," he called out loudly. "But I'm sure everything is just fine. I can assure you that we take very good care of our equipment."

Lindsay fumed as she double-checked several guests' saddlery. How could Nick accuse her so quickly of being totally at fault? Perhaps the bad latigo had been cleaned by Jake and he'd missed the tear in it, or maybe somehow both of them had overlooked that particular saddle, and it hadn't been checked at all. There were many possible explanations. Anyway, she doubted very much that she could have been the one to clean that saddle; she was just too careful about such things.

But wouldn't Jake have been, too? He'd been doing this sort of thing for a long time, and certainly he couldn't have been so careless either. So what had happened?

Lindsay could think of no answers by the time the group reached the chuck wagon and settled down to eat their breakfast. She had half a mind not to even sit by Nick, she was still so furious at him, but he moved to her side as soon as he had his metal plate filled with steak and eggs so she really had no choice. She refused to say anything to him first, though.

"Are you going to keep up this silent treatment all through the meal?" he asked at last when they were about half through eating.

She glared at him. "You owe me an apology."

"Why?"

"Why!" she exploded. "Why do you think?"

He shrugged and took another bite of steak. "You can't blame me for thinking you're at fault for this one. This has never happened in all the years Jake's been at the ranch. You have to admit you're the only logical candidate for the blame."

"But, Nick—" she sputtered.

"Look, as I told that woman, accidents do unfortunately happen. You'll be more careful in the future, I'm sure."

"You know there is the remotest possibility that I'm not responsible for missing that bad latigo yesterday," she told him sarcastically.

"Maybe," he agreed. "But why didn't you catch it when you were saddling?"

"I didn't even saddle that horse today!" she said indignantly. "And you know very well that everybody only tightens the left side of the cinch and doesn't check the off side for something like that. We can only assume since the tack is constantly checked that it must be all right."

He smiled indulgently at her. "You're probably right about that part. I guess whoever saddled that horse this morning is also partly to blame. I doubt whether anyone will jump forward and admit to doing it, though."

"Well, all I know is, it wasn't me," she mumbled stubbornly.

"Okay, okay, let's just forget about it," Nick suggested easily. "No one was hurt, thank God, so there's no sense harping about it."

Lindsay was surprised at how calmly he was actually taking it all. Even though she knew he still blamed her for the accident, he didn't seem terribly angry at her about it. That was something new.

Nick, too, was rather surprised at his reaction. Or rather, his lack of a reaction. He should be more upset at her, or at least more pleased that she had screwed up again. Hadn't he been waiting since the first day she came to the ranch for her to constantly make mistakes? So why was he taking this whole thing so lightly? Deep down, he must either think she wasn't really responsible for those two accidents or else he just didn't care. Neither thought was particularly reassuring.

Nick was silent on the way back to the ranch and let the other guides do the talking. All the guides except for Lindsay, that is. He noticed she wasn't talkative either. When they occasionally passed while making a tight turn on the trail, he found her watching him with a rather peculiar look on her face.

Dammit anyway, why did she have to be so beautiful, so stubborn, so sensitive, so smart? And so different from him? She seemed to be adapting to this life pretty well, yet he had to constantly remind himself that it was only temporary. In a few months she would be gone, back to her life in the city. Maybe even back to some hotshot boyfriend. The thought made his throat tighten uncomfortably.

Irritably he pushed his Stetson farther down on his head. He was going to have to get better control of his emotions. After his disastrous marriage, he'd vowed never to let himself become vulnerable to any woman again. And especially not to one as potentially dangerous as Lindsay. For he wasn't blind enough not to realize he was starting to fall for that lovely green-eyed vixen. He'd never in his entire life felt the things he was feeling for her. Not even for Julie, and at the time, he'd thought that he loved her more than it was humanly possible to love anyone. But with Lindsay, those feelings were even more intense.

It was just plain crazy. He knew he was unquestionably headed for a heartache worse than he'd had over Julie. And yet, he was powerless to try to do anything about ending his relationship with Lindsay. If he had one ounce of sense, he'd quit this job tomorrow and hightail it to another state far away from her.

But he couldn't do that. He was already in too deep. And that's what scared him more than anything.

"Have a nice ride?" Jake asked Lindsay pleasantly while they brushed horses and put them away.

"I guess so," she said, and then paused. "Jake, do you remember cleaning the saddle with that bad latigo?"

He shook his head regretfully. "No, I don't. I sure wish I knew how that could have happened." He rubbed his chin thoughtfully. "You know, I almost think we both missed that one somehow and it didn't get checked at all."

"I was sort of thinking the same thing. Then you don't blame me for it?"

"No. I've seen enough of your work to know how conscientious you are. I give you just as much chance of missing that bad latigo as I do myself."

Lindsay flashed him an appreciative smile. "Thank you. It's nice to know I have someone on my side once in a while."

Jake stopped his brushing and turned to look at her. "Meaning? No, let me guess. Nick thinks it's all your fault."

She sighed. "Of course."

"Nick just doesn't want to believe you're innocent. It's too easy to blame you."

"But why? Why can't he ever think someone else might make a mistake around here besides me?"

Jake turned back to the gelding and continued to brush him with long, sure strokes. "I told you he doesn't want to trust any woman. And you most definitely fit into that category."

"She most certainly does," a deep voice agreed.

Lindsay turned quickly to face Nick, who had suddenly appeared behind her. She flushed as she noticed the very personal way he was eyeing her.

"Talking about me behind my back again, you two?" he asked in an amused voice.

"Yes, and not a thing was good," she teased.

"Figures," Nick grunted.

"Actually, we were discussing those two accidents," Jake explained seriously. "You know, Nick, I don't think we should overlook the fact that maybe neither was really an accident."

"You mean you think someone is deliberately trying to sabotage the ranch?" Lindsay gasped. That idea had never occurred to her.

"You mean," Nick said mockingly, "that someone besides Lindsay is responsible for Tramp getting out and for that broken latigo."

"Come on, Nick, be serious." Jake set down his brush and faced Nick squarely. "You could put aside your own personal bias about this and look at it impartially."

"Okay, okay, don't get so excited," he said with one raised brow. He winked at Lindsay. "I was only being facetious, anyway."

"You could have fooled me," Lindsay muttered.

Nick tipped his hat back on his head and rubbed one temple thoughtfully. "I suppose it is a possibility, although I can't imagine why anyone would want to damage the reputation of the ranch. But I guess we'll just have to keep our eyes open.''

"Well, I don't know about you two, but I'm going to clean up before lunch. See you later,'' Lindsay told them, and quickly hurried out of the barn.

As she headed for her cabin, a cold chill went through her. Could Jake be right? Was someone trying to hurt the ranch and purposely making those accidents look like they were her fault?

No, the whole idea was a long shot. Yet, a tiny nagging voice wouldn't let her forget about the possibility. Well, if there was a chance that such a thing was going on, she was going to have to do a whole lot more than just keep her eyes open. She wasn't about to let someone get away with continuing to make her look like an incompetent idiot. This job, as well as Nick's opinion of her, were simply too important for that.

Chapter Ten

When the next few days passed uneventfully, Lindsay began to hope that no more "accidents" would occur. She hadn't brought up the topic with either Nick or Jake again, and she wondered if they, too, had dismissed the two incidents as freakish and insignificant.

However, Lindsay herself was the victim of an unrelated accident one evening after a trail ride. She was leading one of the horses into the barn when she stopped to say something to Jake. The horse stopped one step later, right on Lindsay's foot.

"Ow!" she screamed in agony, and pushed hard on the mare's shoulder. "Get off of me, you stupid horse!"

The mare finally obliged and shifted her hoof off Lindsay's cowboy boot. Lindsay lifted her foot immediately and gingerly held the end of it in one hand as it throbbed painfully.

"Are you all right?" Jake rushed to her side and took hold of her elbow.

"Ooh," she groaned, "I don't know."

"Here, let me have the clod," he said, pulling the horse's reins from her hand. "I'll put her away before she can do any more damage. She always was one not to watch where she put her feet."

"Now you tell me."

Lindsay hopped over to lean against a stall door. In a moment, Jake returned.

"Can you put any weight on it?"

"I don't know. It hurts too much right now to try." She continued to rub the aching toes as lightly as possible.

"Now you know why Uncle Ross insists on everybody wearing cowboy boots. Just think of the damage that would have been done if you were wearing tennis shoes."

"Remind me to thank him next time I see him," she said through clenched teeth.

"Come on, see if you can walk on it." Jake put his arm around her slender waist to give her some support and pulled her away from the stall.

Lindsay threw her arm around his shoulders and carefully tested her injured foot on the ground. With Jake's help, she could hobble a little.

"I don't think anything is broken," she replied after a minute of limping around. "It's feeling better already."

"Are you sure?" Jake teased, his eyes lighting up merrily. "It's kind of fun helping you walk like this."

Lindsay laughed and squeezed his shoulder with her fingers. "It's just like you to find something pleasurable out of my misery."

He flinched and shrugged his shoulder beneath her pinch. "Okay, okay, I'm sorry. Let go, will you?"

Just as she relinquished her death grip, she looked up to see a very straight-faced Nick watching them from a few feet away. Instantly she dropped her arm from around Jake's shoulder, but to her chagrin, Jake did not do likewise.

"Sorry to interrupt," Nick said coldly, his eyes hard and piercing. "I was looking for you to see if you were ready to go up to supper, but I can see you're otherwise occupied. My mistake." He turned sharply and walked out of the barn.

"Nick!" Lindsay called, pulling away from Jake.

"Oh, let him go," Jake muttered.

Lindsay watched him boldly stride away, and realized she had no other choice. But by the time he was out of sight, her own anger had risen considerably.

"Let's finish the chores," she suggested tightly. In her agitation, she forgot all about her foot, and she stomped around ignoring the tenderness in her toes.

The nerve of that man! she fumed silently as she dumped a can of grain into an anxious horse's bucket. She knew how it must have looked with her and Jake standing there with their arms around each other, but he still should not have jumped to conclusions! He could be so unfair when he wanted to be. She doubted he would ever trust her, the way he constantly thought the worst of her anytime something happened. Well, she would show him his childish behavior would not be tolerated.

A half hour later, when the evening chores were done, Lindsay headed huffily up to the main lodge for supper with Jake. She had insisted on waiting for Jake to finish his work before going up the lodge herself.

"I'm sorry for what happened in the barn," Jake said as they walked.

She flashed him a brief smile. "You don't have anything to be sorry about. It was a perfectly innocent situation. It's not your fault Nick acted like he did."

"Still, I feel partly responsible." He paused and glanced at her out of the corner of his eye. "Usually you don't wait for me to get everything done in the barn. Any special reason you did tonight?"

She shrugged. "Do I need a reason?"

"Don't get me wrong, I think it's great. But I just wondered if there was something significant behind it."

The closer they got to the lodge, the more her anger was quickly being replaced by nervousness at facing Nick. She was having trouble concentrating on Jake's words.

"Significant?" she repeated distractedly. "In what way?"

Jake chuckled quietly without mirth. "Obviously not in the way I was hoping," he mumbled more to himself than to her.

"I'm sorry, what did you say?"

"Nothing." He sighed. "Look, Lindsay, I hope that we are at least good friends. And you know anytime you want to talk or something, I'll be here for you. I'm a good listener."

She glanced over at him and met his warm gaze. She couldn't help but compare his dark blue eyes to Nick's aquamarine ones. Nick's eyes were so much more intense, so much more vivid than Jake's. And they could change without a moment's notice to almost steel gray when he was angry, and then they could just as suddenly match the baby-blue softness and sparkle of the sky.

But there was one bad quality to Nick's eyes—usually they were carefully veiled and unreadable. Jake's eyes were always open and frank, and when he had them turned to her, they were usually affectionate. And right now, they were a little too open and affectionate to suit her.

It struck her then that maybe Jake might want more from her than just friendship, and she wondered if they would have gotten involved if it hadn't been for Nick. Jake was certainly one of the nicest, most dependable men she had ever known, and yet for some reason she had never thought of him in the romantic sense; there was just no spark attracting her to him. With Nick, it had been an instant blaze from the very first time she had looked into his cool, amused, mocking eyes. And even though she knew she would almost certainly be hurt in the end by Nick, she'd been powerless to stop herself from falling deeply, irrevocably in love with him.

"You know, Jake," she said, her voice husky with emotion, "sometimes I wonder how I ever could have got along here without you. You've been a wonderful friend to me."

She had to look away from him then because she saw the disappointed look come over his face when she reaffirmed the word friend. So she had been right after all; Jake did feel something more than just friendship toward her. Dear, sweet Jake! She almost wished she could return his feelings. She knew she could always count on him. With Nick, she just wasn't sure.

The dining room, as usual, was crowded to capacity. It took her several long moments to locate Nick. When she did finally spot him, her heart sank in disappointment. He was seated with three other people at a table for four. She'd already decided to explain what had happened with Jake and try to smooth things over between them. It seemed, however, that Nick was going to do his best to avoid her.

She waited in the food line, her eyes remaining despondently on him. Finally he met her gaze. He studied her for several seconds with no expression at all on his face, then he raised his eyebrows and shrugged slightly. A moment later he turned back to the people at his table and rejoined their conversation.

Judging by the almost apologetic look on Nick's face, Lindsay wondered if perhaps the guests that were seated with Nick had sat down after he did, and Nick had been too polite to tell them one seat was saved for her. Still, she couldn't help but think it had most likely been the other way around—that Nick had sat down last, finishing off the table for four in order to evade her.

"So, are you going to eat with me tonight, too?" Jake asked as they walked away from the food line with heaped plates.

Lindsay flashed him a brief smile. Evidently he had also noticed Nick was already at a full table.

"Sure, why not?" she answered briskly. "If we can find a table."

"That's what happens when you wait for me; you're about the last one to eat." Jake led the way through the maze of tables and people. "I think there's room at one of the tables in the corner."

Lindsay followed him, smiling and greeting several of the guests. It was no coincidence, she was sure, that Jake chose to walk right by Nick's table.

"Evening, Nick." Jake grinned as they went around him.

Nick nodded curtly at Jake, barely glancing at him as he instead watched Lindsay. She met his smoldering blue eyes as they passed, but he did not smile or speak.

When they were finally seated at the end of a long table, Lindsay stared dismally down at her plate and wondered how she would ever get a bite of food down her tightened throat. As she picked at the ham and sweet potatoes, her eyes wandered unconsciously to Nick. He seemed to be enjoying himself immensely in the company of the family of three whose name escaped her. She also couldn't help but notice the attention the attractive and shapely teenage daughter was paying to Nick. She was flirting outrageously with him, laughing often and resting her hand on his arm just as frequently. Her mother was also seemingly entranced with the handsome cowboy at her table, while the father looked decidedly uncomfortable and remained for the most part silent. Lindsay could only stare at Nick and fume.

"Lindsay, I'm sure you'll be able to work things out with Nick," Jake said gently, noticing her agitation. "Do you want me to talk to him?"

She shook her head in answer, her voice suddenly cut off by the constriction of her throat. Pushing her untouched plate into the center of the table, she rose and walked quickly out of the dining room without looking at a single person.

She felt better just getting outdoors and breathing in the fresh, clean air. A ride, that's what she needed, a long ride on Sundance. She hurried to the barn and after hastily brushing and bridling the mare, she jumped up on her bareback. As soon as they were away from the confining corrals and buildings, she squeezed her horse into an easy, ground-covering canter.

The soft breeze lifted her long auburn hair away from her face and whipped Sundance's golden mane back to tangle in her fingers. Lindsay greedily drank in the cool air and the last rays of the setting sun, feeling more sated than if she had eaten.

Without the saddle to impede it, warmth from the mare's body radiated into Lindsay's legs and spread through her entire body. She reveled in the freedom and pleasure she felt at that moment.

After they had loped several miles, Lindsay pulled Sundance down into a relaxed walk. Gradually the exhilaration from the run wore off, and a feeling of melancholy overcame her. She was upset with herself for allowing her feelings to be swayed so easily by just the sight of Nick. Before she'd gone in the dining room, she was ready to indignantly tell him off. But as soon as she met those damn stony blue eyes, she'd melted again. And now all she wanted was to work things out with him. Where was her pride?

Her thoughts turned dejectedly to her future. What was she going to do? Not just with the present misunderstanding with Nick, but with her life in general? Would she be going back to Chicago after the season was over, or would she stay here and work at the ranch? Would Nick, could Nick ever love her the way she loved him?

She sighed and patted the mare's sweaty neck. "Life is just too complicated, lady."

"It certainly is," a deep voice agreed.

"Nick!"

Lindsay stared at him in astonishment. There he was, standing in the pine trees on the side of the trail a few feet in front of her, mounted bareback on his pinto. Where had he come from? He must have followed her out of the dining room, seen where she was headed and gotten here first. The thought that he'd come after her sent a tremor of joy through her.

"You could have at least taken the time to saddle your horse so I could have saddled mine, too." His smile was slightly mocking.

She flushed and looked away, hating herself for reacting to him as strongly as she did. She didn't like to be so transparent, so vulnerable.

"So what was the big hurry?" he asked casually.

She shrugged and tried to match his casualness. "I just felt like going for a ride."

"In the middle of dinner?"

"I get strange urges sometimes," she replied, then wished she could snatch the words back as she realized how they must have sounded.

Nick urged his horse forward and closed up the few steps that separated them. He reached out to lightly stroke her cheek with the back of one tanned, rough hand.

"So do I," he told her huskily.

Lindsay instantly felt more heat in her body than she had moments before while cantering on her warm horse. She trembled with longing for him and had to look away to hide the emotion in her burning eyes.

When she didn't speak, Nick dropped his hand back to his side and turned to move alongside of her. The two horses went forward in a leisurely walk.

"Tell me about you and Jake."

Lindsay stiffened, taken aback by the suddenness of his statement. He certainly wasn't going to beat around the bush. It wasn't even a question, it was more of a quiet order. She felt a prick of irritation at his attitude.

"What do you mean?"

"You know what I mean." His voice held a touch of impatience.

Lindsay stared at the trail in front of them. "There really isn't anything to tell. Jake was just helping me."

"That much was obvious. But helping you do what?"

"Walk."

"Walk?" he repeated curtly. "Will you stop hedging the issue and tell me the truth? Is there something going on between you two?"

"Of course not," she admonished, doing her best to sound offended. "One of the trail mares stepped on my foot while I was putting her away. Naturally it was pretty painful, and Jake was simply helping me walk so I could see how bad it was hurt. And that's all there is to it."

"It didn't look to me like you were experiencing much discomfort," he growled, unconvinced. "And it's pretty damn obvious how Jake feels about you. He follows you around like a lost colt."

Lindsay stared at him, stung by his words. "I think this whole conversation is ridiculous. Even if there was something between Jake and me, what would you care? You've never once given me an inkling of any commitment or any hint as to how you feel about me. I don't think you have any right to say such awful things to me," she retorted furiously.

"A commitment doesn't have to be spoken out loud to exist," he argued. "I thought certain things between us were understood."

"Well, obviously you were wrong."

"Maybe I've been wrong about more than that," he said flatly.

"What is that supposed to mean?"

"You tell me what I should think when I see you and Jake all wrapped around each other like that."

"Is the word 'trust' in your vocabulary, Nick?" she burst out. "All right, so Jake was giving me some support, and to do that he had to have his arm around me. Does that mean we're lovers or something? And maybe he does care about me. Is that my fault? Why do you have to believe the worst about me all the time? You don't see me drooling over him, do you?"

"No, but you looked damned nervous when I caught the two of you," he muttered.

"Speaking of drooling, you were doing a little of that yourself at dinner," she accused.

"That girl was hardly more than a child. And I certainly wasn't encouraging her."

"You certainly seemed to be enjoying yourself, being in the limelight with two attractive females. Why didn't you wait to sit with me?" she challenged him breathlessly.

"I didn't know who you wanted to sit with for supper, but before I could pick anywhere to sit that woman grabbed my arm and insisted I join them. They've been coming here for three years, and I hardly felt like I could politely refuse," he explained gruffly. "You know it's our job to cater to the guests."

"Be nice, but not too nice—isn't that what you told me once?" she reminded him.

"Yes, but," he started out, and then suddenly stopped his horse. "You have a marvelous talent for changing the subject. I wasn't through talking about Jake."

Lindsay stopped her horse and met his hard stare defiantly. "Well, I am through talking about him. I'm tired of having to prove myself over and over to you. Either you trust me or you don't. You'll just have to decide that for yourself."

She kicked Sundance into a canter and left Nick standing there. She held her breath as she waited anxiously for hoofbeats to follow her. It was almost a full minute before she at last heard Nick catching up to her. She watched out of the corner of her eye as he was soon abreast of her, and then all at once he had charged his horse in front of Sundance, cutting her off. She pulled her mare to a sliding stop.

"All right, so maybe I did overreact a little," he offered reluctantly. "You know the old saying: once bitten, twice shy."

Lindsay relaxed a little and gave him an understanding smile. She had won this battle; she only hoped she could win the war.

"I think these two are a bit tired. What do you say we get off and lead them a while?" Nick suggested.

Curious about his motive, Lindsay slid to the ground. Neither horse was breathing very hard and she knew both had had much more strenuous workouts before. She looked over at Nick and then burst out into laughter.

"I'd say your horse isn't quite done shedding for the summer, yet," she giggled, pointing to his jeans.

Nick glanced down at the inside of his legs and turned to look at the seat of his pants. His jeans were covered thickly with damp, white hairs.

"That's why I wanted a saddle," he groaned good-naturedly as he tried to brush away some of the hairs. "This always happens if I ride him bareback in the summer."

"Chestnut horses are more practical," she teased, checking out her own jeans. "You can't see their hair as well."

As she watched him continue to brush off his pants, her smile suddenly faded. He was bent over in front of her, and she stared in fascination at his tight buttocks and his muscled, bulging thighs. The seams on his cotton shirt were strained in their effort to clothe his broad back. Even though he was bent at the waist, not an ounce of fat hung over his belt buckle. His every movement was somehow so sensual that it made her weak, and she had to reach out and hang onto Sundance's mane for support. It never ceased to amaze her just how much she wanted this man.

"I guess it's hopeless," Nick murmured, straightening up. "I've got to ride him back anyway." Then he turned and looked at her.

She wasn't fast enough in masking her raw desire for him; she knew by the sudden burst of flame in his eyes that he had seen through her. He reached out for her and the next thing she knew, she was in his arms and he was kissing her as passionately as she longed for. His mouth devoured hers in a hunger that seemed even stronger than her own.

Unthinkingly, she dropped Sundance's reins to the ground and wrapped both arms tightly around his neck, trying to draw him even closer. Her breasts were crushed against his hard chest as strong hands on her back pulled her urgently against the full length of his body.

"Damn, you feel so good," he whispered, breaking contact from her mouth so they both could gasp for air. He nuzzled her neck, letting his tongue lounge lazily up and down the side of it.

"Lindsay?" His voice was gentle.

"What?" She could barely get the word out, her blood was racing so hard through her veins.

"Your horse is walking away."

It took several moments for his words to sink in. Her hooded eyes flew open wide and she pulled away to run toward the leisurely retreating Sundance.

"Whoa!" she called sternly to her mare over Nick's laughter. The horse stopped obediently and Lindsay walked her back to Nick.

He looked down at her flushed face and smiled tenderly. "I think we better get back to the ranch before it gets dark."

She nodded and they mounted their horses. After a few minutes of silence, Nick spoke again.

"It's probably a good thing I saw your horse when I did. In another minute I would have taken you right there in the grass."

Her heart pounding, Lindsay turned to meet his gaze. "And I would have let you," she replied honestly.

To her disappointment, Nick didn't respond. They rode the rest of the way back without further conversation.

Later, when she was putting Sundance away for the night, she wondered if this would be the night she and Nick stayed together. Surely he must have realized tonight that she was willing now, even eager, for the two of them to make love.

Her fingers shook at the thought as she lightly brushed Sundance.

Several stalls away, another horse was being brushed much more vigorously. Not that the huge pinto minded the grooming, but his owner's agitation was beginning to make the normally placid horse nervous.

Nick's arms were starting to ache from the exertion of the energetic brush strokes he was applying over his horse's body. What was the matter with him, anyway? Why did he suddenly feel as unsettled as a stallion that had been locked inside a stall for days on end?

That look in Lindsay's eyes had almost been too much for him. Tonight had been one of the few times she'd let her desire for him show. In fact, he'd seen it twice tonight. Once when he was trying to clean the horsehair off his jeans, and again when she'd told him she would have let him make love to her back there in the grass.

Could she really have meant it? he wondered. And now that they were back at the ranch, was the moment lost? Would she pull away and fight her feelings for him again? He knew now she wanted him as much as he wanted her. Well, maybe not quite as much. He very much doubted if that were possible.

He swore under his breath as he vividly remembered the sight of Jake with his arm around her, of her laughing with him, her body so close to his. It had felt like a butcher knife had twisted in his gut when he'd walked into the barn and seen them like that. Visions of the past came hauntingly back to him. Visions of his wife, his own damn *wife,* in bed with another man.

That had been almost more than he could take, but tonight, seeing Lindsay with Jake had somehow been even worse. He was extremely proud of himself that he had managed to get out the few harsh words that he had. It sure hadn't been easy. All he really wanted to do at that point was run over and jerk her out of Jake's grasp and hold her tightly to his own body. And shake the words out of her that she loved *him*.

Lindsay love him? He laughed scornfully at the thought. He hardly gave her a reason to even like him most of the time. Even now, as he was starting to realize and accept just how deep his feelings for her were becoming, a part of him still wanted to drive her away. Drive her away before she got any closer and hurt him that much more when she left to go back to Chicago. Or tired of him and found another man.

He had to admit Lindsay had been partially right earlier when she accused him of not having the word trust in his vocabulary. He'd trusted Julie, and where had that gotten him? It irked him that he wanted to trust Lindsay, he really did, but he found somehow he just couldn't. And he shouldn't, he argued with himself. After seeing her with Jake, it was a painful reminder of what it felt like to be vulnerable again, to be made a fool of.

"Oh, hell, it wasn't like she was in bed with Jake," he muttered aloud to the pinto. The horse stirred and stepped away from him to munch noisily on some rich alfalfa hay. Nick leaned against the back of the stall door, his arms crossed over his massive chest, and stared unseeingly at his horse.

Where was she now? he wondered. Was she waiting for him outside? He shook his head as he realized the predicament he now faced. Lindsay just might not turn down his advances anymore. But now that she was possibly willing, he felt more like backing away.

Backing away, hell. He felt more like running away right now. The thought of having her splendid eager body beneath his brought on such a rush of longing and desire that he found it difficult to breath. Yet he now also realized how

costly that could be. Not that long ago, he believed one
night in the sack with her would exorcise her from his
thoughts.

But he wasn't quite foolhardy enough to believe that
anymore. He knew, without a doubt, that one night with
Lindsay would never be enough. Instead of ridding her from
his thoughts, it would permanently brand her into him. He
knew instinctively that it would be so special that as long as
he lived he would never forget it. Or her. Did he want to risk
that now?

No, not tonight. He had to have more time to think, to
make sure of what he was letting himself in for.

He hated himself for his weakness and cowardice, but a
moment later he had silently left his horse's stall and slipped
out the back door of the barn. In two minutes flat, he
reached the safety of his cabin.

Lindsay, my love, forgive me, he whispered to the dark,
empty room. *I don't expect you to understand what I don't
understand myself, but I hope you'll forgive me.*

Chapter Eleven

After waiting nervously for twenty minutes for Nick to show up outside Sundance's stall, Lindsay finally went cautiously looking for him. She was tremendously surprised not to find him in his pinto's stall, or anywhere in the barn, for that matter. She could only deduce that he had gone back to his cabin without her.

She was completely baffled. Why did he suddenly choose to avoid her? He never just left her like this. And just when she'd given him the indication that she wanted to stay with him tonight. It made no sense at all.

As she slowly walked to her cabin alone, she felt more and more like a fool. Maybe she had assumed too much with him. Or maybe he really didn't want her at all. No, she couldn't quite believe that. There was no mistaking his desire for her. She wasn't very experienced in the ways of love, but she wasn't naive either. So why did Nick pull this disappearing act?

The thought occurred to her that possibly he was waiting for her in his cabin, that he expected her to show up there if she was really sure about sleeping with him. She hesitated in front of her door. Should she go to him?

The decision wasn't really that difficult. After considering it for ten seconds she hastily went inside her cabin. No, she couldn't just knock on Nick's door and say, here I am. There was always the chance that he chose to avoid her tonight because he didn't want to make love to her. And if that was the case, there was no way Lindsay could ever face him again after finding that out.

She sighed heavily as she pulled the quilted bedspread over her trembling body. If she lived to be a hundred, she didn't think she would ever find Nick predictable. Nor did she think she would ever stop wanting him so much.

Lindsay stared in amazement and sudden panic at the work schedule posted in the kitchen the next morning. She looked again at her name, which was right after Nick's. That was certainly nothing new, but her assignment for that day was. She was scheduled to be one of the guides on the overnight trail ride.

A slight chill went through her. Usually only the most experienced guides went on the overnight trips. She never expected to be on one of them until maybe late in the summer, if at all. Of course, Nick must have had something to do with getting her on this ride, but it still seemed strange.

It wasn't the ride itself that worried her. She'd heard enough stories from the other guides to know it was usually a fun assignment. She had wished more than once while she listened to them that she might get to go on one before the season was over. But that had been a couple weeks ago, before she'd become involved with Nick.

How in the world was she ever going to spend the night up in the mountains with him with all those other people around? She knew that the guests as well as the guides camped out in sleeping bags under the stars, and not all that far from each other. The guides for the most part stayed in one close group, a short distance from the guests. Good God, how could she possibly ever sleep with Nick only an arm's reach away?

The timing of the ride seemed significant. She had to wonder if Nick hadn't planned this as some sort of torture. Or test. Or something. She was sure there must be more to this than met the eye. And she was going to ask him straight out about it.

A half hour later, sitting at a table for two with him during breakfast, she found her bravado had once again slipped away. She picked at her food, still upset about last night and curious about what was going through that handsome head of his.

"You know, this is getting to be a habit with you," Nick said, motioning with his fork at her nearly untouched plate. "You're not eating again."

"I ate a lot the other morning on that breakfast ride," she reminded him. His casual attitude, as if nothing had happened, was starting to drive her crazy.

"Ah, yes, but if I recall you were quite riled up then." He stopped chewing and gave her a playful smile. "Maybe I should get you riled up more often."

She rolled her eyes. "That won't be necessary, thank you."

Nick turned back to his meal. She seemed upset with him this morning, as he had expected her to be. He wanted to bring up last night, but somehow the words just wouldn't form in his mouth. All he could do was pretend it never happened, and wait for her to get over being steamed at him.

That was one reason he had made the last minute change on the schedule early this morning. The idea of having her up in the mountains next to him all night was tremendously appealing. In fact, he was surprised that he hadn't done it sooner. Oh, he knew it would be hard, damn hard, to get any sleep with her so close. But at least it was one way to spend the night with her, so to speak, without having to worry about any repercussions.

He was almost through eating before he broke the silence again.

"Have you taken a look at today's schedule yet?" he asked casually. He had to know what her thoughts were about it, and it was obvious she wasn't going to bring it up.

"Yes." Lindsay bit her lip and met his guarded eyes. "Isn't it a little uncommon for a new employee to be on an overnighter?"

He shrugged. "Not especially," he hedged. But he knew she knew better. "Don't you want to go?"

The question surprised her. And if she was totally honest, she would have told him no. She would have told him she would much rather spend the night with him in his cabin, or somewhere else under the stars far away from everyone else.

"Well, yes, of course," she lied. "I just wondered if you had some special reason for scheduling me on it."

"No, not really. I just thought you would enjoy it. There's nothing quite like spending the night tucked inside a sleeping bag up in the mountains, next to a dying camp fire. You think it's quiet around here, wait until you get up there. There's not a sound anywhere except the wind and maybe a lonesome animal call here and there."

Lindsay trembled at the emotion evident in his voice. She realized how much Nick loved Wyoming and his way of life. She couldn't take her eyes off him, and she felt such a stirring inside that it was difficult not to reach out, touch him and press her lips against his.

Nick stared back at her, reveling in the way she was looking at him. God, when she looked at him like that, with such passion in her eyes, he felt like anything was possible. Absolutely anything.

"What time do we leave?" she asked breathlessly after a moment. She couldn't remember now what the schedule had said.

"Four."

She nodded and stood up. "Well, I guess I'll see you later then." She picked up her plate and left the table.

She caught Nick's look of surprise and confusion before she turned away, and it pleased her. Let *him* see what it felt like to have someone walk away without an explanation.

Not that that was the reason she was doing it. No, although giving him a little taste of his own medicine was an added bonus, she really just had to get away from him before she said or did something she would regret. For the sexual tension and electricity between them were more than she could handle this morning. Besides, she needed some time away from him to get herself prepared for this evening. It would not be an easy night, of that she was sure.

As the day dragged on, Lindsay became more and more nervous about the upcoming trail ride. She kept thinking of things like how she was going to look in the morning, with her hair all tousled and her mascara smeared. And where was she going to brush her teeth? Unless she took a mirror with her, which was admittedly a rather vain thing to do, she would have no idea what she looked like until they returned to the ranch late in the morning.

By the time the guides were getting the horses ready for the ride, she was completely frazzled and on edge.

"So, you're going on one of our famous overnight rides, huh?" Jake commented to her while they saddled.

"I guess so," she replied glumly.

"You don't sound very excited about it."

"I'm just a little nervous about the whole thing. Being my first time and all." But by the knowing look Jake gave her, she doubted whether he believed that was all there was to it.

"Well, I'm sure Nick will look out for you," Jake said flatly.

Lindsay glanced sharply at him. She'd never heard him use that biting a tone of voice before. But then remembering her earlier suspicions about Jake's true feelings for her, she decided he must be somewhat jealous. She sighed softly. There wasn't a whole lot she could do about that.

Precisely at four o'clock, the group of fourteen guests and six guides set out for the high mountains. Cindy Thompson led the group, while Lindsay brought up the rear. Nick was stationed in the middle of the guests, mounted, as always, on his magnificent pinto. Lindsay was just as glad she was riding Champ on this ride, for she didn't have to pay much attention to the small gelding. He was so experienced that she felt like she was just along for the ride.

At six-thirty, the group reached its destination. The chuck wagon was already waiting for them with thick, juicy steaks cooking on a grill. After the guides secured the horses on a picket line, all twenty people settled down for their dinner.

Despite her nerves, when Lindsay sat down beside Nick she found her appetite to be far from lacking. In fact, she was almost done eating before he was.

"Ah, there's nothing like the steaks on these rides. And there's no better way to heat up beans than over a camp-fire." Nick set his plate down beside him and stretched like a cat.

"I'll have to agree with you there. I've never had a better meal in my entire life," Lindsay said, taking a sip of coffee. She grimaced. "But I don't think I'll ever get used to these metal coffee cups."

"You can get used to anything if you put your mind to it," he said lightly.

"So what happens now?" she asked, quickly changing the subject.

"Well, in a little while the guys will get out their guitars and harmonicas, and we'll have a good old-fashioned sing-along."

"Sing-along?" she repeated, her eyes wide.

"Yeah. What's wrong with that?"

She shook her head and frowned. "I can't carry a tune at all."

He patted her on the back. "Don't worry, neither can I. But that never stopped me before. That's one reason it's so fun. Nobody cares what you sound like."

As Nick had predicted, a half hour later Lindsay found herself sitting nestled in his arms, singing boisterously along with everyone else. When Nick heard her sing for the first time, he had to laugh. She hadn't exaggerated about her abilities. But she had assured him he didn't have any reason to criticize her, the way he sounded.

The group sang until they were hoarse, and then one of the cooks passed around marshmallows. Lindsay and Nick waited until the rest were almost through before they moved closer to the fire to roast theirs.

"I haven't had an honest-to-goodness toasted marsh-mallow since I was a kid," Lindsay told him with a giggle.

"I believe it."

"What's that supposed to mean?" she asked with raised eyebrows.

"I think you've been missing out on a lot of the finer things in life before you came out here."

Lindsay trembled and felt herself drowning in his warm, aquamarine eyes. She stared in fascination at the flames that were mirrored in his eyes. After a long moment, she turned to watch the real fire again.

"I think you're right," she murmured.

"And I think you better pay more attention to that marshmallow," he teased.

"Oh, no!" Lindsay looked down dismally at her now ashen marshmallow. "It's ruined."

"Ruined! That's how they're best!" He laughed. That crestfallen expression on her face made her look like a pouting child. It was with great difficulty that he refrained from reaching out to kiss her.

"Here, I'll trade you then," she offered brightly, holding the smoldering marshmallow in front of his face.

"Don't poke me with the end of that stick!" he warned her.

"Then take it. And give me yours."

"All right, all right." Nick handed her his marshmallow, which was toasted a golden brown. "Come on, let's get away from these flames. I'm getting rather hot."

"I know what you mean," she whispered playfully.

They settled back in their original position with Nick leaning against the trunk of an oak tree while Lindsay curled up in the circle of his arms. Neither spoke until they were through with their marshmallows.

"Boy, this is gooey. How do you get it all off your fingers?" Lindsay said after she had unsuccessfully tried licking her fingers clean.

"You just don't know how to do it right. Let me help you." Nick took hold of her hand and one by one, licked and sucked each of her fingers until they were spotless.

The sensuousness of his action had made her heart start pounding dreadfully hard in her chest, and she felt suddenly as if they were all alone in the wilderness. She was filled with such longing for him that she didn't think she could stand it.

"I'm beginning to wonder if this was a good idea after all," Nick said gruffly, his eyes burning into hers. He released her hand reluctantly. "At least your fingers aren't sticky anymore."

"Thank you," she whispered. She reached up and ran her index finger over his full lips. "Maybe I should get another marshmallow."

"Maybe I should see if your teeth are sticky."

"Mm," she murmured as he bent over and gently touched his lips to hers. "I think they are." She closed her eyes as his tongue tenderly explored her mouth. It was an exquisite moment.

"Hey, you two, don't forget about all of us over here," Cindy called out loudly.

Lindsay flushed and pulled away from Nick as everyone laughed and started applauding.

"You guys go any farther and we could sell tickets," another guide yelled teasingly.

Nick held up his hands and grinned. "Okay, we'll be good. It doesn't look like we have any choice."

"We'd appreciate it," Cindy quipped.

In a minute, when they were no longer the object of everyone's attention, Lindsay relaxed again. "You know for a while, I did forget about being out here with eighteen other people," she told him.

"I know what you mean," Nick agreed smugly. He stroked her cheek with the back of his hand. "For two cents I'd throw you on the back of my horse and gallop all the way back to my cabin."

"Although that doesn't sound like a bad idea, it is pretty heavenly right here."

How she wished this moment could last forever! Never had she felt so happy, so alive. Sitting out here next to Nick under thousands of brilliantly lit stars and a full moon with the air deliciously scented by pine trees was indeed her idea of paradise.

"Why did you really come out here to work?" Nick asked suddenly. He hadn't really meant to say that at all right now, but the words just popped out. It was something he constantly wondered about.

Lindsay pulled off her cowboy hat and shook her long hair until it fell loosely around her shoulders. "I told you once, I needed a break from my job."

"Why? And why come here?"

She didn't want to get into this with him now. She was afraid of spoiling this special evening.

"I saw an ad for the job," she told him at last. "The idea of working on a western dude ranch intrigued me."

"Wasn't it a little hard to leave your family and friends for the whole summer?" *Or your boyfriend?* his mind continued, but his mouth couldn't form those words.

"Oh, I don't have that many close friends, actually. And the only family I had left was my father, and he died about a year ago." Her voice still carried the sadness from her loss.

"I'm sorry," Nick said softly, and pulled her tighter in his arms.

"It's all right." She hesitated. Should she go on? How much did he really want to know?

"But it's still a pretty drastic change to pack up and go out west for a summer. There must be more to it than just following a silly whim."

"A silly whim?" she repeated with a smile. "No, there was a little more thinking involved than that."

"I'd like to know," he said simply.

Lindsay glanced up at him and found his face unreadable. He wasn't going to give her any extra encouragement on this one. She sighed.

"I suppose it's mostly for my father that I decided to take this job." She moved away from the warm encirclement of Nick's arms and hugged her legs to her chest. With her chin resting on her knees, she continued.

"You see, my father loved my mother very much, but he always had the belief that he had to work as hard as he could to save money for their future, for when he retired. So for years he was either working long hours at one job or else working two jobs. And he saved and saved his money."

Her voice caught in her throat as she remembered those days. She and her mother hardly ever saw him back then. It had been a lonely childhood.

"Then one day my mother was killed in a car accident. My father was devastated. Here he'd spent most of his life preparing for their comfortable future, and all of a sudden the one person he had done it all for was gone. I think in some strange way, he blamed himself for her death, even though he wasn't even in the car with her when it happened. So all he had left was his job, and that became his whole life. After a few years of working himself to the point of exhaustion every night, he starting having a lot of health problems. It was inevitable that he die a relatively young man."

"It must have been very hard on you," Nick said gently when she remained silent for a minute.

"I survived," she replied with a shrug. She turned her head to meet his steady gaze. "You know, when I was growing up, both my parents tried to drill into me the value of money. My father's whole philosophy was to work as much as you could while you were young in order to safeguard your future when you're old. I don't think my mother quite agreed with it all, but she always supported him. And then when my father died, one day I realized that his philosophy had become my philosophy. And it scared me."

"I can see why. There's a lot more to life than money."

"That's what's so ironic. My father, right before he died, suddenly realized that. He told me not to make the same mistake he had, that I should enjoy life and take some time out for the fun things."

Lindsay turned to stare at the dying flames of the camp fire again. "That's why I took this job, I suppose. I promised my father I would take his advice. And working out west with horses was something I'd always had in the back of my mind, ever since I can remember. When I saw the ad, I just had to try for this position."

"But just for the summer?" Nick pressed. "You think that will fulfill your promise to your father?"

"I really don't know."

"You have no idea, no plans for your future?"

Boy, did she have plans for the future now. And they all included Nick as a part of them. But she couldn't tell him that.

"Well, you know, for the longest time I guess I just thought I'd work at the insurance company, moving my way up the ladder, getting bigger and bigger raises. It's not exactly a dream of mine or anything, and it's not that the idea of spending the rest of my working days there appeals to me. I suppose I thought it was my only choice, my only practical choice."

"And what about a man? Is there a man in Chicago who fits into your exciting plans for the future?" he asked, his voice carefully controlled. He realized he was holding his breath waiting for her answer.

She scoffed. "No, nothing like that."

He exhaled slowly. "So what happens to Lindsay Jordan after the summer is over? Now that you've gotten a taste of an entirely different way of life, have your ideas changed any?"

Why was he pressing her so much? What did he really want to hear? She wished she knew what the right thing to say was.

"I can't answer that right now," she told him.

At least that was partially the truth. She honestly didn't know what she was going to do anymore. Her whole life had been turned upside down by this handsome, stubborn, arrogant cowboy. She frowned in the darkness. Why did she have to love him so much? It would be so much simpler if she didn't.

They were silent for several minutes, each lost in their own thoughts. Finally, when the silence was starting to become awkward, Nick spoke up.

"It looks like everyone is turning in for the night," he said, noticing several guests were already curled up in their sleeping bags. He slowly got to his feet. "I guess we should hit the sack, too. I'll get our stuff."

Lindsay felt renewed butterflies in her stomach. She was dreading this part. A moment later Nick returned with their packs.

"Where are we going to sleep?"

"What's wrong with right here?" Nick winked at her devilishly. "We're a ways apart from everyone else."

"Okay." She unrolled her sleeping bag and climbed inside. "Well, good night."

"Don't I even get a good-night kiss?" he protested.

She appeared to consider the matter carefully. "Well, I guess it would be all right," she teased.

"Come here, woman," he growled, and pulled her close to him. He brushed his lips lightly against hers. "I'm afraid that's all I can give you if you expect me to stay in my own sleeping bag tonight."

"Considering our present circumstances, I think that would be a very wise idea. See you in the morning, I guess."

He looked at her with one raised eyebrow. "I'll be here."

Out of the corner of her eye, Lindsay watched him struggle to get inside his sleeping bag. When he laid down facing her, she rolled over so that her back was to him. She didn't want him staring at her while she tried to fall asleep, anymore than she wanted to lie awake all night staring at him. She needed some sleep.

Now if only she could convince her aching, tingling body of that, everything would be fine.

When the first pale crimson rays of sunshine appeared on the horizon, Lindsay finally crept softly out of her sleeping bag. She hadn't slept more than an hour the whole night, and she couldn't lie on the hard ground another minute.

After pulling on her boots and her jacket, she stood and stretched. Her body was tired and more than a little stiff from the restless night she'd gone through. She would doze off for a few minutes when an owl would hoot, a horse would nicker, or a coyote would howl off in the distance. Once or twice she'd even been disturbed by someone snoring. It felt like she had been laying on a bed of rocks, and she missed her pillow. Combining all of that with the fact that Nick was only three feet away from her did not add up to a very successful night sleeping.

She gazed down at Nick with a sigh. It felt right waking up next to him. He looked utterly at peace and very vulnerable while he slept, his rugged features softened and relaxed. His breathing was not as deep as it had been an hour ago, and she knew he would be awakening soon.

Lindsay pulled a small compact and a comb out of her pack and headed toward the stream that was nearby. When she reached the bank, she knelt down and splashed water over her tired face. It was very cold, but it did help open her eyes. She let her face dry, then ran a comb through her hair.

She could hear one of the cooks stirring up the camp fire and wrestling with an iron coffee pot. She knew it wouldn't be long before everyone else was up, and probably the first place many of them would come would be this very spot. Well, since she wasn't doing herself any good here, she might as well go see if she could help the cook.

On the way back to camp, she popped a breath mint in her mouth. She may not have a toothbrush, but at least she wouldn't have to worry about facing Nick with bad breath.

"Mornin', Lindsay," Hank, the grizzled old cook, greeted her. "What're you doing up so early? Problems sleeping?"

You don't know the half of it, she thought. "Just an early riser, Hank. Anything I can do to help?"

The old man put her to work instantly, but she was glad to have something to do. Twenty minutes later, just when the guests were starting to rise, they had thick slabs of bacon sizzling in cast-iron pans and coffee heating up over the fire.

"Good morning."

Lindsay jumped as two strong arms pulled her close. She turned and smiled up at Nick.

"Good morning yourself."

He nuzzled her hair. "You smell almost as good as that bacon," he breathed into her ear. "And you certainly look all bright-eyed and bushy-tailed this morning. I take it you slept well?"

"Sure. Why wouldn't I?" she said a little too flippantly. A glance at his face told her he didn't quite believe her.

"Then why the dark circles under your eyes?"

"It's hereditary," she informed him airily. "And I don't have any makeup along to cover them up, so you're just going to have to live with them."

He chuckled and released her. "Come on and help me with the horses."

"Got to go, Hank," Lindsay called. "The horses need tending."

"Thanks for all your help, girl. That dang partner of mine doesn't like to get up until noon," Hank said, laughing, and waved her off.

By the time all the horses were watered and fed, it was time for breakfast. Everyone chatted and joked while they ate, as if they were all old friends and not strangers who had met only a few days before. Lindsay was amazed at the camaraderie that existed among the twenty people, and it made her oddly sad to think they probably would never all assemble together like this again. In fact, in a couple days, most of the guests would return to their regular lives, most of them in the city.

And at the end of her vacation, what would happen to her? Would she go back to Chicago and let her time on the ranch fade away into just a pleasant memory? Would she wave a tearful goodbye and promise to write to all her new friends, knowing she never would?

It made her feel strangely uncomfortable just thinking about leaving here and resuming her job at the insurance company, working from nine to five, wearing dresses, high heels and panty hose and going home alone to an empty apartment. God, it seemed like a lifetime since she had ever done that. And she had thought at the time she was happy. Well, maybe not happy, but certainly content.

Now that she had found what real happiness was like here with Nick, could she ever settle for anything less?

Chapter Twelve

This horse is lame.''

Lindsay stared at Jake in disbelief, but she couldn't deny the swelling in Champ's right front leg.

She had just entered the barn to help with the evening chores when Jake had called her over to Champ's stall.

"But I don't understand," she protested. "He was fine last night and this morning. He was completely sound all the way back to the ranch."

Jake shrugged. "I don't know anything about that. But he's definitely not sound now. Looks like he pulled a suspensory ligament."

Lindsay shook her head. Although the injury wasn't that serious, Champ would have to rest his leg for a couple of weeks. She knew he hadn't shown any signs of being hurt all through the overnight trail ride. And this morning, when they'd come back, he had actually pranced a little when they neared the barn. She was sure the injury must have occurred after they'd gotten back.

"Anything wrong?"

Lindsay cringed at the sound of Nick's voice as he approached them. Was this another so-called accident she was going to be blamed for?

"Take a look for yourself," Jake offered. "It looks like he pulled the suspensory ligament in his right front."

Frowning, Nick joined them in Champ's stall. He picked up the injured leg and went over it with firm, sure fingers. Champ winced in obvious pain when Nick put pressure on one spot.

"I'd have to agree with you, Jake. But it doesn't look too serious." He turned to look at Lindsay. "How did this happen?"

"Why are you looking at me?" she asked defensively.

"You were the last one to ride him. And you know as well as I do that an injury like that happens almost exclusively with a rider on board. Horses just don't hurt themselves like that on their own."

"Well, this one must have." Lindsay walked out of the stall, then turned back to face him. "You know, it doesn't surprise me in the least that you blame me for this. But I check the legs of every horse I ride before I get on, and I am very sensitive to any kind of wrong step or lameness. And you know very well that mostly all we did the whole ride back was walk. A pulled suspensory like this most often occurs during fast or strenuous work."

Mustering up as much of her injured pride as she could, she spun around and stalked off. Let them think what they wanted to, she thought angrily. And let Nick help with the evening chores. She was going to sulk.

As she passed Sundance's stall, her mare nickered a greeting to her. She decided to visit with her horse before she went back and fumed in her cabin.

"Hello yourself, lady," she murmured, stroking the sleek sides. "How's everything going for you?"

Sundance went back to eating her hay, and Lindsay stood for several minutes with her arms crossed over her horse's back. She was just about to leave when she heard steps coming near. The voices belonged to Nick and Jake.

"Do you think this is just another accident?" she heard Jake ask.

"Things like this aren't that uncommon," Nick reasoned. "Besides, I can't believe anyone would purposely hurt a horse."

"It does seem hard to believe, but I'm beginning to wonder," Jake said.

Was Jake starting to doubt her, too? Lindsay wondered. She strained to catch their words as they continued away from her.

"Well, I'll tell you one thing, Jake. You catch more flies with honey than vinegar. I have an idea who might be responsible for these incidents, but I know I won't get anywhere throwing around nasty accusations. I plan on being just as pleasant as possible. Maybe that person will slip up or admit something."

"Do you still think it's Lindsay?" Jake asked, his voice barely reaching her.

Unfortunately, Sundance chose that moment to snort, and Nick's reply was lost to her. Peeking out of the stall, she saw they were at the other end of the barn with their backs to her. She slipped out as quietly as she could and hurried outside.

The nerve of that man! she thought furiously. She had no doubt about how Nick had answered Jake. So he thought if he sweet-talked her, she would admit to her guilt, did he? She had to wonder, though, if he thought she was purposely trying to hurt the ranch, or was just an incompetent idiot. Well, she was going to have to keep trying to prove she was neither. Although if he had any trust in her at all, she shouldn't have to prove anything.

In the meantime, however, she was still faced with the problem of someone intentionally trying to make her look bad. Whether it was just something personal, or whether it was a grudge someone had against the ranch, she did not know. But, like Nick, she was beginning to have an idea about who was responsible for it all. And, as Nick had so unerringly pointed out, you catch more flies with honey than vinegar.

She slammed her cabin door shut. Let Nick think she was the guilty party. If he wanted to use that as an excuse to be nice to her, that was fine, too. Meanwhile, she would find out the truth, and then she would have the extremely pleasant task of demanding a full apology from him.

She smiled despite herself. She was looking forward to that day.

Nick didn't meet Lindsay for dinner that night. He was too preoccupied to face her yet.

He had spent the past two hours restlessly pacing his cabin like a caged animal. The events of the past several days had convinced him of one thing. He was totally in love with Lindsay. He'd been fighting that ever since the first day she had shown up at the ranch, but he couldn't deny it any longer.

He smiled to himself as he remembered how she looked that first day. He'd seen her drive up, of course, but he hadn't approached her until she was sitting on the top rail of the corral, her attention on her horse. He'd watched her for several minutes without her knowing it, she'd been that intent on her mare.

He could remember how taken he was right away at the sight of her. Her long, wavy brown hair, her perfectly molded, trim body, her sparkling emerald eyes—all her physical characteristics had attracted him instantly. Yet there had been something more, something else that had drawn him irresistibly to her side.

He could still see her now, as clearly as if she were standing before him this very minute. He had stared at her in fascination as she watched her lovely sorrel mare galloping around the corral. Her face, her whole expression, had portrayed the love and pride she felt for her horse. He could read it so easily it gave him a chill, as if he were seeing into her very soul.

But what had really startled him, had totally surprised him, was the crazy feeling that emerged in him as he watched her. For somewhere deep inside him came the abrupt speculation of what it would feel like to have her look at *him* like that.

And ever since that day, it had almost been like a personal goal, or actually more like an obsession, to find that out firsthand. It was as if he just had to have her love. And he had succeeded, he knew that last night by the camp fire. He had seen that same glorious look in her eyes then, and it had felt wonderful. She was in love with him, he was sure. What he didn't plan for, or want to happen, though, was to fall victim to her charms.

After all, he'd managed for years not to get close to any woman. But he'd made the fatal mistake of thinking he could get involved with Lindsay and still stay cool and detached. He cursed out loud and shook his head. He should have known better. He really should have.

So now he was faced with a dilemma, and a rather serious one at that. It was as if the past were cruelly replaying itself again. He had tried once before to make a city girl change and adapt to his way of life, and that had been disastrous. How could he set himself up to make the same mistake again?

Nick stopped pacing to stare out the window at the full moon. He took a deep breath and let it out slowly. There was only one solution to his problem, but it did not please him very much. Still, he couldn't see that he had much choice.

Lindsay had not yet voiced any plans of maybe staying on at the ranch permanently, even though he'd casually brought up the subject several times. Instinctively he felt that if he asked her to stay with him, she would agree. But that wasn't good enough. He needed her to decide to stay on at the ranch regardless of how she felt about him. Only then could he be sure she wouldn't have any regrets later.

Grabbing his Stetson, Nick left his cabin. There was just one way he could find out what he needed to know. He would hate himself for what he would be putting her through, but it was for both of them. He could only hope that when it was over, she would forgive him and understand.

Lindsay jumped at the sound of a quiet knock on her door. She glanced at the clock. It was after ten. Who could it be at this hour?

Her heart started to pound as she walked to the door. Maybe it was Nick. But why would he avoid her at dinner and then show up here so late? Well, she'd find out soon enough, she told herself as she opened the door. She wasn't really surprised to see it was, in fact, Nick.

"Yes?" Her voice was deceptively calm.

He didn't wait for an invitation, but merely strode through the doorway and into her living room.

"Aren't you going to shut the door?" he said lightly when she just stood there looking at him without moving.

In answer, she closed the door and then leaned against it. She crossed her arms over her chest. "What do you want?"

He didn't answer right away. His eyes roamed over her body appreciatively, taking in her short cotton robe, which barely covered a light-blue silk nightie. Could he really do this to her? he wondered fleetingly. But he knew he had to. Anyway, this would be the easy part.

"Just to talk a little," he said at last. He plopped down on the couch. "Are you going to stand way over there?"

"Why not?" she countered warily. What was he up to? She sensed a tenseness in him and it made her uneasy.

He motioned to the spot next to him. "Could you please come over and sit next to me? I hate to shout."

She decided to compromise and sat down in the easy chair next to the couch.

"Why are so suspicious of me all of a sudden?" he asked curiously.

"Why are you here?"

"That's no answer."

"Where were you at dinner?"

"I had some thinking to do."

"Oh? About what?" *Probably about how to get me to admit my conspiracies against the ranch,* she thought.

"Different things." He paused and focused his attention on the floor. "I guess you're ticked off at me for accusing you of being responsible for Champ's lameness."

"Bingo."

"I'm sorry, Lindsay. But you could look at it from my side, too. What else am I supposed to think when these things keep happening and you're always the one who's closest to it all?"

"You could think that maybe they're coincidental," she retorted, her eyes flashing. "Or maybe that someone else could be setting me up. Or maybe even that someone else around here is extremely careless besides me."

"You're right, and I have considered all those possibilities. But I'm afraid that when something new happens, my first thought is always the most obvious one."

"Meaning me?" she challenged.

"Yes," he admitted. "But if it's any comfort, I don't think you had anything to do with those accidents. Any of them."

She stared at him in surprise. "You don't?" she repeated.

"No."

"Then who do you think is behind it all?" she asked carefully. She wondered if this was all a snow job, or if he really did have suspicions about someone else.

"I'd rather not say right now," he hedged, and met her gaze squarely again. "But I'm sure it wasn't you. Okay?"

She relaxed a little and felt her guard start to slip. "Okay."

He stared at her a moment longer, and then got to his feet. "Well, that's all I wanted to say, so I guess I should turn in. I just wanted to straighten things out between us."

"Thank you," Lindsay said, and rose also. She walked him to the door. Was this really all he wanted?

As he was about to open the door, he turned toward her.

"There is just one other thing," he told her huskily.

"What?" Her voice was barely a whisper.

"This."

He lowered his mouth slowly to cover hers in an easy, gentle kiss. She felt her blood instantly fire to life as it raged through her veins, making her weak and dizzy. Damn him, she thought. One little kiss and I'm totally lost.

But soon it wasn't just a little kiss anymore. The passion and desire they both felt took control almost immediately, and they clung to each other, their lips and tongues doing erotic dances.

His hands on her back pressed her closer to his body, and she instinctively put her arms around his neck in an effort to bring herself even closer to his strong body. She could feel all his hard, rigid muscles through her thin nightie and robe, and it made her feel soft and fragile in comparison.

"You know," Nick murmured brokenly as he trailed kisses down the side of her delicate throat, "there aren't any other people a few feet away from us tonight. We're all alone."

Her head fell back to expose more of her burning flesh to his teasing lips. "Maybe we should take advantage of that while we can," she told him breathlessly.

Nick didn't wait for any further encouragement, and the next thing she knew, she was in his arms and he was carrying her into the bedroom. When they reached the bed, he slowly let go of her legs until she was standing before him.

His demanding lips pried her mouth open and his tongue boldly sought hers again. His hands began exploring her body, and soon one hand was inside her lace bodice caressing her small, firm breasts. Her nipples were already hard, but he toyed with them anyway, pinching and squeezing them lightly until Lindsay moaned from equal pain and bliss. Her body was on fire; she hardly realized he was pulling off her robe and easing the thin straps of her nightie off her shoulders. He broke away from her mouth then, and bent his head to kiss first one of her taut breasts and then the other. Lindsay was so weak with desire that she had to hang on to him to keep from crumbling in his arms.

Finally unable to stand the sensations he was causing her to feel, she pulled his head back up to her mouth and kissed him ardently. Longing to feel his bare chest against hers, she pulled at the buttons on his shirt until they were all free. She slid her hands deliciously over his broad chest and back, reveling in the splendor of his body. He tore his mouth away from hers again, and pulling her crushingly against him, he buried his face in her long, tangled hair.

"Damn, you are so beautiful," he told her in a voice that sounded almost tortured. "And you smell so good. You have no idea what you're doing to me."

She trembled uncontrollably and kissed and nibbled on his earlobe. He moaned something incoherent and lifted her into his arms again. His lips covered hers hungrily, and he slowly lowered her onto the bed.

When her body touched the cool sheets, a jolt of panic went through her. What was she doing? A few minutes ago she had been very upset with Nick, and she still doubted his sincerity concerning her innocence of the accidents. Was this just a scheme of his to try to get a confession out of her?

What would happen to their relationship if she made love to him now? Oh, she knew she had vowed to go through with it the next time she had the opportunity, but now that the time was here, she was suddenly scared. Scared of losing him, scared of him not being happy with her, scared that in her inexperience she would not be able to satisfy him.

If only he would whisper words of love to her, words of commitment, words that would ease some of her doubts. If only...

But she could think rationally no more. The needs of her body were completely overpowering the thoughts in her mind. She could only hope everything would work out all right and that she wouldn't live to regret this night.

Nick had shed his clothes and was working on pulling off her cotton panties. She helped him to hurry along the process, and he dropped back beside her. For a moment they simply lay together, nearly motionless, each cherishing the feel of the other's naked body. But then their passion became strong again, and they began a zealous exploration of each other's skin.

Nick's hands seemed to be everywhere at once, and Lindsay arched against him. Finally unable to put off her tremendous need to feel him inside her, she rolled over with him until he was on top of her.

"No, not yet," he told her breathlessly as she squirmed beneath him.

"Nick, please," she moaned. "Now, please now."

But he went over her body again with his lips and tongue until she thought surely she would burst. At last he couldn't keep himself from her any longer, and he quickly entered her. She cried out from the suddenness of it, and instantly he pulled back, entering her again more gently. They began moving together in a rhythm that only their bodies could hear, until soon Lindsay was pushing against him, wanting him to join with her deeper and deeper...

The next thing she knew, she was crying out again, only this time not in pain. She felt herself dropping over the edge of the mountains in an explosion of brilliant passion, and she clung to Nick, her fingers digging into his back, carrying him with her. She heard him cry out, too, and then they were both shakingly drifting back to the ground, to reality, to each other. It was a reality Lindsay was reluctant to come back to.

Nick rolled gently off of her and pulled her protectively against his chest. He gave her one more light kiss before they both fell into a deep, exhausted sleep, wrapped intimately in each other's arms.

Lindsay could feel Nick's hand arousing her body again, kissing her, caressing her. She smiled and turned over to kiss him, but then suddenly she awoke with a start. She was alone.

At first she thought everything had been a dream, but as she looked down at the tangled bedsheets and her own still glowing body, she knew it had really happened. She and Nick had indeed made love. She smiled to herself, remembering how exquisite it had been. It had been more wonderful than she had ever imagined. She remembered how perfectly their bodies molded together, how easy it had been to please each other.

Suddenly she stiffened. Where was Nick? She looked around the room quickly, but his clothes were gone from the floor. She didn't bother to call out because she knew he had left. But why? Why did he have to rush off without waking her? How could he just leave her without a word after what they had shared? A chill ran through her, and she stood up and wrapped a blanket around herself.

She sat numbly on the couch for several minutes before sensible thoughts started to run through her mind. She glanced at the clock, and then stared at it in horror. Eight-thirty! She was scheduled for a nine o'clock trail ride, as was Nick, she remembered nervously.

What would he say to her? she wondered. Would things change now? Things had certainly changed for her. Her love for him ran even deeper and stronger than before, and she knew that never again in her life would she find someone who could make her feel the way Nick did. But how did he feel?

She showered and dressed quickly, and as she made her way to the barn, her stomach growlingly reminded her that she'd missed breakfast. Feeling ravenous, she changed her route and headed to the kitchen. There were usually cinnamon rolls left over after breakfast, and one or two of them might tide her over until lunch.

The rolls were still deliciously fresh, and she downed three of them with a glass of milk. She then hurried out to the barn to help saddle the trail horses they would be using. She was late, and she hoped no one had noticed.

When she arrived at the saddling area, she saw that only a few horses were left to be done. As she rushed into the tack room to help, she almost ran headlong into Jake.

"Whoa, there." He smiled, shifting the saddle he was carrying onto one hip. "And where have you been?" he asked pleasantly with one raised eyebrow.

Lindsay flushed, suddenly feeling the whole world must be able to see right through her and know exactly what she had done last night.

"I overslept," she offered lamely.

He studied her carefully, and she looked away from his knowing eyes. "Sure," he said after a moment. "Whatever you say."

Lindsay brushed past him to get a saddle, glad he hadn't pressed her any further. A few minutes later, all the horses were ready and the riders were being given final instructions. They were almost ready to mount when Lindsay spotted Nick for the first time. He came striding out of the barn, leading his pinto, walking in that easy, confident swagger that was unique to him.

She trembled as her eyes followed him, her body remembering all too vividly their lovemaking only a few hours earlier. She was frozen to the spot, waiting with held breath for him to at least look at her. She would know by that first glance how things were going to be.

Nick didn't look at her until she was adjusting the stirrups for one of the guests. His eyes suddenly lifted over the saddle and locked into hers for one brief moment. Then he returned his attention to the task at hand and turned to speak to the rider.

Lindsay felt a stab of disappointment. His eyes had been cool and indifferent, even at this distance. Surely he could have at least smiled at her, she thought resentfully. Something, anything but the controlled way he had looked at her.

She bit her lip and felt tears sting her eyes. So he had been unmoved by their lovemaking. It had meant nothing to him. That's why he had left early this morning. She turned away and shut her eyes tightly for an instant. *You will not let him see you cry,* she told herself fiercely. *He's humiliated you enough already, and you will act as unaffected as he is.*

She had to walk by him to take her place at the front of the group, as she was going to be the leader on this ride. She felt his eyes on her as she passed him, but she stared straight in front of her, not trusting herself to be able to handle the mocking look she was sure he would have on his face.

She led the group of happy, talkative people, forcing herself to partake in their conversations as if she was as cheerful as they were. Inside, her heart felt like it had been wrenched out of her body. How could he do this to her?

By the time they stopped for a break at a bubbling creek, anguish had turned to anger. Who did he think he was, anyway? He had no right to treat her this way, and she intended to tell him so. But moments later when Nick casually walked up to her, leading his horse, she felt such a lump in her throat that at first she couldn't speak. She stared defiantly at him instead, wondering what it was that he wanted to say.

"You were almost too late for the ride," he said calmly.

Her eyes widened. Was he kidding her? No, he appeared serious. "I wonder why," she muttered, boldly meeting his gaze.

His jaw hardened, and he looked away from her accusing eyes. "Lindsay..." he began, then stopped.

"Why did you just leave without saying goodbye?" she whispered. She hadn't meant to say that at all; she didn't want to reveal how badly he was hurting her. But the words were out before she even realized it.

He shrugged noncommittally. "I had work to do."

She longed to shake him. How could he act so totally unemotional? It was like last night hadn't happened. Even now, his nearness left her quivering with desire to feel his lips on hers again, to feel his hands tenderly exploring her body, to feel...

"Lindsay," he began again.

She could tell by the set look on his face that his words would not be good. She couldn't bear to hear what he was going to say. It was taking all her strength now not to burst into tears of hurt and humiliation.

"Just leave me alone," she lashed out, her voice frosty. Before he could reply, she swung quickly into the saddle.

"Time to get going," she called out loudly to the guests. She kicked the horse she was riding into a trot and resumed her position at the front of the group without once looking back.

Chapter Thirteen

Lindsay was sitting with Jake and Cindy at dinner when Ross approached their table and told her he wanted to see her in his office after dinner. After he left, Jake winked at her. Maybe Ross wanted to talk to her about staying on at the ranch. The idea didn't excite her.

She hadn't seen Nick after they'd gotten back from the trail ride that morning, nor did he show up at supper. It had taken every ounce of her strength to get herself in here, since all she really wanted to do was stay in her cabin and cry out her frustration and humiliation. But she'd decided acting that way would get her nowhere, so she'd forced herself to act normally.

She waited for Jake and Cindy to finish eating before she left them to go to Ross's office. Despite her tumultuous emotions over Nick, a little nervousness started to nag at her. Maybe Jake was wrong about what Ross wanted to discuss. Maybe he was going to blame her outright for all those accidents, or maybe even fire her. Well, if he did, at least it would take away her problem of deciding what to do. Somehow having Ross decide her future for her didn't seem like a bad idea right now.

The door to Ross's office was open, so Lindsay walked in. He looked up from the papers sprawled all over his desk and smiled.

"Come on in and sit down, Lindsay," he offered, motioning her into a padded leather chair. "I'll be with you in just a second."

While she waited, Lindsay's eyes traveled around the room. The office was huge, nearly as large as her cabin. The wall behind Ross held one huge window that faced the west. Along two other walls were shelves and shelves of books, many of which were about horses, Lindsay noted. There was a dark leather sofa off to one side of the desk, while two leather chairs and a small round coffee table faced Ross. The desk itself was immense, made out of rich mahogany, and the eye-catcher in the room.

"Okay," Ross began, shuffling his papers into one neat pile, "I'll get right to the point. I'm quite pleased with your work here, even though there have been scattered unpleasant incidents that have occurred, which may or may not be your fault. My nephew seems thoroughly convinced you're quite a responsible worker and not in the least careless, so I'm ready to give you the benefit of the doubt."

"Thank you," Lindsay replied offhandedly, her attention on the gorgeous streaks of crimson, gold and orange that lit up the sky as the sun set behind Ross. How could he ever get any work done at this time of day with that breathless view behind him? she wondered.

"Anyway, I'm going to be a little short of help this winter, with Nick leaving at the end of the season and all, and

I'd like to know if you're interested in a full-time, year-round position here.''

It took several moments for Ross's words to sink in. When they did, her eyes flew to his face in stunned disbelief. "Nick is leaving?" she repeated numbly.

"Yes." He smiled pleasantly. "I thought you knew that. He's finally saved up enough money to buy back his mother's ranch, north of here. I hate like hell to lose him, but it's what he's been working for for years, so I can't really blame him. Matter of fact, that's where he left for this afternoon. He had some business to take care of up there, so he'll be gone for a week or so."

Lindsay could only stare at him. She felt a lump rising in her throat and her eyes started to sting with the pressure of unshed tears. Nick leaving after the summer was over? He must have known from the very beginning that this was his last season on the ranch. Why did he keep that from her? How could he be so deceitful? And she had thought he'd hinted a few times about her staying on at the ranch. Why did he bother if he wasn't going to be around himself?

There was one logical explanation for it all, of course. Only she did not want to accept it or even think about it. But it was there like a slap in the face. Nick must have lied to her and led her on from the very beginning, with only one goal in mind. And he had accomplished that goal last night. She shut her eyes briefly. If she'd felt like a fool this morning, she felt like a complete imbecile now.

"Lindsay?" Ross's concerned voice broke into her anguished thoughts. "Are you feeling all right? You look rather pale."

She managed a weak smile. "I'm fine. But I'm afraid I can't give you an answer right away about working here over the winter. I'll have to think about it first."

Ross nodded. "I can understand that. It's quite a change from what you used to do. I'd appreciate knowing in a couple weeks, though. If you don't want the position, I'll have to try to find someone else."

"Yes, of course," she said absently. "Well, I'll let you get back to your paperwork." She rose on unsteady legs. "And thank you for the offer."

Ross nodded again and waved her out the door. Her heart pounding, she nearly ran all the way to her cabin.

Her mind was in a whirl by the time she reached her living room. How could Nick do this to her? And he'd left today without a word. Without even a goodbye. *Without an explanation of any kind.* And last night, she had thought they had finally reached a very special point in their relationship. She had even thought . . .

She took a deep, shaky breath. She had actually thought by the way Nick had been last night that maybe he was falling in love with her. How could he make such sweet, passionate love to her without caring about her at all? Could she misjudge him that badly?

Lindsay sank down into the easy chair and hugged her knees to her chest. She felt like such an idiot, falling for Nick the way she had. After all, hadn't her instincts cautioned her from the very beginning about getting involved with him? Who did she really have to blame but herself? And she'd known perfectly well last night what might happen in the morning, but she'd gone ahead and slept with Nick anyway.

Thinking about that still made her pulse quicken and her skin tingle, despite everything else. As hurt and furious as she was right now, somehow she didn't really regret making love to Nick. Even if she knew then what she did now, she wouldn't have done it any differently. Being with him had meant too much to her, even if it hadn't touched him at all. It would certainly give her a wonderful, if bittersweet, memory to take back to Chicago with her.

Chicago? She frowned. In her agitation over Nick, she'd already forgotten about Ross's offer. But she knew she would have to give it some consideration. A week ago, she believed she would have accepted a full-time job on the ranch without hesitation. But now...

Now everything seemed to have changed. It was very hard to imagine working here without Nick around. He seemed to be such an integral part of the ranch. But obviously she was going to have to get used to the idea of her life going on minus one Nicholas Leighton.

Tomorrow she'd think about it all. Maybe then she would be able to consider Ross's offer with a clearer mind. Right now, her thoughts were clouded with memories. Memories of a handsome, stubborn, passionate cowboy who could make her tremble with desire with just one kiss.

She got her nightie on, but found she couldn't face sleeping in her big empty bed alone. There were some memories that were just too painful for her to deal with tonight. Irritated at herself almost as much as she was at Nick, she pulled a blanket out of the closet, grabbed her pillow and stretched out on the couch for what she knew would be a sleepless night.

Nick paced the confining walls of the hotel room. He'd ordered a bottle of Scotch from room service, but even after downing half of that in the hope that it would dull his emotions, he still felt too much.

He couldn't get the image of Lindsay's lovely sleeping face out of his mind. The hardest thing he'd ever done in his life was to sneak out of her warm bed this morning. It had been all he could do not to touch and caress her soft naked body until she woke up as aroused as he was. The memory of her made his body ache with lust even now.

If only all he felt for her was lust, he would be all right. But if anything, being with her last night only reinforced the deep love he'd already felt for her. Never had he experienced such exquisite sensations in his entire life. Just knowing he wouldn't see her for a whole week was already driving him crazy. He wanted nothing more than to spend the rest of his life loving her.

He took another large swallow of Scotch. He had to do it this way, he tried to convince himself. No matter how much he hated himself, no matter how much he felt like a total bastard, he had to go through with this. Both his and Lindsay's futures depended on it.

At least in the morning he'd be able to leave this damn hotel. He had to give Lindsay some time alone to make her own decisions, and in the meantime it was as good an opportunity as any to talk to George Parker again about his mother's ranch. He had it figured out that if he was very careful with his money, in another two years he ought to be able to buy the land back from George.

Two more years and he'd be able to make his dream a reality. He could only hope that a certain green-eyed, sharp-tongued woman would be there to share it with him.

Lindsay was up at the crack of dawn riding Sundance. She got back to the ranch just in time to help with the morning chores. An hour of riding had done little to relieve the emptiness she felt inside her.

"You were certainly up early this morning," Jake commented as they gave the horses in the barn their grain.

"Sundance can always use the exercise."

"Oh. I thought maybe you and Nick had some kind of fight," Jake said shrewdly. "He seemed a little preoccupied before he left yesterday."

Lindsay kept her eyes riveted on the grain bin. "Did you know this was going to be his last year at the ranch?" she asked as casually as she could.

Jake hesitated a moment. "Sure. Didn't you?"

She looked over at him and noticed he looked decidedly uncomfortable. Like he was lying. With the way Jake felt about her, she didn't believe he wouldn't have told her if he'd known.

"No, I didn't. Why didn't you tell me?"

"Why didn't Nick tell you?" he countered.

"You didn't really know, did you?" she asked softly.

Jake raised his eyes to meet hers. "No."

"Why did you make all those accidents look like my fault?"

"What?"

"Please tell me the truth, Jake," she pleaded. "In each one of those accidents, if I didn't do them, there was only one other person who could have. And that's you."

Jake looked away from her knowing eyes. "I'm sorry," he said after a minute.

"But why did you do it?" Even though he'd admitted to it, she still could hardly believe it. She had really hoped she was wrong about it all, but she'd had a gut feeling that her suspicions were correct.

He tossed the can of grain he'd been holding back into the bin. His voice took on a touch of bitterness. "When Julie first came to the ranch, Nick wasn't the only one captivated by her. I fell for her, too, but she only had eyes for him. As it turned out, I guess it was for the best that she chose him, because I'm sure I couldn't have made her happy either. And I was over her long before she ever hurt him."

He turned to face her, his eyes begging for understanding. "When you came here, it was the same thing all over again. I saw myself losing another woman to Nick."

"But why the accidents?"

"I swear that Tramp getting out really was an accident. I gave him fresh water late that night, and I guess my mind was on you. When he got out, I knew it was my fault, that I must not have secured his latch." He paused and shook his head. "Then when Nick instantly accused you and got so upset about it, I just couldn't admit it was my fault. It was such a good opportunity to put some distance between you two."

"But Jake, that broken latigo!" she said in horror. "Someone might have gotten hurt! How could you do such a thing? And Champ's leg! How could you hurt him?"

"Wait a minute," he protested quickly. "I could never hurt Champ like that, or any other horse. He did that on his own out in the paddock after you rode him. And I did see that damaged latigo while we were cleaning the tack that day. But I knew by the way it was torn that it would give out when anyone put their weight in the stirrup to mount."

Lindsay stared at him like he was a stranger. Here she'd thought he was one of her best friends on the ranch, and now she wondered how well she really knew him.

"Don't look at me like I'm some kind of a monster," Jake said lightly. "I know it was wrong, but I know Nick so well. I know that he hates incompetence in any person, especially a woman. I was sure he wouldn't get involved with you if he thought you were like Julie."

Lindsay took a deep breath and tried to digest all that he had told her. She didn't want to admit to him that his plot may have worked.

"But you told me once you thought I might be the one to get through to Nick. In fact, you said you hoped I would," she accused.

"Well, I still do think you may be the only woman who could ever turn him around. But it wasn't exactly true that I hoped you would."

"Then why did you lie to me about that, too? Why did you tell me those things at all?"

"I guess I told you what I knew you wanted to hear," he admitted reluctantly. "I knew I wasn't going to stop you from falling for Nick, so I could only hope he wouldn't fall for you. Then when he broke your heart, I'd be right here to pick up the pieces. And you wouldn't feel threatened by me because I was always supportive about your relationship with Nick."

"Oh, Jake," she began, but he cut her off.

"Of course I did make one fatal mistake," he went on with a touch of bitterness. "I should have known you could never want that kind of relationship with me. That if you couldn't have Nick, you wouldn't want anybody. Am I right?"

"Jake, you're one of the nicest, most decent men I've ever known—at least I thought you were until I found out about all of this," she added. Her eyes narrowed.

He gave her a lopsided grin. "But?"

"But even though I care a great deal about you, all it could ever be is like brotherly love. I just can't change what I feel for Nick."

"And you're sure in time that you couldn't feel even a little of that for me?" he asked pleadingly.

She shook her head reproachfully. "I'm afraid not."

"Well, you can't blame a guy for trying," he said with a poor attempt at cheerfulness. "At least I hope you can't."

She smiled. "So what happens now?" she asked.

"I promise you, there'll be no more accidents, unless they're honest-to-goodness ones," Jake said sheepishly. "And I did convince my uncle that you weren't responsible for any of them. Although I didn't go into the details about exactly how I knew that. I, uh, know it's a lot to ask, but I would appreciate it if you wouldn't tell him either."

"All right," she agreed. She could see no point in telling Ross as long as it was all over with now. "But what about Nick?"

"I'll tell him everything when he gets back, if you want me to. It's the least I can do."

"No, that's all right," she said, thinking better of it. "I don't think that'll be necessary. Let him believe what he wants to believe."

"Are you sure?"

She nodded. If the time came to tell him, she would do it herself.

"Lindsay?"

"Yes?"

"Do you think you can ever forgive me?"

"I suppose I should be flattered in a way. You did go through an awful lot because of me." She paused, and her voice became stern. "I'll forgive you if you swear to me you'll never do anything like this ever again."

"I give you my word," he said solemnly.

"Come on then," she said more lightheartedly than she actually felt. "Let's get done with these chores before we're late for breakfast."

Exactly eight days after Nick had left, he suddenly returned. Lindsay was in the barn doing evening chores when she heard the pickup drive in. Irrationally, her heart leapt into her throat before she was even sure it was Nick.

In the week he had been gone, Lindsay had come to terms with their relationship, or lack of it. She still didn't quite understand it all, or believe that Nick couldn't feel something for her. But he obviously felt nowhere near the depth of emotions she felt for him. The hurt had eased a bit, but her sense of loss hadn't.

Eight days of constant mind battles had brought her no closer to a decision about whether she should stay on at the ranch. But she had made one decision. Nick wasn't going to get away with not explaining a few things to her. In the time he'd been gone, her numbness and shock had slowly been replaced by indignation and anger. She was going to face him and demand the truth about everything, no matter how painful it might be to hear it. He owed her that much.

As she peeked out at him from behind the barn door, she knew immediately that if anything, she loved him even more. Her heart was beating wildly and she knew her face was flushed with emotion as she watched him get out of the truck and walk to his cabin. His trim waist seemed even leaner than ever below the massive chest that was testing the strength of the cotton T-shirt he wore.

He strode unhurriedly to his cabin door, an army duffle bag in one hand and a backpack in the other. When he got to the door, he dropped the pack to the ground and reached out to twist the knob. But a moment before he did, he turned and looked directly at the barn.

Lindsay gasped and jumped back out of sight. She closed her eyes, willing her heart to beat normally. Although Nick was perhaps fifty yards away, she knew with absolute certainty that he had looked right at her. How had he known where she was? She felt like a child who had gotten caught with her hand in the cookie jar.

It was several minutes before Lindsay dared risk another peek around the door. When she did, she found Nick's gear gone and his cabin door shut. Evidently he had gone inside. She breathed a sigh of relief and hurried to get back to her chores. But she couldn't keep her hands from shaking or her knees from being almost too weak to support her. Damn him anyway, she swore to herself, he probably hadn't given her a second thought while he was gone, and here she was, so much in love with him she could hardly function.

Tonight, she decided, she would be early for dinner. She knew she wouldn't have the courage to walk up to Nick and sit with him if he was there before her and sitting alone. So she would get there first and see what happened.

The only problem was, she was so nervous and excited about seeing him that she couldn't keep her mind on what she was doing, and several times she caught herself about to feed the horses wrong amounts. By the time she was finally through, she was not early for dinner. Especially since she had to stop in her cabin first to freshen up. Nick hadn't seen her in more than a week and she wanted to look her best.

Hurriedly, she touched up the little makeup she always wore and brushed her long hair until the auburn waves glowed. She left her hair down, the way Nick liked it, or used to like it, anyway, she corrected herself. She changed into a clean, short-sleeved yellow blouse that accented the deep tan she had gotten over the summer and complemented her slim figure. Anxiously satisfied at last, she made her way quickly to the main lodge.

She was greatly unnerved to find Nick already there and alone at a table for two in the corner, *their corner.* Was it an unspoken invitation? she wondered. She tried to meet his gaze to get some clue as to his mood, but he would not look at her. Gathering up all her courage, she decided it was now or never, and she walked slowly up to his table carrying a plate of food she knew she wouldn't be able to eat.

"Mind if I sit down?" she asked in a trembling voice when she at last reached him.

Cool, amused blue eyes rose to look at her, revealing nothing.

"Suit yourself," Nick answered simply.

Lindsay bit her lip and felt her courage making a fast departure. She'd had a feeling he wasn't going to make this very easy for her.

"Thanks," she muttered with a touch of sarcasm, and before she had a chance to change her mind, she sat down beside him.

"Well?" he said flatly when she didn't speak for a moment. He prayed she wouldn't see through him, that he could conceal his churning emotions and the almost overpowering urge to pull her into his arms and kiss her. He'd missed her so much. But if he could live through those eight days without her, he could live through anything. He had too much at stake to weaken now.

"What did you want to say to me?" he pressed.

Lindsay swallowed nervously. She'd been practicing this for days, but now that her chance was here, she didn't think she could say what she wanted to. It would certainly help if he wasn't looking at her in such a detached way.

"How was your time off?" she said at last, stalling in hopes that a wave of bravado would hit her.

"Fine."

"Ross said you went to check on your mother's ranch. What did you find out?"

"Everything's in order," he said impatiently. "Is that all you wanted to talk to me about?"

"No." She looked unseeingly at her food, not wanting to face the indifference in his eyes. "Why didn't you tell me this was your last season working here?" There, it was out at last, and she waited with held breath for his response.

He shrugged carelessly. "I didn't see any point in telling you."

"You didn't see any point?" she repeated, her eyes wide. "Don't you think something like that would be important to me? Why did you have to lie about it?"

"Why should it matter to you?"

"Because," she sputtered, her temper starting to rise. But she couldn't really tell him. She just couldn't. "You know why."

"Why is it any different if I'm leaving here at the end of the season? You'll be leaving too."

"At least I never made any secret of that fact! I was straight with you from the beginning."

"Were you?" Nick jeered. His stomach tightened. That wasn't what he hoped she would say. "Just what is it you want from me, Lindsay?"

"Only the truth," she whispered, her eyes pleading.

"The truth of the matter is, my dear, that it's been a pleasant summer. I've enjoyed the time I spent with you. Especially one certain night not too long ago."

He paused a moment when he saw the stricken look on her face. He wished fervently that he couldn't tell so easily what she was feeling. Intentionally hurting her like this was even harder than he'd thought it would be.

He took a deep breath, gathering his strength for the final blow. "But it's over now," he went on calmly. "You have your life to live and I have mine. So let's just leave it at that, all right?"

It took her several minutes to find her tongue. She felt like he'd ripped her entire heart out of her body. How could she have meant so little to him? How could she have misjudged him so terribly? She felt like crawling into a hole, but she'd be damned if she'd let him know that.

"You're right," she purred coldly. "This summer has been a rather pleasant diversion for me. I don't regret a minute of it. I always wondered how the other half lived, so to speak. I'm glad I had a chance to experience it for a few months."

God, were those things really coming out of her mouth? She knew she'd regret the words later, but for now her pride was so injured that she had to lash out at him, to try to make him feel some of the pain she was feeling.

"You know," she went on, ignoring the dangerous glint in Nick's eyes, "one of my friends in Chicago told me once you haven't lived until you've made it with a real live western cowboy. And she was right. I can't wait to get home and compare notes with her."

His eyes narrowed, and she felt some smug satisfaction that at least his face was no longer emotionless. He was livid.

"Well," he said with barely suppressed fury, "I'm glad we both got what we wanted then. And since we've both already accomplished our respective goals, then we really have no need to continue seeing each other. Or to continue this conversation." He stood up and tipped his hat. "Nice knowing you, Lindsay Jordan."

Completely stunned, Lindsay watched him walk to another table. She made no motion to stop him. She'd be damned if she would run out of the dining room this time like a heartbroken teenager, even though she could think of nothing she felt more like doing at the moment.

Forcing herself to lift the fork to her mouth, to chew and swallow, she finished her meal slowly and sat sipping her coffee until he left the room first. Only after he had been gone for ten minutes did she rise to go outside.

The cool evening air refreshed her immediately. Already she was sorry for the things she said to him. Not that he didn't really deserve to hear those awful things, but lying to him and acting like a scorned child didn't make her feel any better now.

In fact, she felt rather foolish at the moment. Surely Nick had gotten to know her well enough that he knew the things she said weren't true and that she'd only said them out of spite and frustration. She sighed. She'd tried her best to act haughty, but she doubted whether he actually bought it.

It was rather ironic, she thought, that she never even got the chance to tell him who had been behind all those accidents, that none of them had been her fault at all. It probably wouldn't have mattered anyway, but she did wish she could have set the record straight about that. She'd most likely never have the chance again now. She couldn't exactly see them just chatting together after the things they'd just said to each other.

She felt numb, like she was in a state of shock. Was it really over between them? She never would have guessed it would end quite like this. Well, she would just have to learn to live without him—somehow.

Chapter Fourteen

This darn rain," Cindy muttered, staring outside from behind the half-open barn door. "I'm so sick of it!"

"I know what you mean," Lindsay agreed. She, too, had had enough of the rain that had been coming down almost steadily for three days. All outdoor activities had been temporarily discontinued, and after seventy-two hours of being mostly inside, everyone was on edge.

"Well, at least it looks like it's clearing up a little." Cindy sighed and put the hood of her rain slicker over her head. "Ready to make a dash for the lodge?"

Lindsay nodded, and together they dodged puddles and raindrops until they reached the front door of the main lodge. Cindy took off her rain gear and shook the water off of it before going inside.

"You're going to get sick if you keep going out in that rain with nothing on your head," she scolded.

"Thanks, Mom," Lindsay said, rolling her eyes.

"Hey, I speak from experience," Cindy defended herself.

"Come on, let's go in." Lindsay chuckled. Actually, the rain had been suiting her mood perfectly, and she had no desire to try to keep dry. The rain seemed an extension of her feelings, and as long as the sky kept crying, somehow she didn't need to.

They stood in the doorway of the dining room for a moment, taking in the activities. People at several tables were playing cards, some were playing checkers or backgammon, while others just sat around talking while they drank coffee.

"It looks pretty dull in here," Lindsay whispered, noticing Nick was at one of the tables playing backgammon. "I think I'll turn in early."

"Oh, don't be antisocial," Cindy protested. "In a little while, they're going to get the guitars and harmonicas out and have a sing-along."

Lindsay forced a smile. She vividly remembered the last time she was at a sing-along with Nick. The memory of their closeness as they sat companionably together by the camp fire was too painful to think about. "I know, but I'm pretty tired. I'll see you tomorrow."

Lindsay was almost out the door when Ross Browning stopped her.

"Say, Lindsay," he said, walking up to her. "This damn rain is supposed to stop tonight. If it does, I want you to take the north trail first thing in the morning as far as you can go and see what kind of shape it's in. I've got to get these people out riding. Some of our other trails I'm sure will need a couple days to dry out, but that north trail usually isn't as bad as the rest. But I've got to have a report on the condition of the trail before I can send greenhorns out on it."

"All right." She smiled. She was glad he had chosen her. Three days without riding was driving her crazy, and the sooner she was back on the trail, the better.

"Oh, and by the way," Ross said, his face suddenly serious. "I'm expecting an answer from you soon on your plans for the winter. If you aren't going to stay, I've got to get someone else lined up to take your place."

Her smile faded. "I understand. I'll let you know by the end of the week." Seemingly satisfied, Ross went back into the dining room.

By the end of the week, Lindsay mused as she walked back to her cabin, *I'll have made up my mind.* This was Tuesday, so that left her three days to come to a decision. Three more days to make one of the most important decisions in her life.

The first thing Lindsay did when she woke up the next morning was to look outside. To her delight, the rain had stopped. Judging by the amount the grass had already dried around her cabin, it must have quit sometime during the night. Even though it was still overcast, it looked like it would be clearing up later in the day.

A half hour after she was done bolting down her breakfast, Lindsay was mounted on Champ, heading for the north trail. She'd almost taken Sundance to check on the trail, but at the last minute she decided if she did run into adverse conditions, she'd be better off on Champ. The old gelding's leg had healed up fine, and he had twice the surefootedness on mountain trails as her horse.

For the first several miles, Lindsay did not encounter any difficulties. The beginning of the trail was alternately rocky and sandy, and had dried fast after the rain. However, as the mountain path took a turn downward into a canyon, the going became more arduous. The footing there was usually dirt, but after being saturated for three days, it had turned into mud.

Still, Champ didn't seem to be having much of a problem, so Lindsay went on. But as she got to the bottom of the canyon, the gelding began to slip and slide. Although she was now convinced this part of the trail would have to dry up more before the inexperienced guests could ride it, she wanted to see what the rest of the trail was like, and she carefully urged Champ on.

The game little gelding had almost made it safely to the bottom of the canyon when he stumbled, his front feet going out from under him. He fell forward hard onto his knees. As he struggled to regain his feet in the thick mud, Lindsay realized her weight was impairing him to the point that she thought he was going to slip over the side of the narrow trail.

Acting on instinct rather than any rational thought, she kicked her feet out of the stirrups and jumped out of the saddle over Champ's left shoulder. What she hadn't accounted for, however, was the slickness of the trail, and as she tried to land on her feet, she slid and fell. The next thing she knew, she was going over the edge. She half fell, half rolled down the steep decline twenty feet to the canyon floor.

She hit the bottom with a thud and everything went black.

Lindsay groaned and tried to sit up. She was aware of a throbbing in her head, and she had to sit up very slowly to keep from passing out again. She looked in confusion at her muddy clothes and her surroundings, and it took her several minutes to remember what had happened. Her first thought after that was Champ. What had happened to him and where was he? She looked carefully around, but she couldn't see any sign of him.

She took a deep breath and tried to stand. She couldn't find Champ or get back to the ranch while sitting here. But she was only half on her feet when she felt an excruciating pain in her right ankle, and she sat back down.

Biting her lip to keep from crying out in pain, she gingerly touched her ankle. It was very tender and felt swollen inside her boot. She wanted to see what it looked like, but she was afraid if she took off her boot, she'd never get it on again. So she left it alone, and tried once more to get to her feet.

By not putting any weight on the ankle, she was able to stand. Walking was another thing all together. It was too painful to move even one step.

"This is just great," she grumbled out loud. What was she going to do now?

First she would have to find Champ. She had to know if he was okay. If he was, she hoped she could get on him to ride back to the ranch. That was an awful lot of ifs, she thought dismally.

Determined to find the horse, Lindsay picked up the stoutest stick she could find near her, and using it as a cane, she was able to slowly hobble around. She couldn't really imagine Champ being as energetic and disloyal as Thundercloud had been when he'd ran back to the ranch after she fell off him, so she thought Champ must be somewhere near. The most likely place to look, she decided, was where she'd last seen him. The problem was, that was twenty feet straight up. She would have to find the end of the trail where it opened into the canyon.

The trail was fifty yards from where she was standing, and it took her almost fifteen minutes to go that far. When she at last made it to the trail, sweat was pouring out of her from the exertion. Her ankle throbbed with every step, and her head pounded with a dull ache that did nothing to help her progress.

She had to stop and rest. As she sat there catching her breath, she wondered how she would ever have the strength to find Champ if he wasn't right where she'd parted company from him. And if she couldn't find him, that left her only one alternative—waiting for someone to come and find her. No one would expect her to return for several more hours, so that meant it would be hours after that before anyone would worry enough to look for her. It was even possible she might be out here all night.

Pushing that upsetting thought from her mind, Lindsay pulled herself to her feet and once more made her way shakily up the trail.

Her progress was slow due to the slippery mud that covered the trail. She felt like she was taking one step forward and two steps backward. It seemed like hours had passed before she at last spotted Champ's familiar chestnut rump. She called out to him with joy, and watched him turn his head around toward her and nicker softly.

Lindsay felt a stab of worry as she slowly hobbled the rest of the way to the gelding. Champ stood patiently watching her come; he was not moving at all. Surely if he was all right he would at least walk toward her.

Closing up the last few feet that separated them, Lindsay's eyes automatically scanned Champ's body. His legs and stomach were covered with mud, but she couldn't see any blood on him. But then she reached his head, and she looked down at his front legs.

"Oh, Champ!" she cried out in dismay. One of the gelding's knees was swollen to twice its normal size, and a slow trickle of blood was seeping through the mud down his cannon bone and to his hoof. She hadn't been able to see it when she'd walked up from behind him.

The first thing she would have to do was clean the wound up so she could get a better look at it. She pulled her canteen off the saddle, then hesitated. What was she going to use to wash out his knee? She couldn't just pour the water over it. Yet there was nothing else around that would serve as a rag.

An old western movie suddenly popped into her mind. A cowboy's horse had been hurt, and he ripped his own shirt to use as a bandage and a tourniquet. Lindsay gazed down reluctantly at her own green plaid cotton blouse. It was one of her favorites, but what else could she use? Besides, she consoled herself, it was already muddy and torn in several places from her fall. It probably wouldn't be wearable again anyway.

She paused for a moment, wondering what part to tear off. When someone did finally find her it would probably be a man, and she didn't want to be indecent. Maybe Nick would be the one to rescue her. She wouldn't have to worry about him seeing her less than completely clothed, as he'd already seen every naked inch of her. The thought sent her pulse into double time.

No, you can't think about him now, she scolded herself, you've got to take care of Champ. Deciding at last just to rip off a sleeve, she pulled at one of the tears just below her left shoulder. The material gave easily, and in moments she had the sleeve in her hand. She doused it with water and began washing off Champ's knee.

The mud had become dry, and it was difficult to get off. When she finally got it cleaned out, she was disconcerted to find there was a deep cut right in the center of his knee. Luckily it had almost stopped bleeding, so it must have missed an artery. But she couldn't get the inside of the cut cleaned out because it was deep and swollen. Not knowing what else to do, she wrapped her sleeve snugly around Champ's knee and tied the ends in a knot.

She stood back, surveying her work. Not a very professional looking bandage, she had to admit, but it was the best she could do. Champ had been a trooper through it all, hardly moving.

"Well, boy," she said, patting his neck affectionately, "let's just see if you can put any weight on your leg."

She picked up his reins and tried to pull Champ forward. It wasn't easy because she herself had to hop, but after much encouragement, Champ reluctantly took two steps forward. That was enough to show Lindsay that he wouldn't be able to walk back to the ranch on his own, let alone with her on his back. He walked just like she did, scarcely putting any weight on his bad leg.

Sighing, she removed his saddle and pads. They only weighed thirty pounds, but she thought he would be more comfortable without any weight on his back at all. Then she sat heavily down on a tree stump near Champ's head.

"Looks like we'll be here for awhile, boy," she told the gelding wearily. Champ stretched his nose out to nuzzle her bare left arm. His whiskers were rough on her skin, but she made no move to push him away.

With absolutely nothing else to do, her mind turned inevitably to Nick. It had been a week since he'd come back from his trip, and still he hadn't spoken to her unless duty had forced him. Even then there was a tenseness, a guarded tone to his voice.

She sighed audibly again, wondering for the thousandth time whether she should stay on at the ranch for the winter or return to Chicago. If only Nick wasn't going to be leaving, she would definitely stay. She just couldn't imagine life at the ranch without him around. He was such an integral part of this place. But with him gone, what did that leave her with? Memories, pleasant as well as painful, at every corner. Could she handle that?

On the other hand, what did she really have in Chicago? A high-paying job, an empty apartment and Sundance boarded at a stable that was twenty miles away from her. She had no close friends there, and certainly no men in her life. Not that she would ever want another man in her life. Who could possibly ever compare with Nick?

Even though the salary here was much less than at the insurance company, this job was much more satisfying. She enjoyed being with the guests, and a job working with horses had been her secret dream since childhood. Ross Browning was a nice, fair man, and all of his employees were pleasant, fun people to work with. And the location—well, the location was paradise. Even though she'd only been here a couple of months, she already had a hard time visualizing the dirty, busy, traffic-filled streets of the city, despite the fact that she'd lived there all her life.

Her father's face came back to her, along with his parting advice to her. *Don't make the same mistakes I did, honey. Don't work yourself into an early grave.* Wouldn't that be just what she would be doing if she returned to Chicago? Working day after day with her only goal being the almighty dollar?

Was that really all she wanted in her life? Was that all that mattered to her?

Lindsay shifted position on the stump and gazed out through the trees into the canyon below. Yes, it would be very hard to leave the mountains. And she knew now that money wasn't that important to her. What had taken her father a lifetime to realize, she had learned while she was still young, before it was too late to do something about it.

She smiled at Champ and reached out to pat his neck. Nick or no Nick, she was staying on at the ranch. She couldn't help but wish things had turned out differently between them, though. It was going to be hard to adjust to life without him. But what other choice did she have? She couldn't force him to love her. If only Nick...

After an indeterminable amount of time, she dozed off. She hadn't even been aware that she had slept. She awoke with a start. She looked around and noticed the sun was starting on its downward journey in the sky, so it must be past noon. And she'd left at eight o'clock this morning. She stretched her arms out over her head and groaned. How much longer would it take for someone to find her?

A sound from somewhere up the trail made Lindsay sit up straight, straining to identify the noise. A similar sound must have woken her up, she realized. She glanced at Champ. His head was raised, his ears pricked forward. So he had heard something, too. It wasn't her imagination.

Please let it be Nick, she prayed silently. Maybe out here alone and away from the ranch we can finally talk to each other.

A moment later, there was a whinny that sounded very close. Champ instantly returned the call, and shifted impatiently on his feet.

Lindsay realized she had been holding her breath when she saw a large black and white pinto with a tall, powerfully built rider coming toward her. A burning in her lungs made her expel her breath. So it was Nick who would find her after all. Why wasn't she surprised?

She could see him urging the pinto to walk faster when he saw her. Still, she said nothing until he pulled up in front of her.

"What took you so long?" she said lightly, her voice amazingly steady despite her pounding heart and the sudden dizzy feeling that had come over her.

He glared at her with a look that she couldn't quite decipher. His eyes took in her disheveled appearance before he turned to Champ.

"My God, what happened to you two? You look like you were mud wrestling."

"And the mud won." She was giddy with relief at being rescued at last, and that her Nick was her rescuer. Her happiness was short-lived.

"You crazy fool, what were you doing bringing him down this trail, anyway? Ross wanted a report of the condition of it, not a demonstration of its dangers," he said harshly. "And where's his saddle? Don't tell me you were stupid enough to ride him out here bareback."

Lindsay bristled. "The saddle is over there. And Champ was handling the trail just fine until he got to this point. He tripped on something. Besides, Ross told me to take the trail as far as I could, and I—"

"What happened to his leg? It's all swollen!" he exploded. He jumped off the pinto and bent to feel Champ's leg.

"I know," she snapped. Damn him, why didn't he give her a chance to explain?

"At least you got the bleeding stopped." He threw a glance in her direction, his eyes dark and angry. "It looks like you got thrown off again, huh?"

"No, I didn't get thrown," she said tartly. She felt like she had during her first few days at the ranch, when Nick had argued with everything she said, always implying she was incompetent. It infuriated her just as much now as it had then.

"When he stumbled and couldn't get his balance, I jumped off so he could regain his feet without my weight to impede him," she informed him icily.

He snorted. "Sure you did." He looked back at Champ's leg grimly. "He certainly can't walk back to the ranch like this."

"Why do you think I'm just sitting here?" she asked sarcastically.

"Because you're too lazy to walk back on your own?" he returned coolly. Then his eyes narrowed and his expression became even stormier, and he shook his head slowly. "If this was all some big production to show me that you're not like my ex-wife, you've wasted your time. I don't buy it."

He was being rough on her and he knew it. But he'd been so angry with her the past few days. Angry that she evidently didn't want to stay on at the ranch, angry that she didn't try to talk to him again since the day he'd gotten back, and especially angry over the things she'd said to him that day. He'd tried very hard to convince himself that she didn't mean any of those god-awful words, that she'd just been hurt and retaliated any way she could think of at the time. But nagging doubts had haunted him, making him wonder if he hadn't been wrong about her all along and that she had, after all, made him the fool.

He'd been so worried about her when she didn't come back today. He'd called himself a million nasty names for doing all this to her without maybe having the chance to explain it. The thought that he might never see her again had nearly driven him insane. His tremendous relief at finding her at last was causing him to be unnecessarily harsh in order to cover up his true feelings.

He stared at her now as she digested his cruel words, wanting desperately to pull her into his arms, yet not daring to.

It was several moments before the meaning of Nick's words sank in. Lindsay was tired and hungry and dirty, and her body ached all over, not to mention her heart, which now felt like lead in her chest.

"Damn you, Nick," she spat, jumping furiously to her feet. "After all this time, don't you know me any better than that? How could you possibly think this whole thing was a ploy? That I could care so little about a horse that I could ride him when he's lame? You've got a hell of an ego if you think I did all this just to get on your good side. What makes you think I care what you think anyway?''

''Get off it, Lindsay,'' he retorted. ''You're more like Julie than you want to admit. You couldn't be happy living on this ranch any more than she was. You're city born and bred and you could never be any different. You're really inconsiderate for not telling Ross right away you don't want to stay here when you know very well you don't want this job full-time. You told me yourself you couldn't wait to get home again.''

''Well, that just shows how little you really know me,'' she spat, her cutting words rushing out at a furious rate. ''I've decided to take Ross up on his offer. I'm just glad I won't have to worry about seeing you all the time. In fact, finding out you were leaving made my decision a lot easier. Now, why don't you just go back to the ranch and leave me alone? I'll wait for someone else to rescue me. I'd rather crawl back than ride with you anyway.''

She whirled around, meaning to stomp off haughtily away from him. But in her anger, she had forgotten her ankle. The first step she tried to take brought a cry of pain to her lips and she reached blindly to catch herself to keep from crumbling to the ground.

''You're hurt!'' Nick exclaimed, his voice sounding faintly accusing.

''So what do you care?'' she retorted over her shoulder. She bit her lip, willing her ankle to support her weight as she tried a bit more cautiously to walk. But all she got for her efforts was a bloody bottom lip. She just couldn't step on her foot. Hours of sitting had made it stiffen and hurt even more than it had before.

Tears of frustration and pain stung her eyes. She quickly wiped them away, furious with herself for letting Nick get to her like this. She would *not* let him see her cry.

"Lindsay?"

His voice was soft and husky. And close. In her agitation, she hadn't heard him come up behind her.

"Lindsay?" he said again. Strong hands touched her shoulders.

She tried to pull away. "Don't touch me," she whispered in a halting voice. Already her anger had started to dissipate. One gentle word and touch and she melted. She was irritated with herself for being so easily moved by him.

He ignored her request and pulled her body against his. She had decided to stay on at the ranch despite him! He couldn't believe it. He felt that a tremendous burden had been lifted off his chest. He had no reason to go on with this charade any longer. Now if only he could get her to understand and forgive him for his test. Considering her words a minute ago, that might prove a little difficult, he thought ruefully. But he knew she had to still love him. And he would make her see she did, too.

His arms moved to firmly encircle her waist. "I'm sorry, Lindsay. I'm being an ass. Let's pretend I just got here and start over."

His breath was warm against her hair, and it tickled her ear. She swayed against him, relishing the feel of his strong, tight body behind her back. *If he lets go of me right now,* she thought, *I know I'll fall to the ground in a heap.*

"By the way, where's your cowboy hat?" he teased lightly.

Her hand went automatically up to her head, even though she could tell her hat was not there. "It's probably down there." She pointed to the bottom of the canyon.

She could feel him stiffen. "How would it get down there?"

Lindsay hesitated. She just wanted to lean against him and let him hold her. She didn't want to talk and risk arguing again.

"Well," she began at last, "when I jumped off Champ so he could get his balance, I slipped in the mud and sort of went over the side."

"Sort of? You either did or you didn't." His voice was tense but not mocking.

"Okay, so I did. Anyway, I must have lost my hat down there. I never noticed it until now."

"And your leg? What did you do to that?"

She shrugged. "I must have hurt my ankle rolling down. It all happened so fast, I really don't remember."

"Did it hurt as soon as you landed at the bottom?"

"I don't know. I was out awhile right after I fell."

Nick moved back enough to loosen his hold. Then he turned her around to face him. "How did you ever get back up here?" he asked softly. His eyes had lost that cool, impersonal look that had been there for so long.

Lindsay stared up at him, weak with sudden desire. When he looked at her like that, it was hard for her to concentrate on his words. She trembled, unable to break her eyes away from his.

"I hobbled with a stick," she said breathlessly.

Nick smiled. "I'll bet you did," he said gently. He reached up and caressed her cheek lightly with rough, callused fingers. "Does it hurt much?"

She shivered again, all her senses brilliantly alive and tingling. "Not right this minute it doesn't," she told him truthfully. How could she feel pain when her body was one mass of nerve ends waiting to be further ignited by his touch?

After what seemed eons, Nick lowered his mouth to cover hers in what started out as an easy, gentle kiss. In seconds, she was responding so hungrily and urgently to his mouth that the kiss became a blazing, demanding expression of need. She wrapped both arms around his neck and clung to him as if he were her lifeline.

After a few minutes, Nick broke his mouth away from hers. "I have missed you," he said, his breath ragged.

Lindsay closed her eyes briefly, wishing they could just stay like this forever. But she couldn't keep that nagging voice inside of her quiet, and it reminded her of how Nick had been treating her lately, how he had treated her when he first found her today. It was obvious he was still attracted to her physically, but she couldn't open herself up to being hurt again from another sexual encounter with him. As blissful as it would be to make love to him again, the pain of his detachment afterward was not worth it.

"Nick," she began, reluctant to bring her feelings into words.

He pulled away enough to look into her eyes, and successfully read the message there. "Sh," he whispered before she could go on, and covered her mouth with his.

It was another long moment before Lindsay could draw enough strength to break away. If she didn't stop him now, if she didn't talk to him and get a few things straight, she knew she'd be lost again. Already her body was on fire, and the tremendous need she felt for him was making her weak.

"No, stop it." Her voice was harsher than she'd meant it to be, but at least it got her the desired reaction from Nick. He released her from his arms, and stood watching her and waiting, a wary expression in his eyes.

"What's wrong?" he asked when she didn't speak right away.

"What's wrong?" she repeated incredulously, the anguish she had suffered ever since they had made love coming through in her voice. She saw him wince, and felt a small gleam of satisfaction.

"You finally get me into bed only to give me the cold shoulder the next morning. Then you take off without a word for eight days. Then you come back and give me a big speech about what a pleasant but unmeaningful conquest I was. Now here you are, suddenly being nice again, kissing me like you used to, like you . . ."

Her voice broke, and she had to pause to regain her composure. She took a deep breath and continued. "I can't take this up-again, down-again relationship anymore, Nick. You can't have it both ways. And since you're leaving after this season, I don't really see the point in continuing any kind of a relationship at all."

He had been studying her carefully the whole time she spoke, but now he looked away, staring off into the canyon behind her. "You're right," he said quietly after a moment. "It isn't fair to you, I realize that. It does have to be one way or the other."

Lindsay stared at him, knowing by the strange look on his face that he was going to say something important. Suddenly she wished she hadn't said the things she'd just said. What if he said, you're right, we'll just forget it all? Even though she'd come to believe that was the way it was going to be, she didn't think she could handle hearing him tell her that again. But she couldn't take back her words, either, so she stood there holding her breath and waiting for him to continue.

Nick shoved his hands into his pockets. "I'm not very proud of some of the things I've said to you lately, or the way I treated you when you first came here. I'd been fighting the inevitable so long, I guess I just took out my frustration and anger at myself on you. I thought once I divorced Julie, I'd be able to control my emotions from then on. In fact, I didn't even think I had any emotions left after I divorced her. Until I met you.''

Lindsay trembled, not daring to even think about what his words might be leading up to. She was suddenly aware of how tired her good leg was from supporting all her weight and the throbbing of her hurt ankle became painful enough to break into her blurred mind and loudly remind her of her injury. She sank down heavily onto a nearby rock.

''Your ankle!'' Nick rushed to her side and bent down beside her. ''I forgot all about it. Let me look at it.''

Lindsay didn't protest as he raised the leg of her jeans, revealing her painfully swollen ankle. He ran his sure fingers up and down her boot, and she couldn't keep a sharp cry of pain from escaping when he pressed down too hard.

''I hope it's not broken,'' he muttered. ''We don't dare take off that boot yet. It's the only support we can give it for now.''

Lindsay nodded. ''That's why I left it on, even though I'd like to see what it looks like.''

Nick flashed her a grin. ''Smart girl. There may be hope for you yet,'' he teased gently. Then his face became grim again. ''I'm sorry for what I said about you plotting this to show me you're not like Julie. You're not like her at all. But I must admit, it sort of took me until a few minutes ago to be totally convinced of that,'' he said apologetically.

Lindsay's heart was beating crazily in her chest. Did she dare believe him?

''Lindsay, I'm not leaving the ranch at the end of the summer.''

She could only stare at him, her mouth open in total shock. ''What?'' she finally squeaked.

He reached out and trailed one finger up and down her bare arm. "I'm not leaving here at the end of the summer," he repeated softly. "In fact, by my calculations, I'll be working here two more years yet."

"I don't understand," she began, shaking her head. "Why did you lie about that?"

He took a deep breath and met her confused and guarded eyes squarely. "I had to find out how badly you really wanted to work here. I had to know if you would stay on at the ranch even if I wasn't around."

"But why? Why this elaborate scheme?"

"When I married Julie, she gave up her life in the city to live out here with me. She knew I would never leave Wyoming, so she gave in to what I wanted. But in hardly a year she was so miserable here that she was looking for some excitement elsewhere. I guess I can't really blame her because I know how I would hate living in the city. You just can't expect a person to completely change a life-style they've been born and raised with."

Her eyes narrowed suspiciously. "You had it planned all along to leave that day after we slept together, didn't you? Was making love to me some sort of test too?"

"In a way, I suppose," he admitted reluctantly. "Actually making love to you that night accomplished two purposes. One, I knew that if I scorned you afterward it would make you mad as hell at me and that it would help you make your decision about staying here that much less influenced by any feelings you had for me."

"Assuming I had any feelings for you," she snapped. The knowledge that he had played with her emotions for his own purposes did not please her. "And the second purpose sleeping with me accomplished?"

"If you did decide to go back to Chicago, then at least I would always have that very special memory of you to keep with me forever. Even though all it's done to me since then is keep me awake every night from wanting you again so much."

These were the words she had been longing to hear for so long, yet still she couldn't erase these last two weeks of doubt and hurt from her soul that easily.

"How could you leave me without even saying good-bye?" she asked in a trembling voice, her anguish from that morning still fresh.

He looked away uneasily. "When I woke up and saw the peaceful, beautiful way you were sleeping, I wanted nothing more than to wake you up and make love to you again. But I knew if I didn't leave right then and there, I'd never be able to. So I snuck out."

She started to speak but he cut her off, anticipating her next words. "Later, when we were on the trail ride, I wanted to grab you and kiss you and tell you how great it had been, but I just couldn't. Then you were so damned cool and unemotional, I thought maybe I'd been a stupid fool all along, that I really had misjudged you and our making love hadn't meant anything to you."

She smiled slowly and shook her head. "I thought that's how you felt, like it wasn't anything special to you. That's not how I felt, Nick. It was..." She stopped, still feeling too vulnerable to voice her feelings to him.

"It was what?" he persisted, his fathomless eyes demanding an answer.

She licked her lips. He was coming clean, at last telling her what she hoped was the truth. Maybe if she just opened up a little...

"It was everything," she said simply, holding his eyes.

He leaned forward to lightly brush his lips against hers. "It was to me, too," he murmured huskily. "And I'd like nothing more than a repeat performance right now, but I better get you back to the ranch and get that ankle taken care of."

"And Champ's knee," she reminded him, feeling a stab of disappointment when he stood up and pulled her to her feet. She knew he was right, but she wanted him so much it was hard to deny her body the pleasure it was screaming for.

"Yes, Champ's knee, too." He looked around, frowning. "Do you think you can ride my horse if I lead Champ on foot? I don't really know how else to get him back up the trail. If I go first, I'm sure my horse won't give you any trouble."

"I'm sure I can handle him," she retorted stiffly. Here he was, back to his old superior self again, doubting her ability to ride a horse. Maybe he would never change.

"Look, Lindsay," he said with a touch of impatience. "I know you could handle him just fine if you were healthy. I'm worried about your ankle. And your head. You've got an awful bump up there."

"Oh," she said, feeling foolish. "I'm sorry. Old habits die hard, I guess."

"I've probably given them reason to," he grudgingly admitted. "Here, I'll help you up."

Nick had to almost lift her into the saddle, but she finally made it up. Using the left stirrup was out of the question, so she kept her right foot out so she wouldn't be off balance. With a good deal of persuasion, Nick was able to pull Champ in front of the pinto and they started slowly up the trail.

With the first step, Lindsay wondered instantly if she'd be able to make it. Even though the jolt was in actuality very slight, it felt like someone was hitting her ankle with a hammer every time the pinto took a step. But she knew there was no other way to get back up the mountain, so she gritted her teeth and tried to think of something else.

Her eyes glued on Nick's back, it was easy to think about him and the conversation they had just had. Did Nick really care about her? No, it was too much to hope for. Her heart had been on a roller-coaster ride for too long to become level again so soon. She would just have to keep a tight rein on her emotions until she found out his true feelings. But at least he wasn't leaving! She couldn't help but be thrilled by that.

Time passed by in a blur, and Lindsay was almost delirious when they finally reached the top of the trail and Nick stopped. The severe pain in her ankle had given her a pounding headache as well, and she was near the point of falling off. She was thankful the pinto merely followed Nick and Champ without any direction from her. She didn't think she had the strength to control him.

As soon as Nick stopped, he turned to say something to Lindsay. But when he saw her white, pinched face he swore and hurried to pull her off the horse.

"Why didn't you tell me how much it was hurting?" he scolded her. He sat down in the grass with her wrapped in his arms.

Lindsay rested her head gratefully against his strong chest, her headache receding somewhat almost immediately. It felt so good to be held by him.

"Are you sure you won't miss the city?" he asked, kissing the top of her head lightly.

"Positive. I haven't missed it once all summer. I love it here, Nick. I can't imagine ever being happy in Chicago again."

He cocked one eyebrow curiously. "Then why have you waited so long to give Ross an answer?"

"I guess you're right about people having a hard time changing the life-style they've been raised with," she told him truthfully. "But it isn't impossible. Although, believe it or not, I always imagined myself someday with a little place in the country where I could keep Sundance and some more horses."

She paused and reached up to trace a line down his firm jaw with trembling fingers. "It really threw me when Ross told me you were leaving here. I take it he was in on your little ploy?"

"He wasn't too thrilled by it, but he did agree to help me."

"Did anyone else know the truth?"

"Like who?"

"Jake."

He stiffened. "Why do you ask?"

"I just wondered."

"No. No one else knew."

"Speaking of Jake..." she began.

"Yes?"

"He's the one responsible for those accidents," she told him quietly.

"He admitted that?" Nick sounded surprised.

"Of course," she said defensively. "You don't think I'd tell you something like that without proof."

He sighed. "I had a feeling it was him." His gaze swept over her intimately and possessively. "I don't have to ask what his motives were either."

"Well, he promised to never do anything like that again. And I promised not to tell Ross about it."

"I guess it really doesn't matter anymore," he agreed grudgingly.

"He was a good friend to me when you were acting like you hated me."

Nick pulled her tightly into his arms. "Never again, love. Besides, I never hated you, you know."

"Oh, no? You sure gave a convincing performance."

"So I missed my calling as an actor," he said lightly. Then he relaxed his hold just enough so that he could tip her chin up and look thoughtfully into her eyes. "I could never hate you, Lindsay. In fact, I tried like hell not to love you, but God help me, I do. I think I have since the very first day you showed up here looking frazzled but so very sure of yourself. It sounds silly, but when I saw the way you looked at your horse galloping around the corral with such love and admiration in your eyes, all I could think of was what it would be like to have you look at me like that."

Her heart skipped a beat, and for a moment she couldn't speak. Surely she must be so delirious she wasn't hearing right.

"What?" she whispered breathlessly. "What did you say?"

"You heard me. Why do you think I had to put you through all of that the past two weeks? I had to make sure you made an unbiased decision to stay here. I couldn't have you staying here just because of me. It had to be what you wanted," he told her earnestly.

"It was still kind of a lousy thing to do to me." That much was true, but if he really did love her, she knew she'd get over the injustice of it in no time.

"I know. But please try to understand, I just couldn't make the same mistake twice. And I love you too much to ever give you up once I really have you."

She squinted up at him. "Okay. I guess you're off the hook."

He smiled and kissed her lightly on the tip of her nose. "Isn't this where you're supposed to gush out that you love me, too?" His voice was teasing but she knew by the trace of reserve still on his face that his question was serious.

She laughed and kissed the side of his neck. So the roller coaster had leveled out after all.

"Nick, you crazy fool, I've loved you for so long, I can't remember when I didn't."

He pulled her so tightly into his arms, she had a hard time breathing. He murmured her name several times, his voice husky with emotion against her ear.

Nick held her for several minutes before releasing her. "I hate to say it, but we probably should get going back to the ranch. I think we better leave Champ tied here, though. He's favoring that leg. We should be able to get a truck and trailer this far. I'll ride with you the rest of the way on my horse. I don't want you passing out on me and falling off. Besides, the rest of the trail is pretty good so my horse shouldn't have any trouble carrying both of us."

"He did it once before, remember?" she said playfully.

"How well I do remember. It just about drove me crazy having your body that close to mine."

She flushed, the memory of what his body did to hers fresh in her mind, too. She watched him stand, secure Champ's reins around a tree and pull the saddle off his horse. As he came back to her and lifted her on the horse, he had a devilish look on his face.

"You know, with that ankle, you're probably going to have to stay indoors a lot of the time to let it heal."

She groaned and wondered why that seemed to please him so much. "You're right. It's going to be very boring."

"Oh, I don't know about that." He gave her a lecherous grin. "I can think of one indoor activity that will keep you pretty busy and far from bored."

"Oh?" She feigned innocence, but the flush of color on her face gave her away. "And what is that?"

Nick jumped up to sit behind her on the horse and reached one hand around to tantalizingly stroke her breast. "I'll show you when we get back."

Her blood raced through her burning body, and she could feel Nick's heartbeat, as wild and unsteady as hers was. "Promise?"

"Promise," he said, nibbling her ear. He urged the pinto forward into an easy walk.

"Lindsay?" he asked, his voice suddenly thoughtful.

"Yes?"

"Where do you want to get married?"

She laughed, delirious this time from joy instead of pain. "Is that a proposal, Mr. Leighton?"

"It certainly is, Mrs. Future Leighton. How about an answer?"

She turned her head to kiss him fully, passionately on his mouth. "How's that for an answer?" she asked, breaking away.

He shrugged in mock confusion. "A simple yes or no will do."

"Yes, you idiot, I'd love to marry you."

"Calling me names already. I guess there's only one way to keep you quiet."

He had a dangerous gleam in his eyes as he lowered his mouth on hers once more, demanding and possessive. It was a kiss that expressed more than words ever could.

The sun was just starting to set behind the mountains in front of them as they slowly made their way back to the ranch, their bodies pressed close together, aware only of each other and the wonder of the love they felt.

* * * * *

Silhouette Intimate Moments

COMING IN OCTOBER

SEA GATE
by
MAURA SEGER

Atlantis . . . land of the imagination. Or is it real?

Suppose a man of our world were to meet a woman who might not be exactly what she seemed. What if they found not only love, but a way to cross bridges that had never before been crossed?

Travel with them in SEA GATE, a very special love story about two very special people. Coming next month, only from Silhouette Intimate Moments.

Don't miss it!

IM209-1

ATTRACTIVE, SPACE SAVING BOOK RACK

Display your most prized novels on this handsome and sturdy book rack. The hand-rubbed walnut finish will blend into your library decor with quiet elegance, providing a practical organizer for your favorite hard-or soft-covered books.

Only $9.95

Approximately 16" x 8" when assembled

Assembles in seconds!

To order, rush your name, address and zip code, along with a check or money order for $10.70* ($9.95 plus 75¢ postage and handling) payable to *Silhouette Books.*

Silhouette Books
Book Rack Offer
901 Fuhrmann Blvd.
P.O. Box 1396
Buffalo, NY 14269-1396

Offer not available in Canada.

BKR-2A

*New York and Iowa residents add appropriate sales tax.

Silhouette Special Edition

COMING NEXT MONTH

#409 A CERTAIN SMILE—Lynda Trent
Impulsive widow Megan Wayne and divorced father Reid Spencer didn't have marriage in mind, but what harm could come if their friendship turned into something stronger? Reid's two teenage daughters didn't intend to let them find out....

#410 FINAL VERDICT—Pat Warren
Prosecutor Tony Adams's upbringing had built him a strong case against lasting love. Could attorney Sheila North's evidence to the contrary weaken his defenses and free his emotions from solitary confinement?

#411 THUNDERSTRUCK—Pamela Toth
Crew member Honey Collingsworth accepted the risks of hydroplane racing. Still, when her brother and dashing defector Alex Checkhov competed, churning up old hatred, she feared for their lives...and her heart.

#412 RUN AWAY HOME—Marianne Shock
Proud landowner Burke Julienne knew that to restless vagabond Savannah Jones, the lush Julienne estate was just another truck stop. Yet he found her mesmerizing, and he prayed that one day Savannah would trade freedom for love.

#413 A NATURAL WOMAN—Caitlin Cross
When farmer's daughter Vana Linnier abruptly became a sophisticated celebrity, she desperately needed some plain old-fashioned horse sense to cope with her jealous sister and her disapproving but desirable boss, Sky Van Dusen.

#414 BELONGING—Dixie Browning
Saxon Evanshaw returned home to a host of family fiascos and the lovely but stealthy estate manager, Gale Chandler. Who was she really? Where were the missing family treasures? And would Gale's beauty rob him of his senses?

AVAILABLE THIS MONTH:

Starting in October...

SHADOWS ON THE NILE

by

Heather Graham Pozzessere

A romantic short story in six installments from best-selling author Heather Graham Pozzessere.

The first chapter of this intriguing romance will appear in all Silhouette titles published in October. The remaining five chapters will appear, one per month, in Silhouette Intimate Moments' titles for November through March '88.

Don't miss "*Shadows on the Nile*"—a special treat, coming to you in October. Only from Silhouette Books.

Be There!

IMSS-1